— GalFed —

Here are stories of the Galactic Federation, which encompasses most of the intelligent life in the galaxy—from the residents of Sol III (known to them as "Earth") to the great cats of Ungruwarkh, to a certain stiff-necked people on Tau Ceti IV.

All from Phyllis Gotlieb, one of science fiction's liveliest and most original voices!

PHYLLIS GOTLIEB

SON OF THE MORNING

AND OTHER STORIES

ACE SCIENCE FICTION BOOKS
NEW YORK

SON OF THE MORNING
AND OTHER STORIES

An Ace Science Fiction Book / published by arrangement with
the author and her agent, Virginia Kidd

PRINTING HISTORY
Ace Original / December 1983

ISBN: 0-441-77221-8

Ace Science Fiction Books are published by
The Berkley Publishing Group,
200 Madison Avenue, New York, New York 10016.
PRINTED IN THE UNITED STATES OF AMERICA

— Acknowledgments —

"Tauf Aleph" © 1981 by Phyllis Gotlieb from *More Wandering Stars*, Doubleday and Company, Inc., edited by Jack Dann, © 1981 by Jack Dann.

"Sunday's Child" from *Cosmos*, September 1977, © by *Baronet Publishing Company*.

"The Military Hospital" from *Fourteen Stories High*, edited by David Helwig and Tom Marshall, © 1971 by *Oberon Press,* Canada, and from *The Magazine of Fantasy and Science Fiction,* May 1974, © by *Mercury Press, Inc.*

"Gingerbread Boy" from *IF Science Fiction*, January 1961, © 1960 by *Digest Publications Corporation*.

"Blue Apes" from *The Berkley Showcase*, Vol. 4, © 1981 by *Berkley Publishing Corporation*.

"Phantom Foot" from *Amazing Science Fiction*, December 1959, © by *Ziff-Davis Publishing Company*.

"A Grain of Manhood" from *Fantastic Science Fiction Stories*, September 1959, © by *Ziff-Davis Publishing Company*.

"ms & mr frankenstein" and "was/man" from *The Works: Collected Poems* by Phyllis Gotlieb, *Calliope Press*, Canada, © 1978 by Phyllis Gotlieb.

"Son of the Morning" from *The Magazine of Fantasy and Science Fiction*, June 1971, © by *Mercury Press, Inc.*, and from *A Judgment of Dragons*, by Phyllis Gotlieb, © 1980 by *Berkley Publishing Corporation*.

Many thanks
    to H. L. Gold who recommended my work
    to Harry Altshuler who first sold it
    to Cele Goldsmith Lalli who first published it
    and particularly to Virginia Kidd
    who keeps it alive and growing

— Table of Contents —

− Tauf Aleph −

Samuel Zohar ben Reuven Begelman lived to a great age in the colony Pardes on Tau Ceti IV and in his last years he sent the same message with his annual request for supplies to Galactic Federation Central: *Kindly send one mourner/gravedigger so I can die in peace respectfully.*

And Sol III replied through GalFed Central with the unvarying answer: *Regret cannot find one Jew yours faithfully.*

Because there was not one other identifiable Jew in the known universe, for with the opening of space the people had scattered and intermarried, and though their descendants were as numerous, in the fulfillment of God's promise, as the sands on the shore and the stars in the heavens, there was not one called Jew, nor any other who could speak Hebrew and pray for the dead. The home of the ancestors was emptied: it was now a museum where perfect simulacra performed 7500 years of history in hundreds of languages for tourists from the breadth of the Galaxy.

In Central, Hrsipliy the Xiploid said to Castro-Ibanez the Solthree, "It is a pity we cannot spare one person to help that poor *juddar*." She meant by this term: body/breath/spirit/sonofabitch, being a woman with three tender hearts.

Castro-Ibanez, who had one kind heart and one hard head, answered, "How can we? He is the last colonist on that world and refuses to be moved; we keep him alive at great expense already." He considered for some time and added, "I think perhaps we might send him a robot. One that can dig and speak recorded prayers. Not one of the new expensive ones. We ought to have some old machine good enough for last rites."

O/G5/842 had been resting in a very dark corner of Stores for 324 years, his four coiled arms retracted and his four hinged ones resting on his four wheeled feet. Two of his arms terminated in huge scoop shovels, for he had been an ore miner, and he was also fitted with treads and sucker-pods. He was very great in size; they made giant machines in those days. New technologies had left him useless; he was not even worthy of being dismantled for parts.

It happened that this machine was wheeled into the light, scoured of rust, and lubricated. His ore-scoops were replaced with small ones retrieved from Stores and suitable for grave-digging, but in respect to Sam Begelman he was not given a recording: he was rewired and supplemented with an almost new logic and given orders and permission to go and learn. Once he had done so to the best of his judgment he would travel out with Begelman's supplies and land. This took great expense, but less than an irreplaceable person or a new machine; it fulfilled the Galactic-Colonial contract. O/G would not return, Begelman would rest in peace, no one would recolonize Tau Ceti IV.

O/G5/842 emerged from his corner. In the Library he caused little more stir than the seven members of the Khagodi embassy (650 kilos apiece) who were searching out a legal point of intra-Galactic law. He was too broad to occupy a cubicle, and let himself be stationed in a basement exhibit room where techs wired him to sensors, sockets, inlets, outlets, screens, and tapes. Current flowed, light came, and he said, LET ME KNOW SAMUEL ZOHAR BEN REUVEN BEGELMAN DOCTOR OF MEDICINE AND WHAT IT MEANS THAT HE IS A JEW.

He recorded the life of Sam Begelman; he absorbed Hebrew, Aramaic, Greek; he learned Torah, which is Law: day one. He learned Writings, Prophets, and then Mishna, which is the first exegesis of Law: day the second. He learned Talmud (Palestinian and Babylonian), which is the completion of Law, and Tosefta, which are ancillary writings and divergent opinions in Law: day the third. He read thirty-five hundred years of Commentary and Responsa: day the fourth. He learned Syriac, Arabic, Latin, Yiddish, French, English, Italian, Spanish, Dutch. At the point of learning Chinese he experienced, for the first time, a synapse. For the sake of reading marginally relevant writings by fewer than ten Sino-Japanese Judaic poets it was not worth learning their vast languages; this gave him pause: two nanoseconds: day the fifth. Then he plunged, day the sixth, into the literatures written in the languages he had absorbed. Like all machines, he did not sleep, but on the seventh day he unhooked himself from Library equipment, gave up his space, and returned to his corner. In this place he turned down all motor and afferent circuits and indexed, concordanced, cross-referenced. He developed synapses exponentially to complete and fulfill his logic. Then he shut it down and knew nothing.

But Galactic Federation said, O/G5/842, AROUSE YOURSELF AND BOARD THE SHIP *Aleksandr Nevskii* AT LOADING DOCK 377 BOUND FOR TAU CETI IV.

At the loading dock, Flight Admissions said, YOUR SPACE HAS BEEN PREEMPTED FOR SHIPMENT 20 TONNES *Nutrivol* POWDERED DRINKS (39 FLAVORS) TO DESERT WORLDS TAU CETI II AND III.

O/G knew nothing of such matters and said, I HAVE NOT BEEN INSTRUCTED SO. He called Galactic Federation and said, MOD 0885 THE SPACE ASSIGNED FOR ME IS NOT PERMITTED IT HAS BEEN PREEMPTED BY A BEING CALLED *Nutrivol* SENDING POWDERED DRINKS TO TAU CETI INNER WORLDS.

Mod 0885 said, I AM CHECKING. YES. THAT COMPANY WENT INTO RECEIVERSHIP ONE STANDARD YEAR AGO. I SUSPECT SMUGGLING AND BRIBERY. I WILL WARN.

THE SHIP WILL BE GONE BY THEN MOD 08 WHAT AM I TO DO?

INVESTIGATE, MOD 842.

HOW AM I TO DO THAT?

USE YOUR LOGIC, said Mod 0885 and signed off.

O/G went to the loading dock and stood in the way. The beings ordering the loading mechs said, "You are blocking this shipment! Get out of the way, you old pile of scrap!"

O/G said in his speaking voice, "I am not in the way. I am to board ship for Pardes and it is against the law for this cargo to take my place." He extruded a limb in gesture toward the stacked cartons; but he had forgotten his strength (for he had been an ore miner) and his new scoop smashed five cartons at one blow; the foam packing parted and white crystals poured from the break. O/G regretted this very greatly for one fraction of a second before he remembered how those beings who managed the mines behaved in the freezing darkness of lonely worlds and moons. He extended his chemical sensor and dipping it into the crystal stream said, "Are fruit drinks for desert worlds now made without fructose but with dextroamphetamine sulfate, diacetylmorphine, 2-acetyl-tetrahydrocannabinol—"

Some of the beings at the loading gate cried out curses and many machines began to push and beat at him. But O/G pulled in his limbs and planted his sucker-pods and did not stir. He had been built to work in many gravities near absolute zero under rains of avalanches. He would not be moved.

Presently uniformed officials came and took away those beings and their cargo, and said to O/G, "You too must come and answer questions."

But he said, "I was ordered by Galactic Federation to board this ship for Tau Ceti IV, and you may consult the legal department of Colonial Relations, but I will not be moved."

Because they had no power great enough to move him they consulted among themselves and with the legal department and said, "You may pass."

Then O/G took his assigned place in the cargo hold of the *Aleksandr Nevskii* and after the ship lifted for Pardes he turned down his logic because he had been ordered to think for himself for the first time and this confused him very much.

The word *pardes* is "orchard" but the world Pardes was a bog of mud, foul gases, and shifting terrains, where attempts at terraforming failed again and again until colonists left in disgust and many lawsuits plagued the courts of Interworld Colonies at GalFed. O/G landed there in a stripped shuttle which served as a glider. It was not meant to rise again and it broke and sank in the marshes, but O/G plowed mud, scooping the way before him, and rode on treads, dragging the supplies behind him on a sledge, for 120 kilometers before he came within sight of the colony.

Fierce creatures many times his size, with serpentine necks and terrible fangs, tried to prey on him. He wished to appease them, and offered greetings in many languages, but they would only break their teeth on him. He stunned one with a blow to the head, killed another by snapping its neck, and they left him alone.

The colony center was a concrete dome surrounded by a forcefield that gave out sparks, hissing and crackling. Around it he found many much smaller creatures splashing in pools and scrambling to and fro at the mercy of one of the giants who held a small being writhing in its jaws.

O/G cried in a loud voice, "Go away you savage creature!" and the serpent beast dropped its mouthful, but seeing no great danger dipped its neck to pick it up again. So O/G extended his four hinged limbs to their greatest length and, running behind the monster, seized the pillars of its rear legs, heaving up and out until its spine broke and it fell flattened in mud, thrashing the head on the long neck until it drove it into the ground and smothered.

The small beings surrounded O/G without fear, though he was very great to them, and cried in their thin voices, "Shalom-shalom, Savior!"

O/G was astonished to hear these strangers speaking clear Hebrew. He had not known a great many kinds of living persons during his experience, but among those displayed in the corridors of the Library basement these most resembled walruses. "I am not a savior, men of Pardes," he said in the same language. "Are you speaking your native tongue?"

"No, Redeemer. We are Cnidori and we spoke Cnidri before we reached this place in our wanderings, but we learned the language of Rav Zohar because he cared for us when we were lost and starving."

"Now Zohar has put up a barrier and shut you out—and I am not a redeemer—but what has happened to that man?"

"He became very ill and shut himself away because he said he was not fit to look upon. The food he helped us store is eaten and the Unds are ravaging us."

"There are some here that will ravage you no longer. Do you eat the flesh of these ones?"

"No, master. Only what grows from the ground."

He saw that beneath the draggling gray moustaches their teeth were the incisors and molars of herbivores. "I am not your master. See if there is food to gather here and I will try to reach Zohar."

"First we will skin one of these to make tents for shelter. It rains every hour." They rose on their haunches in the bog, and he discovered that though their rear limbs were flippers like those of aquatic animals, their forelimbs bore three webbed fingers apiece and each Cnidor had a small shell knife slung over one shoulder. All, moreover, had what appeared to be one mammalian teat and one male generative organ ranged vertically on their bellies, and they began to seem less and less like walruses to O/G. The prime Cnidor continued, "Tell us what name pleases you if you are offended by the ways we address you."

"I have no name but a designation: O/G5/842. I am only a machine."

"You are a machine of deliverance and so we will call you Golem."

In courtesy O/G accepted the term. "This forcefield is so noisy it probably has a malfunction. It is not wise to touch it."

"No, we are afraid of it."

Golem scooped mud from the ground and cast it at the forcefield; great lightnings and hissings issued where it landed. "I doubt even radio would cross that."

"Then how can we reach Zohar, Golem, even if he is still alive?"

"I will cry out, Cnidori. Go to a distance and cover your ears, because my voice can pierce a mountain of lead ore."

They did not know what that was, but they removed themselves, and Golem turned his volume to its highest and called in a mighty voice, *"Samuel Zohar ben Reuven Begelman turn off your forcefield for I have come from Galactic Federation to help you!!!"*

Even the forcefield buckled for one second at the sound of his voice.

After a long silence, Golem thought he heard a whimper, from a great distance. "I believe he is alive but cannot reach the control."

A Cnidor said, trembling, "The Unds have surely heard you, because they are coming back again."

And they did indeed come back, bellowing, hooting, and striking with their long necks. Golem tied one great snake neck in a knot and cried again, *"Let us in, Zohar, or the Unds will destroy all of your people!!!"*

The forcefield vanished, and the Cnidori scuttled over its border beneath the sheltering arms of Golem, who cracked several fanged heads like nutshells with his scoops.

"Now put up your shield!!!" And the people were saved.

When Golem numbered them and they declared that only two were missing among forty he said, "Wait here and feed yourselves."

The great outer doorway for working machines was open, but the hangar and storerooms were empty of them; they had been removed by departing colonists. None had been as huge as Golem, and here he removed his scoops and unhinged his outer carapace with its armor, weapons, and storage compartments, for he wished to break no more doorways than necessary. Behind him he pulled the sledge with the supplies.

When his heat sensor identified the locked door behind which Zohar was to be found, he removed the doorway as gently as he could.

"I want to die in peace and you are killing me with noise," said a weak voice out of the darkness.

By infrared Golem saw the old man crumpled on the floor by the bed, filthy and half naked, with the shield control resting near his hand. He turned on light. The old man was nearly bald, wasted and yellow-skinned, wrinkled, his rough beard tangled and clotted with blood.

"Zohar?"

Sam Begelman opened his eyes and saw a tremendous machine, multi-armed and with wheels and treads, wound with coiling tubes and wires, studded with dials. At its top was a dome banded with sensor lenses, and it turned this way and that to survey the room. "What are you?" he whispered in terror. "Where is my kaddish?"

He spoke in *lingua,* but O/G replied in Hebrew. "You know you are the last Jew in the known universe, Rav Zohar. There is no one but me to say prayers for you."

"Then let me die without peace," said Begelman, and closed his eyes.

But Golem knew the plan of the station, and within five

minutes he reordered the bed in cleanliness, placed the old
man on it, set up an i.v., cleansed him, and injected him with
the drugs prepared for him. The old man's hands pushed at
him and pushed at him, uselessly. "You are only a machine,"
he croaked. "Can't you understand that a machine can't
pray?"

"Yes, master. I would have told that to Galactic Federation, but I knew they would not believe me, not being Jews."

"I am not your master. Why truly did you come?"

"I was made new again and given orders. My growth in
logic now allows me to understand that I cannot be of use to
you in exactly the way Galactic Federation wished, but I can
still make you more comfortable."

"I don't care!" Begelman snarled. "Who needs a machine?"

"The Cnidori needed me to save them from the Unds when
you shut them out, and they tried to call me Savior, Redeemer,
master; I refused because I *am* a machine, but I let them call
me Golem because I am a machine of deliverance."

Begelman sniffed. But the sick yellow of his skin was gone;
his face was faintly pink and already younger by a few years.

"Shmuel Zohar ben Reuven Begelman, why do you allow
those helpless ones to call you Rav Zohar and speak in your
language?"

"You nudnik of a machine, my name is not Samuel and certainly not Shmuel! It is Zohar, and I let myself be called Sam
because *zohar* is 'splendor' and you can't go through life as
Splendor Begelman! I taught those Cnidori the Law and the
Prophets to hear my own language spoken because my
children are gone and my wife is dead. That is why they call
me Teacher. And I shut them out so that they would be forced
to make their own way in life before they began to call *me*
Redeemer! What do you call yourself, Golem?"

"My designation is O/G5/842."

"Ah. Og the giant King of Bashan. That seems suitable."

"Yes, Zohar. That one your Rabbi Moshe killed in the land
of Kana'an with all his people for no great provocation. But O
is the height of my oxygen tolerance in Solthree terms; I cannot work at gravities of less than five newtons, and eight four
two is my model number. Now Zohar, if you demand it I will
turn myself off and be no more. But the people are within

your gate; some of them have been killed and they must still be cared for."

Zohar sighed, but he smiled a little as well. Yet he spoke slowly because he was very ill. "Og ha-Golem, before you learn how to tune an argument too fine remember that Master of the Word is one of the names of Satan. Moshe Rabbenu was a bad-tempered man but he did very greatly, and I am no kind of warrior. Take care of the people, and me too if your . . . logic demands it—and I will consider how to conduct myself off the world properly."

"I am sure your spirit will free itself in peace, Zohar. As for me, my shuttle is broken, I am wanted nowhere else, and I will rust in Pardes."

Og ha-Golem went out of the presence of the old man but it seemed to him as if there were some mild dysfunction in his circuits, for he was mindful—if that is the term—of Begelman's concept of the Satan, Baal Davar, and he did not know for certain if what he had done by the prompting of his logic was right action. How can I know? he asked himself. By what harms and what saves, he answered. By what seems to harm and what seems to save, says the Master of the Word.

Yet he continued by the letter of his instructions from Galactic Federation, and these were to give the old man comfort. For the Cnidori he helped construct tents, because they liked water under their bellies but not pouring on their heads. With his own implements he flensed the bodies of the dead Unds, cleaned their skins, and burned their flesh; it was not kosher for Begelman and attracted bothersome scavengers. He did this while Rav Zohar was sleeping and spoke to the people in his language; they had missed it when he was ill. "Zohar believes you must learn to take care of yourselves, against the Unds and on your world, because you cannot now depend on him."

"We would do that, Golem, but we would also like to give comfort to our Teacher."

Og ha-Golem was disturbed once again by the ideas that pieced themselves together in his logic and said to Begelman, "Zohar, you have taught the Cnidori so well that now they are capable of saying the prayers you long for so greatly. Is there a way in which that can be made permissible?"

The old man folded his hands and looked about the bare

and cracking walls of the room, as Golem had first done, and then back at him. "In this place?" he whispered. "Do you know what you are saying?"

"Yes, Zohar."

"How they may be made *Jews*?"

"They are sentient beings. What is there to prevent it?"

Begelman's face became red and Og checked his blood-pressure monitor. "Prevent it! What is there to them that would make Jews? Everything they eat is neutral, neither kosher nor tref, so what use is the law of Kashrut? They live in mud—where are the rules of bathing and cleanliness? They had never had any kind of god or any thought of one, as far as they tell me—what does prayer mean? Do you know how they procreate? Could you imagine? They are so completely her-maphroditic the word is meaningless. They pair long enough to raise children together, but only until the children grow teeth and can forage. What you see that looks like a penis is really an ovipositor: each Cnidor who is ready deposits eggs in the pouch of another, and an enzyme of the eggs stimulates the semen glands inside, and when one or two eggs become fertilized the pouch seals until the fetus is of a size to make the fluid pressure around it break the seal, and the young crawls up the belly of the parent to suckle on the teat. Even if one or two among twenty are born incomplete, not one is anything you might call male or female! So tell me, what do you do with all the laws of marriage and divorce, sexual behavior, the duties of the man at prayer and the woman with the child?"

He was becoming out of breath and Og checked oxygen and heart monitors. "I am not a man or woman either and though I know the Law I am ignorant in experience. I was thinking merely of prayers that God might listen to in charity or appreciation. I did not mean to upset you. I am not fulfilling my duties."

"Leave me."

Og turned an eyecell to the dripping of the i.v. and removed catheter and urine bag. "You are nearly ready to rise from your bed and feed yourself, Zohar. Perhaps when you feel more of a man you may reconsider."

"Just go away." He added, snarling, "God doesn't need any more Jews!"

"Yes, they would look ridiculous in skullcaps and prayer

shawls with all those fringes dragging in mud . . ."

Zohar, was that why you drove them out into the wild?

Og gathered brushwood and made a great fire. He cut woody vines and burnt them into heaps of charcoal. He gathered and baked clay into blocks and built a kiln. Then he pulled his sledge for 120 kilometers, and dug until he found enough pieces of the glider for his uses. He fired the kiln to a great heat, softened the fragments, and reshaped them into the huge scoops he had been deprived of. They were not as fine and strong as the originals, but very nearly as exact.

He consulted maps of Pardes, which lay near the sea. He began digging channels and heaping breakwaters to divert a number of streams and drain some of the marshes of Pardes, and to keep the sea from washing over it during storms, and this left pools of fresher water for the Cnidori.

Sometimes the sun shone. On a day that was brighter and dryer than usual Begelman came outside the station, supporting himself on canes, and watched the great Golem at work. He had never seen Og in full armor with his scoops. During its renewal his exterior had been bonded with a coating that retarded rust; this was dull gray and the machine had no beauty in the eyes of a Solthree, but he worked with an economy of movement that lent him grace. He was surrounded by Cnidori with shovels of a size they could use, and they seemed to Begelman like little children playing in mud piles, getting in the way while the towering machine worked in silence without harming the small creatures or allowing them to annoy him.

Og, swiveling the beam of his eyecell, saw an old, white-bearded Solthree with a homely face of some dignity; he looked weak but not ill. His hair was neatly trimmed, he wore a blue velvet skullcap worked with silver threads, black trousers, and zippered jacket, below which showed the fringes of his *tallith katan*. He matched approximately the thousands of drawings, paintings, and photographs of dignified old Jews stored in Og's memory: Og had dressed him to match.

Begelman said, "What are you doing?"

"I am stabilizing the land in order to grow crops of oilseed, lugwort, and greenpleat, which are nourishing both to you and the Cnidori. I doubt Galactic Federation is going to give us anything more, and I also wish to store supplies. If other

wandering tribes of Cnidori cross this territory it is better to
share our plenty than fight over scarcity."

"You're too good to be true," Begelman muttered.

Og had learned something of both wit and sarcasm from
Begelman but did not give himself the right to use them on the
old man. His logic told him that he, the machine, had nothing
to fear from a Satan who was not even a concept in the
mainstream of Jewish belief, but that Zohar was doing battle
with the common human evil in his own spirit. He said,
"Zohar, these Cnidori have decided to take Hebrew names,
and they are calling themselves by letters: Aleph, Bet, Gim-
mel, and when those end at Tauf, by numbers: Echod,
Shtaim, Sholosh. This does not seem correct to me but they
will not take my word for it. Will you help them?"

Begelman's mouth worked for a moment, twisting as if to
say, What have these to do with such names? but Cnidori
crowded round him and their black eyes reflected very small
lights in the dim sun; they were people of neither fur nor
feather, but scales that resembled both: leaf-shaped plates the
size of a thumb with central ridges and branching radials;
these were very fine in texture and refracted rainbow colors on
brighter days.

The old man sighed and said, "Dear people, if you wish to
take names in Hebrew you must take the names of human
beings like those in Law and Prophets. The names of the
Fathers: Avraham, Yitzhak, Yaakov; the Tribes: Yehuda,
Shimon, Binyamin, or if you prefer female names, the
Mothers: Sarai, Rivkah, Rakhael, Leah. Whichever seems
good to you." The Cnidori thanked him with pleasure and
went away content.

Begelman said to Og, "Next thing you know they will want
a Temple." Og suspected what they would ask for next, but
said, "I believe we must redesign the forcefield to keep the
Unds out of the cultivated areas. Perhaps we have enough
components in Stores or I can learn to make them."

He had been scouting for Unds every fourth or fifth day and
knew their movements. They had been avoiding the Station in
fear of Og and the malfunctioning forcefield but he believed
that they would attack again when the place was quiet, and
they did so on the night of that day when the Cnidori took
names. The field had been repaired and withstood their batter-

ing without shocking them; their cries were terrible to hear, and sometimes their bones cracked against the force. They fell back after many hours, leaving Og with earthworks to repair and two of their bodies to destroy.

In the morning when he had finished doing this he found Begelman lying on a couch in the Common Room, a book of prayers on his lap, faced by a group of ten Cnidori. All eleven spoke at once, Begelman with crackling anger in his voice, the Cnidori softly but with insistence.

Begelman cried out when he saw Og, "Now they tell me they must have surnames!"

"I expected so, Zohar. They know that you are ben Reuven and they have accepted your language and the names of your people. Is this not reasonable?"

"I have no authority to make Jews of them!"

"You are the only authority left. You have taught them."

"Damn you! You have been pushing for this!"

"I have pushed for nothing except to make you well. I taught nothing." Within him the Master of the Word spoke: This is true, but is it right?

Begelman in anger clapped shut his book, but it was very old and its spine cracked slightly; he lifted and kissed it in repentence. He spoke in a low voice, "What does it matter now? There is no surname they can be given except the name of convert, which is ben Avraham or bat Avraham, according to the gender of the first name. And how can they be converts when they can keep no Law and do not even know God? And what does it matter now?" He threw up his hands. "Let them be b'nei Avraham!"

But the Cnidori prime, who had taken the name Binyamin, that is, Son of the Right Hand, said, "We do not wish to be b'nei Avraham, but b'nei Zohar, because we say to you, Og ha-Golem, and to you, Rav Zohar, that because Zohar has been as a father to us we feel as sons to him."

Og feared that the old man might now become truly ill with rage, and indeed his hands trembled on the book, but he said quietly enough, "My children, Jews do not behave so. Converts must become Jews in the ways allowed to them. If you do not understand, I have not taught you well enough, and I am too old to teach more. I have yielded too much already to a people who do not worship God, and I am not even a Rabbi with such small authority as is given to one."

"Rav Zohar, we have come to tell you that we have sworn to worship your God."

"But you must not worship me."

"But we may worship the God who created such a man as you, and such teachings as you have taught us, and those men who made the great Golem." They went away quickly and quietly without speaking further.

"They will be back again," Begelman said. "And again and again. Why did I ever let you in? Lord God King of the Universe, what am I to do?"

It *is* right, Og told the Master of the Word. "You are more alive and healthy than you have long been, Zohar," he said. "And you have people who love you. Can you not let them do so?"

He sought out Binyamin. "Do not trouble Rav Zohar with demands he cannot fulfill, no matter how much you desire to honor him. Later I will ask him to think if there is a way he can do as you wish, within the Law."

"We will do whatever you advise, Golem."

Og continued with his work, but while he was digging he turned up a strange artifact and he had a foreboding. At times he had discovered potsherds which were the remnants of clay vessels the Cnidori had made to cook vegetables they could not digest raw, and this discovery was an almost whole cylinder of the same texture, color, and markings; one of its end rims was blackened by burn marks, and dark streaks ran up its sides. He did not know what it was but it seemed sinister to him; in conscience he had no choice but to show it to Zohar.

"It does not seem like a cooking vessel," he said.

"No," said Begelman. "It does not." He pointed to a place inside where there was a leaf-shaped Cnidori scale, blackened, clinging to its wall, and to two other burn marks of the same shape. Strangely, to Og, his eyes filled with tears.

"Perhaps it is a casing in which they dispose of their dead," Og said.

Zohar wiped his eyes and said, "No. It is a casing in which they make them dead. Many were killed by Unds, and some have starved, and the rest die of age. All those they weight and sink into the marshes. This is a sacrifice. They have a god, and its name is Baal." He shook his head. "My children." He wept for a moment again and said, "Take this away and smash it until there is not a piece to recognize."

Og did so, but Zohar locked himself into his room and would not answer to anyone.

Og did not know what to do now. He was again as helpless as he had been on the loading dock where he had first learned to use his logic.

The Cnidori came to inquire of Golem and he told them what had happened. They said, "It is true that our ancestors worshipped a Being and made sacrifices, but none of that was done after Zohar gave us help. We were afraid he and his God would hold us in contempt."

"Both Zohar and his God have done imperfect acts. But now I will leave him alone, because he is very troubled."

"But it is a great sin in his eyes," said Binyamin sorrowfully. "I doubt that he will ever care for us again."

And Og continued with his work, but he thought his logic had failed him, in accordance with Zohar's taunts.

In the evening a Cnidor called Elyahu came writhing toward him along the ground in great distress. "Come quickly!" he called. "Binyamin is doing *nidset!*"

"What is that?"

"Only come quickly!" Elyahu turned back in haste. Og unclipped his scoops and followed, overtaking the small creature and bearing him forward in his arms. They found Binyamin and other Cnidori in a grove of ferns. They had built a smoky fire and were placing upon it a fresh cylinder: a network of withy branches had been woven into the bottom of it.

"No, no!" cried Og, but they did not regard him; the cylinder was set on the fire and smoke came out of its top. Then the Cnidori helped Binyamin climb over its edge and he dropped inward, into the smoke.

"No!" Og cried again, and he toppled the vessel from the fire, but without violence so that Binyamin would not be harmed. *"You shall make* no *sacrifices!"* Then he tapped it so that it split, and the Cnidor lay in its halves, trembling.

"*That* is *nidset*, Golem," said Elyahu.

But Golem plucked up the whimpering Cnidor. "Why were you doing such a terrible thing, Binyamin?"

"We thought," Binyamin said in a quavering voice, "we

thought that all of the gods were angry with us—our old god
for leaving him and our new one for having worshipped the
old—and that a sacrifice would take away the anger of all.''

"That confounds my logic somewhat.'' Og set down
Binyamin, beat out the fire, and cast the pieces of the cylinder
far away. "All gods are One, and the One forgives whoever
asks. Now come. I believe I hear the Unds again, and we need
shelter close to home until we can build a wider one.''

Then the Cnidori raised a babble of voices. "No! What
good is such a God if even Zohar does not listen to Him and
forgive us?''

It seemed to Og for one moment as if the Cnidori felt
themselves cheated of a sacrifice; he put this thought aside.
"The man is sick and old, and he is not thinking clearly either,
while you have demanded much of him.''

"Then, Golem, we will demand no more, but die among the
Unds!'' The shrieking of the beasts grew louder on the night
winds but the Cnidori drew their little knives and would not
stir.

"Truly you are an outrageous people,'' said Golem. "But I
am only a machine.'' He extended his four hinged arms and
his four coil arms and bearing them up in their tens raced with
them on treads and wheels until they were within the safety of
the forcefield.

But when he set them down they grouped together closely
near the field and would not say one word.

Og considered the stubborn Zohar on the one side, and the
stubborn b'nei Avraham on the other, and he thought that
perhaps it was time for him to cease his being. A great storm
of lightning and thunder broke out; the Unds did not approach and within the forcefield there was stillness.

He disarmed himself and stood before Zohar's door. He
considered the sacrifice of Yitzhak, and the Golden Calf, and
how Moshe Rabbenu had broken the Tables, and many other
excellent examples, and he spoke quietly.

"Zohar, you need not answer, but you must listen. Your
people tell me they have made no sacrifices since they knew
you. But Binyamin, who longs to call himself your son, has
tried to sacrifice himself to placate whatever gods may forgive
his people, and would have died if I had not prevented him.
After that they were ready to let the Unds kill them. I pre-

vented that also, but they will not speak to me, or to you if you do not forgive them. I cannot do any more here and I have nothing further to say to you. Good-bye."

He turned from the door without waiting, but heard it open, and Zohar's voice cried out, "Og, where are you going?"

"To the storeroom, to turn myself off. I have always said I was no more than a machine, and now I have reached the limit of my logic and my usefulness."

"No, Golem, wait! Don't take everything from me!" The old man was standing with hands clasped and hair awry. "There must be some end to foolishness," he whispered. "Where are they?"

"Out by the field near the entrance," Og said. "You will see them when the lightning flashes."

The Holy One, blessed be His Name, gave Zohar one more year, and in that time Og ha-Golem built and planted, and in this he was helped by the b'nei Avraham. They made lamps from their vegetable oils and lit them on Sabbaths and the Holy Days calculated by Zohar. In season they mated and their bellies swelled. Zohar tended them when his strength allowed, as in old days, and when Elyahu died of brain hemorrhage and Yitzhak of a swift-growing tumor which nothing could stop, he led the mourners in prayer for their length of days. One baby was stillborn, but ten came from the womb in good health; they were gray-pink, toothless, and squalled fearfully, but Zohar fondled and praised them. "These people were twelve when I found them," he said to Og. "Now there are forty-six and I have known them for five generations." He told the Cnidori, "Children of Avraham, Jews have converted, and Jews have adopted, but never children of a different species, so there is no precedent I can find to let any one of you call yourself a child of Zohar, but as a community I see no reason why you cannot call yourselves b'nei Zohar, my children, collectively."

The people were wise enough by now to accept this decision without argument. They saw that the old man's time of renewed strength was done and he was becoming frailer every day; they learned to make decisions for themselves. Og too helped him now only when he asked. Zohar seemed content, although sometimes he appeared about to speak and remained silent. The people noticed these moods and spoke to Og of them occasionally, but Og said, "He must tend to his spirit for himself, b'nei Avraham. My work is done."

He had cleared the land in many areas around the station, and protected them with forcefields whose antennas he had made with forges he had built. The Unds were driven back into their wilds of cave and valley; they were great and terrible, but magnificent life-forms of their own kind and he wished to kill no more. He had only to wait for the day when Zohar would die in peace.

Once a day Og visited him in the Common Room where he spent most of his time reading or with his hands on his book and his eyes to the distance. One peaceful day when they were alone he said to Og, "I must tell you this while my head is still clear. And I can tell only you." He gathered his thoughts for a moment. "It took me a long time to realize that I was the last Jew, though Galactic Federation kept saying so. I had been long alone, but that realization made me fiercely, hideously lonely. Perhaps you don't understand. I think you do. And then my loneliness turned itself inside out and I grew myself a kind of perverse pride. The last! The last! I would close the Book that was opened those thousands of years before, as great in a way as the first had been . . . but I had found the Cnidori, and they were a people to talk with and keep from going mad in loneliness—but Jews! They were ugly, and filthy, and the opposite of everything I saw as human. I despised them. Almost, I hated them . . . that was what wanted to be Jews! And I had started it by teaching them, because I was so lonely—and I had no way to stop it except to destroy them, and I nearly did that! And you—" He began to weep with the weak passion of age.

"Zohar, do not weep. You will make yourself ill."

"My soul is sick! It is like a boil that needs lancing, and it hurts so much! Who will forgive me?" He reached out and grasped one of Og's arms. "Who?"

"*They* will forgive you anything—but if you ask you will only hurt yourself more deeply. And I make no judgments."

"But I must be judged!" Zohar cried. "Let me have a little peace to die with!"

"If I must, then, Zohar, I judge you a member of humanity who has saved more people than would be alive without him. I think you could not wish better."

Zohar said weakly, "You knew all the time, didn't you?"

"Yes," said Og. "I believe I did."

But Zohar did not hear, for he had fainted.

He woke in his bed and when his eyes opened he saw Og beside him. "What are you?" he said, and Og stared with his unwinking eye; he thought Zohar's mind had left him.

Then Zohar laughed. "My mind is not gone yet. But what are you, really, Og? You cannot answer. Ah well . . . would you ask my people to come here now, so I can say good-bye? I doubt it will be long; they raise all kinds of uproar, but at least they can't cry."

Og brought the people, and Zohar blessed them all and each; they were silent, in awe of him. He seemed to fade while he spoke, as if he were being enveloped in mist. "I have no advice for you," he whispered at last. "I have taught all I know and that is little enough because I am not very wise, but you will find the wise among yourselves. Now, whoever remembers, let him recite me a psalm. Not the twenty-third. I want the hundred and fourth, and leave out that stupid part at the end where the sinners are consumed from the earth."

But it was only Og who remembered that psalm in its entirety, and spoke the words describing the world Zohar had come from an unmeasurable time ago.

O Lord my God You are very great!
You are clothed with honor and majesty,
Who covers Yourself with light as with a garment,
Who has stretched out the heavens like a tent,
Who has laid the beams of Your chambers on the waters,
Who makes the clouds Your chariot,
Who rides on the wings of the wind,
Who makes the winds Your messengers,
fire and flame Your ministers . . .

When he was finished, Zohar said the *Shema*, which tells that God is One, and died. And Og thought that he must be pleased with his dying.

Og removed himself. He let the b'nei Avraham prepare the

body, wrap it in the prayer shawl, and bury it. He waited during the days in which the people sat in mourning, and when they had gotten up he said, "Surely my time is come." He traveled once about the domains he had created for their inhabitants and returned to say good-bye in fewer words than Zohar had done.

But the people cried, "No, Golem, no! How can you leave us now when we need you so greatly?"

"You are not children. Zohar told you that you must manage for yourselves."

"But we have so much to learn. We do not know how to use the radio, and we want to tell Galactic Federation that Zohar is dead, and of all he and you have done for us."

"I doubt that Galactic Federation is interested," said Og.

"Nevertheless we will learn!"

They were a stubborn people. Og said, "I will stay for that, but no longer."

Then Og discovered he must teach them enough *lingua* to make themselves understood by Galactic Federation. All were determined learners, and a few had a gift for languages. When he had satisfied himself that they were capable, he said, "Now."

And they said, "Og ha-Golem, why must you waste yourself? We have so much to discover about the God we worship and the men who have worshipped Him!"

"Zohar taught you all he knew, and that was a great deal."

"Indeed he taught us the Law and the Prophets, but he did not teach us the tongues of Aramaic or Greek, or Writings, or Mishna, or Talmud (Palestinian and Babylonian), or Tosefta, or Commentary, or—"

"But why must you learn all that?"

"To keep it for others who may wish to know of it when we are dead."

So Og surrounded himself with them, the sons and daughters of Avraham and their children, who now took surnames of their own from womb parents—and all of them b'nei Zohar —and he began: "Here is Mishna, given by word of mouth from Scribe to Scribe for a thousand years. Fifth Division, *Nezikin*, which is Damages; *Baba Metzia*: the Middle Gate: 'If two took hold of a garment and one said, "I found it," and the other said, "*I* found it," or one said, "I bought it," and the other said, "*I* bought it," each takes an oath that he claims not less than half and they divide it . . .' "

In this manner Og ha-Golem, who had endless patience, lived a thousand and twenty years. By radio the Galaxy heard of the strange work of strange creatures, and over hundreds of years colonists who wished to call themselves b'nei Avraham drifted inward to re-create the world Pardes. They were not great in number, but they made a world. From *pardes* is derived "Paradise" but in the humble world of Pardes the peoples drained more of the swamps and planted fruitful orchards and pleasant gardens. All of these were named for their creators, except one.

When Og discovered that his functions were deteriorating he refused replacement parts and directed that when he stopped, all of his components must be dismantled and scattered to the ends of the earth, for fear of idolatry. But a garden was named for him, may his spirit rest in justice and his carapace rust in peace, and the one being who had no organic life is remembered with love among living things.

Here the people live, doing good and evil, contending with God and arguing with each other as usual, and all keep the Tradition as well as they can. Only the descendants of the aboriginal inhabitants, once called Cnidori, jealously guard for themselves the privilege of the name b'nei Zohar, and they are considered by the others to be snobbish, clannish, and stiff-necked.

— Sunday's Child —

The cloud lowered till it rested on the tips of the scraggy pines; lightning forked through it and thunder ricocheted between cloud and ground.

Nadja's eyes sharpened out of their stupor. She lay unmoving in the bunk and stared upward through the dome roof: a few autumn branches tapped it, beckoning. The plexiglass triangles stared back at her. Their shutters had been folded back because of the darkening sky, and the sharp locking triangles became one faceted eye. One became many and many became one and again many. Eyes.

They watched. Eyes. I's. Eye. Watch.

She screamed. "Stop!" And again, "Stop! No, no!"

She leaped and ran screaming through the partition doorway, down the hall, out the door, Mandros gaping, David frozen with a hand reached to grab her. Barefoot in the cold wind, the wet earth; her tattered nightgown billowed and her feet splattered mud at every step. "No! Don't!"

Lightning probed before her eyes, split a dead tree that burst into flames. Weeping, Nadja flung herself in its crèche, fainted, and lay like an animal roasting in coals.

David and Mandros pulled her out and dropped her on the ground; her hair was burning, and David tore off his jacket, squeezed out the flames with it. She lay snorting with her face half in mud, the rags of her black hair tangled in white ash.

"God damn it, never know what she'll do." David shoved his arm into the muck under her shoulders and lifted her.

Mandros took her by the stick legs and said nothing. The downpour began again, drenching the fire, and combed the thin dark hair straight down Mandros's skull, caught in globules through David's hair and beard. They hauled her inside, a dead weight, bruised and filthy.

Stella was waiting. "She badly hurt?"

"A few bruises, her hair got burned," David said. "I think she fainted."

He took the weight from Mandros and carried her to the small infirmary in the service complex. The skinny body hung over his shoulder; tears and raindrops fell from Nadja's face, with a flake of ash, a drop of blood from the bruised cheek, saliva from her open mouth. One wet red leaf was plastered on the side of her neck. He put her on the bed, took off his glasses and wiped them with thumb and fingers. "She shouldn't be here."

"Yeah." Stella ripped off the old nightgown in one powerful sweep. "Wash that and save it for patches."

"That *is* patches." He touched Nadja's face, gently turned her body over and back again. "Just needs a bit of antiseptic."

They bathed the gaunt pale shape, trimmed the singed hair, daubed the bruises. Nadja stirred and muttered, protested with feeble hands.

When she was settled they stood looking at her for a moment without pride in their pathetic handiwork. There might have been beauty in her with health and vigor. And sanity, Stella said to herself. That's not asking much. "You're right. She shouldn't be here."

David said morosely, "Try moving her and she'll fight like a cat in a sack." He left, and Nadja lay as she had done most of the days and nights, shifting sometimes to short intervals of lucidity or bursts of mania.

She had battered the door one midnight a couple of years earlier, howling a tale of beating, rape, pursuit. No one had pursued. David and Joseph Running Deer had picked up her trail through mud and scrub for a kilometer, and except for a fox and two rabbits no other tracks had crossed her path. She was haunted down the crazy labyrinth of her mind by imaginary furies; because of her terror they had let her stay, and she had never left.

"What is it?"

Nadja was trying to whisper. She licked her lips and swallowed.

"What?"

"Send . . . send . . ."

"What?" Stella lifted the blue-veined wrist, its pulse thready and vulnerable.

"Send Mandros. Here." Nadja's head whipped from side to side. "Mandros!"

"Him? Why do you want—"

"Mandros!" Her voice rose to a shriek.

"All right! Stay quiet and I'll get him."

She opened the door, and stepped back. Mandros was standing there, waiting, hair still falling in lines down his forehead, lower lip hanging loose from his teeth. His brown eyes narrowed, shifted from side to side like Nadja's head. Stella licked her lips. "She wants you."

"Alone," Nadja croaked.

Stella looked at her, and then at Mandros in the checked flannel shirt still so wet it clung to his shoulders. "Try to keep her calm." Mandros said nothing. She passed him, the door closed. She pulled herself away from it uneasily and through the triangles watched David outside in the rain rescuing what was left of his jacket.

In the common room Ephraim Markoosie was sorting out his tackle box. His hair too was black, but his slant brown eyes were merry. "She gone wild again?"

"Yeah. Burnt half her hair off this time."

He shook his head. His wife Annabel was warming her feet by the tiny gas heater, knitting a scarf from yarn scraps; she had tied the ends of her braids with blue and red strands. Because they lived less outdoors, the Markoosies did not have the deeply weathered faces of most Inuit.

Stella sat on the braided rug, picked pieces of yarn from the tangle in the sugar sack, and began to splice them.

After a long silence, Ephraim asked, "You not feeling well?"

"I was wondering where Mandros came from."

"Better not ask," said Annabel. "You make yourself sick with too much of that."

Stella shrugged. She had no memory of anything before finding herself in front of the dome five years ago, and no strength of will or tortuous effort could push her memory further. She crossed her legs and kept on splicing.

David flung the sodden tattered jacket in the middle of the floor. "Have I got a job for somebody!"

Ephraim put aside the tackle box. "Ha. Mister Medicine Man, how come you sew up people all right and you can't fix clothes?" He picked up the jacket and began to pluck at the charred edges of the holes. "We got plenty of rabbit skins."

"I'm not a plastic surgeon."

Ephraim chuckled. Stella got up and took her coat off the hook.

"You going outside?" David asked.

"A few minutes. The rain's let up."

"There's a rough wind."

"I won't be long."

To the church again? he asked with his eyes. She lowered her own.

Joseph Running Deer was setting out on his patrol of the power line, and nodded as she passed. Pushing aside thorny bushes and whipping branches, she went a score of meters along the path to the church, a path she had worn mainly by herself, and paused to look back.

The dome's triangles reflected the sullen sky. Joseph in his yellow slicker, pieced into the shapes of leaves through the black branches, receded and dwindled. Five kilometers southward, Leona Cress from the next dome would be patrolling the line to the transformer; when they met they would make the small exchanges for which they did not waste radio time or helicopter fuel: greetings, gossip, letters, packages. Across the boreal forest stood dome after dome.

From the zenith of each a watchtower rose: its inhabitant read pollution monitors and pressed reports on button panels. Sometimes a mine, well, or processing plant fifty or a hundred kilometers away would shut down for a day if the air got too thick. Whatever the reading, the air stank excrementally of sulphur and caught the throat; on blue days the grey always bordered the horizon.

The machines did not grope, crush or boil as frantically as they had once done. There were fewer people and fewer demands. Southward the cities on the lakes sat choked in their own detritus and their inhabitants lived in domes much larger than the ones manned by the northern watchtowers, but still in domes with filtered air; every year fewer children were born in them, and every year more young adults lifted off Earth for the bleaker domes of planets and moons. The equatorial zones rippled with sands and sparse grasses, most of their lung-plantations hacked away, the rest withering. The lakes shrank and thickened with algae and the watersheds leached the increasingly treeless soil and carried the salt of the earth and its pollutants into more and more bitter seas. The icecaps had diminished, and the forests pulled their borders back from the temperate zones and retreated toward the tundra, narrowing and thinning over the Precambrian shield; the trees gnarled.

No starships lifted.

Five years earlier the first tentative but desperate few to break the boundary of the solar system had reported a ring of alien ships appearing without warning from the void. Then in turn the radio of each venturer blurted half an hour of garbled hysteria and went dead. Tracking satellites lost them. Twelve strange ships orbited the system half a million kilometers beyond Pluto. Signals beamed at them in millions of combinations were unanswered, and after seven or eight months Earth gave up. Three new ships lifted toward the Pole star and died.

Earth sat and considered herself, walled-in and choking. Astronomers considered the ships and asked themselves: Alpha Centauri, Sirius—or Procyon? The ships had appeared instantly in orbit. There were no directions to adduce. One day someone said, as if it were a datum: Procyon—why, when the others were nearer?—and the twelve had become the aliens of Procyon, hostile by nature but of what shape no one could guess, except in the wild imaginings of the newly formed sects that prayed to them.

Stella climbed the path to the clearing where the church stood on a rock of pinkish granite, one of many that rose from the soil, some angular, deep red or grey, some like the heads or limbs of giants waking to split the thin skin of earth like an amniotic membrane. The church had been built by some group long vanished; it was a weathered shell, outer paint worn off, shingles falling or askew, steeple frail with rust. There was nothing inside: some believer had stolen the crucifix, and the pews and paneling had been removed for use in the dome. It had no denomination, no creed, and Stella did not know why she came there, because she did not pray, but she stood in its windy doorway and watched the land from the height of the rock, rather than from the dome's tower with its winking lights and smutty windows.

Sometimes, with her inner eye, she watched herself from the ships of Procyon: through telescope, past port or viewscreen, cutting silver circles of orbit: Pluto, Neptune, Uranus, Saturn, past looping comets and asteroid gravel to the third planet, the dying world: stratosphere, atmosphere, cloud, and Stella. Big woman with a weathered granitic face and body solid down to the feet flat on the bone-colored rock, the multibillion-year-old granite. She did not know her age; certainly she was no longer young. She had long fair hair of the sort that grows grey imperceptibly, a wisp gathered from each temple and drawn back into a thin braid tied with string. Ephraim had made her a long sky-blue buckskin coat lined and bordered with rabbit fur; she rubbed cornmeal on it to keep it clean, a small vanity.

"Here I am," she told the Procyons. Because of her amnesia she had often had the terrifying fantasy that the aliens had formed her and set her in the dome for some awful purpose; she spent black hours scouring her mind and driving her memory; she went at her tasks with almost as much mania as Nadja's to drive out irrational guilt. One midnight in bed she had forced herself to tell David of the fear, shaking and sweating, pushing the words out.

He had lit the lamp and stared at her for a long while, and she crouched before him in her naked soul, jeering at herself because her hands were trembling. "No, I'll never believe that," he said at last, and turned out the light. The black hours separated themselves and diminished. She accepted them.

The hour was blue now, evening rising under the shadow of

the world. The dome was lit in a filigree of light through its
shutters.

Branches crackled: David came up the path, stumbling a
little and cursing under his breath. His hands and arms were
the essence of grace, and the rest of him heavy and clumsy as a
dancing bear. He stopped at the base of the rock and looked
up at her. "You all right, love?"

"Yes. I'm all right."

He reached out his hand and she came down and took it. A
fine soft rain began.

Nadja's appetite improved; she ate broth, bread, stew. The
hollows of her body filled out a little. She did not sleep quite
so much, and her mania became subdued, but she giggled
often on a note just below hysteria, and spoke in rhyming
snatches.

The winter closed down.

The men set traps and caught lean foxes and their prey, the
scrawny rabbits. The flesh of the foxes was left to placate the
wolves and wild dogs who had joined the packs; the bigger
animals had been overhunted and were scarce. The women
chopped firewood and burned charcoal for the water-filter.
Snow turned dirty before it reached the ground and glittered
only in the brightest sunlight.

David, coming back with a brace of rabbits hung over his
shoulder, stopped to watch Stella chopping wood; his hands
were too valuable to gather calluses from an axe handle. "It
makes me sweat to look at you."

"I'm sweating," she said between hacks.

Nadja drifted through the half-open doorway, singing and
twirling to some imaginary orchestra.

"Oh God, there she goes again." David started toward her,
and paused.

She was standing, arms stretched high, face to the sun and
full of ecstasy.

"At least she put on some weight," said Stella.

"Yes . . . she has . . . hasn't she?" David was staring at the
slender ankles in the snow, the thin arms rising from the
sleeves of the shapeless faded gown. He dropped the rabbits
and approached her with a stalker's caution. "Nadja dear,

come inside with me. It's too cold for you. . . ." He pulled down one of her arms slowly and gripped her hand. "Come on, sweetheart." She went with him, skipping barefoot in the snow, singing one of the odd little tunes of the young child or the mad.

Stella's sweat turned cold. She put the axe on the stacked wood and followed.

David persuaded Nadja to lie on her bunk, squatted beside her and put his hand on her belly. She giggled and tickled his neck. He raised his head to Stella and the flat outer planes of his glasses shone with sunlit triangles. "How long since she menstruated?"

"I don't know . . . she's so irregular—we keep her clean, but it's hard to keep track." Her voice rose. "You think she's pregnant?"

"Don't get excited! Look," he smoothed the cloth over Nadja's stomach, "not much swelling, but it's where she put most of the weight. You can feel—"

"No—" she stepped backward. *Send Mandros.* "You're sure."

"Yes. I'm sure."

"You knew it outside. You saw something."

"Yes," said David. "I saw it move."

The fire had not yet been built, and the common room was cold and bleak. David knocked his pipe on the fender and stuffed it with tobacco. "Last ten years, only three babies in the domes I know of . . . two of them taken south. . . ."

Stella rolled a cigarette she did not want because she felt nauseated. "How far gone is she?"

David struck fire from a lighter, touched it to the kindling, and lit pipe and cigarette. "Three months and a bit. Early for it to move, but not impossible."

"She didn't throw up or anything."

"It's not necessary."

"You think she was raped?"

"I doubt it. She'd have probably raised hell and been knocked around."

"How could it happen, then? Who would do that?"

"I don't know. I haven't seen any of the men hanging around her."

"Mandros . . . when she ran out in the rain—'Send Mandros,' she said—oh God, I wish I hadn't . . . but he was waiting, I was afraid she'd go wild again . . . and—and David, I think he's impotent."

"Yes . . . I've thought that. He doesn't go near anyone, seems to be shrinking inside. Gives everybody the same look, blank. I'd swear he has no sexual feelings at all—but he's the only man we know was alone with her."

"Maybe he had feelings, once."

"Or somebody else did, on some wild impulse, when nobody was looking. . . ." He shuffled his feet. "It wasn't me."

"I know that . . . I can read your face too." She licked her lips. "Should we ask her?"

"What's the use? It could be God, the devil, the Procyons, the Sasquatch, the Wendigo . . ."

"If we tell the others they'll be upset and insulted, a woman so sick being victimized. The men will be tense, and the women will start wondering. . . ."

"No, we'd better not tell. She's hardly showing, and she wears those loose nightgowns. . . . We'll have a fuel allowance built up soon and we'll call for the chopper, send her off on some excuse. It'll take a lot of doing, but we can't care for her properly up here anyway."

"We'll have the man here. It'll still be a horrible puzzle."

"I don't think we'll solve it."

She dropped her cigarette into the fire. "The atmosphere will be poisoned."

"It *is* poisoned, love."

Mandros went about his work: patrolled the line, butchered meat, took his turn at the cooking pots and in the tower. Said perhaps ten words a day, mainly *yes, no, okay, uh-huh;* his eyes were blank. He did not go near Nadja.

Nadja ate heartily; her weight-gain balanced out the slow thickening of her belly.

Once, on a clear day, she said, "I like the blue sky," and smiled.

Stella's heart clenched, and relaxed. Maybe it would be all right; in the south Nadja would become well, the baby would be loved. Her black hour paled a little.

The dome's life went on quietly as ever with its slow air of winding down. The radio brought no news of great disasters and did not mention the Procyons. In the evenings, tasks done, Billy and Clyde sometimes put away their checkers, Billy brought out his battered fiddle and he and Clyde played and sang old loggers' songs; the flames shook to the stamp of their feet. They were wiry men with red weathered faces and crosshatched necks, friends for thirty years and perfectly suited to each other, without heat or passion. The late March snow thickened on the windows.

"It's like this, Dave, eh?" Clyde scraped one sole on the side of the other boot and stared at the worn leather. Billy stood half behind him, nodding at every phrase. "We used to work in the woods, eh? an there ain't been no fuckin woods since we were young bucks, so we come out here, eh?" Billy nodded and Clyde paused and looked up as if he expected David to read his mind.

"What are you getting at, Clyde?"

Clyde tightened his fists, twisting the question between them. "Up here we been workin, doin whatever had to be done. I think we pulled our weight, eh?"

"You mean you want to go? Clyde? Billy?"

Billy nodded.

"Yeah. I didn' want to say it just like that."

"After twelve years . . ."

"Then I guess it's about time, eh? We're gettin older . . . if there's a place that's clean enough we'll fish an trap, an if not they need manpower down south with all them leavin an dyin off."

"But—"

"You wouldn feel bad if we left, Dave? We done our share an all."

"You're my friends! I can't help feeling bad. And—and I just—God damn it, I just don't understand!"

"Well . . ." Clyde struggled and Billy pursed his mouth and shook his head. "It's a queer thing, Dave, and I don't think I understand either. We been talking about it, ain't we, Billy? Something here doesn't feel right, we dunno what, but we want to leave." He added, simply and with finality, "That's all it is."

David gave in. "At least let me call for the helicopter. We'll have enough fuel soon."

"No thanks, Dave. We got snowshoes. If we can take a hatchet an a frypan an maybe a couple of lighters, we'll make it on our own."

Fiddle, stamping feet, bawdy song . . . those longtime friends.

But—Nadja . . . could they? No, not those old bachelors, bent and dry as the wood they stacked.

The early April snow fell thickly and melted fast. In two weeks David would send for the helicopter. He set trap lines with Joseph and Ephraim. They spoke of Clyde and Billy with mild regret.

Stella found it strange that no one seemed to notice how swollen Nadja was becoming. Perhaps they were occupied with their own thoughts.

One evening Joseph calmly announced that he and Anne-Marie Corbière were leaving in two days for Manitoulin Island to stay on the reservation with his family. Jenny Bellisle, whose father lived in the Métis commune there, said she would go with them. Once again David offered the helicopter, and they refused.

"I didn't even bother asking them if they felt funny." David turned the pipe in his fingers; flecks of ash scattered on the floor.

Ephraim sat punching holes in a piece of leather. Annabel squatted on the floor, propped against his back, knitting. Except where it concerned Nadja, David did not guard his tongue with them; he was tired of strange feelings.

Stella was sewing moccasins from cut pieces prepared by Ephraim. "Annabel, what's that you're knitting?"

The scarf had been finished long ago; Annabel held up a small multicolored piece. "Second sleeve of jacket. For the baby. Nadja's."

"Annabel," Stella whispered, "who else knows?"

"Maybe everybody. Or nobody. They don't talk. Maybe they don't want to know." She turned the needle and started a new row. "She's getting pretty big . . . you think it's Mandros?"

"We don't know. We didn't want to talk about it because we'd upset everybody."

"They got upset from something, eh? Mandros, he don't look like he's leaving."

"I wish he would," said David. "Oh God, I wish we'd never kept her here!"

"Ephraim? Annabel? How about you?"

"I don't feel funny," said Ephraim. "Yet."

Stella ploughed through the wet snow to the church and stood in its door frame under the dripping eaves and rotting shingles. Through the branches she saw David as a shadow in the tower, Ephraim beginning his long walk down the line, Joseph with Anne-Marie and Jenny shouldering their packs and moving away forever.

"David, Ephraim, Annabel, Nadja, Mandros, and I. Procyons, why are you waiting? . . . and why did I say that?"

"David, let's all leave in the helicopter." She was curled about his body, breathing against his warm stout back.

"Zat?" He jerked awake in the middle of a snore.

"I said let's get out of here in the helicopter."

"Unh. Won' take all if dome's empty."

"Who cares about domes? We're just puppets pushing buttons. We can't be kept here."

"Maybe don' wan' all go . . ." Not having been quite awake, he slept.

Maybe. Ephraim and Annabel who had come here to ease their old age a little—settling in the barren south? They would rather go north and die.

If we leave now it will be like sending them north to die.

The thaw quickened and little rivulets stirred, waiting for blackflies. The snow turned to grey rains that streaked the glass.

On the day David planned to call for the helicopter the cloud lowered and lightning forked it. Stella shuddered; Nadja had run out into the fire on such a day. She kept close watch, but Nadja was quiet, kneeling on the rug in the common room building towers with Clyde's abandoned checkers, red upon black upon red. The child kicked visibly in her belly, her own movements were slow and deliberate.

"You won't get the copter today," said Stella.

"Yeah." David tugged fingers through his ginger beard. "They couldn't reach here before nightfall even if the storm let up."

Nadja grinned, swiped wildly at the tower and checkers flew everywhere. Her face shifted abruptly, mouth turned down at the corners, and her eyes filled with tears.

"All right, Nadja. . . ." David squatted, gathered the checkers with his quick hands and rebuilt the tower.

Nadja clapped her hands and laughed, the child writhed in her belly and he turned his eyes away.

Ephraim came and sat down, unrolled a piece of leatherwork; he was ready to take his place on the line as soon as Mandros returned.

Silently Mandros appeared in the doorway watching Nadja; water ran down his face, dripped from his oilskin and pooled at his feet.

For a moment the room seemed to echo with the banter of lost friends, filled with their shadows.

David's eyes were fixed on Mandros. Words came without control. "You see her, Mandros? Do you? a madwoman? Why? Why her? Tell me, hey?" His voice was almost pleading. "Mandros?"

"I don't know what you are saying," said Mandros. He stood, boots puddling the floor, a glove held in each upturned hand like an offering. "What do you mean?" His eyes were blank, not shifting, his lower lip hung.

He turned and left.

Nadja, unmoved, went on playing with checkers.

David rubbed sweat off his forehead with the palms of his hands. "I shouldn't have done that."

Ephraim sighed and got up, rolled his piece of leather and put it on a table. His jacket was checkered in red and black like a big game-board. He zipped it, took his oilskin off its hook and shouldered it on. The sky was darkening, wind whipped rain against the glass.

"Ephraim, don't bother about the line," Stella said.

"Nobody's going to be attacking it tonight."

Ephraim shrugged. "I promised Tom Arcand some skins and I'll have a talk with him down there. In here is cold as Ellesmere Island." He took mittens from his pocket. "Maybe I'll go there."

"I'm sorry, Ephraim," David whispered.

Ephraim grunted. The outer door thudded behind him.

David pounded his fist on his knee in an agony of embarrassment.

"What's the matter, David? There was nothing wrong in asking."

His shoulders twitched. "We've lost the others. . . . I don't want Ephraim to . . ."

Nadja looked up, and her hand, in the act of placing the last checker, paused above the tower. Her eyes were calm. She was bent forward slightly, and the drape of the gown over her belly hid the child's movement. She had been well cared for; her hair was clean and fell in soft waves to her shoulders, her dark eyes were unshadowed, her skin smooth; the bone structure of her face showed clearly, but without gauntness.

She's pretty, Stella thought. At last, and so what? "How's the baby, Nadja?" she asked, to fill the silence. "Which do you want, a boy or a girl?"

Nadja looked, somewhere, not at her. "It is a male. Its name is Aesh." She placed the last checker. "In our language."

"In our language? What . . ." Stella and David stared at each other in a strange fear.

David raised his hand as Stella was about to speak again. "That's enough," he said. "Forget it."

Annabel came down from the tower and headed for the kitchen, and Stella in turn climbed the iron spiral.

The tower stood much higher above ground than the church, but Stella had never found it peaceful. Lights flickered over the panel map, the radio whispered of the deaths of continents; the stars had been obscured by pollution, and at night nothing could be seen through the windows except sometimes a dirty moon. The panes reflected the watcher and the objects inside, and Stella, who never flinched before a mirror, did not like the grim face the glass returned to her.

The shades and frames on the roof got in the way of the light below, but Stella in imagination observed David smoking his pipe by the fire and trying to find reason in Nadja; Annabel moving about among the cooking pots; Mandros perhaps sitting on the edge of his bunk sewing up the split finger of a glove. . . .

White light slammed the dome, the rock, the world.

From the sudden darkness came a hiss intense as a scream. Stella cried out in echo. . . .

When her blinded eyes cleared she saw the small beam of the emergency lantern, grabbed it out of its clamp with one hand and with the other dragged down on the switches of the wind generator and its power line.

The lights trembled and then surged.

"Stel-ell-ella!" David was yelling over the intercom.

"I'm all right!" She was gripping the lantern, thoughts ricocheting wildly; the flash-beam swung over the dead blank panel, her heart jumped in rhythm with *no-loss, no-loss, no-loss,* beating so fiercely it took her a moment to realize that the radio had also gone dead. Wireless. She said confusedly, "But how—"

"—ella!"

"I'm coming!" She ran down the stair. "David, the radio's dead! The line—"

He was in his coat, cramming his hat down over his ears. "Ephraim! If he was around when it blew—"

Nadja was hunched on the floor, weeping. Annabel, in silence, watched David yanking on his boots. Mandros was waiting, dressed for outdoors. Stella found that her hand was locked around the lantern. She held it out, Mandros took it and went into the darkness with David. The door thudded. Annabel picked up the scroll of leather and gripped it with both hands. Rain swept against the glass.

Nadja flung herself into a rigid backward arch as if she were in tetany and began to scream.

The power line was laid along the ground, flowing between hewn rock faces and over old stream beds; it was cased in flexible plastic, a twenty-centimeter cable that shifted naturally with seasonal erosion and withstood flooding and rockfalls. It could not break and had not been broken. It had been sheared by a terrific force that left the ends ten meters apart, coiling like pythons, wiring fused into lumps of solder.

Ephraim was lying in the pounding rain beside the charred track of its furious burning. He was dead, one arm rag and bone, one side blackened to cinder. The bag of skins for Tom Arcand lay beside him.

David doubled up, vomiting, and wondered dimly why he was not surprised.

He straightened, spat, turned his face away from Ephraim, and Mandros. "Too far . . . to bring him in . . . until the rain . . ."

"I am sorry," said Mandros.

David shook his head.

Mandros said, "Tomorrow I will make a travois."

"Yes," said David. "You do that." Blindly he headed north against the rain.

As they came within sight of the dome they heard the muffled screaming under the driving wind. David ran ahead, sloshing, dragged the door open. "Stella! Annabel!"

"Infirmary, David!"

They were holding the screaming Nadja down on the bed, one to each pair of limbs as the body arched, the child writhed. Nadja's gown was flecked with blood.

"You give her anything?" David struggled with soaked clothes.

"Only the usual. I was afraid, I didn't know what—" Her voice was trembling. "I'm afraid the baby—"

"I'll hold her, you give her a double dose, intravenous."

Nadja did not turn quiet under increased medication; her voice sank two octaves into a steady moan. Her body flattened on the bed. Annabel let go of the small tight fists and raised her eyes to David.

They were very still; they were the stillest things in the room.

"Ephraim is dead," he whispered. "I think lightning . . ." Lightning? Whatever tore that line apart like a piece of string.

Annabel looked down and brushed the hair from Nadja's wet forehead. Her hand moved in a series of little jerks. "You bring him in?"

"Couldn't . . . half a kilometer away . . . tomorrow—" He pulled in a deep breath, exhaled on half a sob and hurried to the lavatory to wash.

Nadja's moan shifted to a sound that was half giggle and half snarl of pain. "Ephraim's away," she croaked, "he's gone to stay, he won't be back another day. . . ."

Annabel pulled back her hand as if it had been burnt, and stared at the twisted face. Then slowly reached out again to lift the wrenching body so that Stella could change the gown and bedding. Nadja was bleeding in a thin steady stream.

David's primitive hospital gave him a few drugs, instruments, bandages, a clean shirt and surgical gloves.

"Only six months, David! Is—is she—"

"Aborting, maybe . . . can't be sure it's six, though. . . ." He rested his hand on Nadja's belly. "Or whether it happened that day. . . ." The dome shape tightened itself into a peak. "But it's way low down, contracting and . . ." one hand on the humped curve, he explored with the other, "my God, fighting like hell—dilated—head's right up at the top—" Blood spurted around his hand. The red stream ran off the bed and dripped on the tiled floor. "Got to bring it on, it's the only way to stop—"

The screaming rose.

"Another needle?"

"Not yet—we'll need the—" sweat ran down his face and caught in globules through his beard, "need the—the—"

"Christ, David, the blood!"

"I know, God damn it! Need anesthetic and we've hardly got—" bearing down on the squirming hump with one hand, he forced with the other, "never had such a tough . . . ah . . ." The waters broke and flowed, the red paled for a few moments, and deepened again. David's face was so dark red it seemed he would sweat blood. "Never had such a—get the instrument and anesthesia packages off the shelf above—" groping through blood, heaving desperately at the hidden shape in the flesh envelope to bring the head on aim with the world. "That's it—first the relaxant . . ."

And fighting like hell. Why does he?

He?

All right, then, pull him out hind-end first, anything to make the womb tighten and close, stop the blood. . . . "That's better . . . place the cone so she can breathe, and tape it—Jesus, we've got enough equipment to pull a hangnail!'' He was panting. He knew what to do well enough, and had almost nothing to do it with. "See if you can get Mandros to raise Central Eastern Hospital."

"I told you, David, the radio's dead."

He said nothing, aimed his blade to enlarge an opening for the stubborn and furious child. His teeth were chattering. Annabel wiped his face. Nadja was quiet and pale.

"Her pulse is weak," Stella said.

"She has a murmur, I'm scared of that—oh, I can't go on this way, it has to be cesarian."

He raised the blade.

The belly humped and a red bubble swelled out of its peak and broke; from within a sharp thing had punctured it. "What's that?" The pointed thing caught the harsh light, began to tear a ragged line down the skin. A claw.

"Oh, my God!" David howled, and sliced. Divided the shredded membranes, reached in and pulled away the dark squirming creature, held it up, it was received.

Deaf, dumb, blind, David. Knife on floor in darkening red.

Stitch on stitch, he sewed.

"David . . . she's dead, David. . . ."

Tears joined sweat rivers falling in blood.

"I know," he said, and kept on sewing.

It was male. *His name is Aesh.*

"In our language," David muttered. In our language, what?

Aesh was covered with fine dark hairs, not thickly, but like the arm of a hairy man. Ears very small, high on the head, eyes sharp and black, slanting a little. His nails were sharp translucent claws with a fine blood vessel running through each almost to the tip. In his armpits were small webbings of hairy goose-pimpled skin extending from halfway down the inside of the upper arm across to the vicinity of the sixth rib. His penis was short and tubular, without glans, like a section of aorta, and his one testicle was the size and color of a chestnut, covered with the long dark hairs that reminded Stella, hysterically, of the hair plastering itself in straight lines down Mandros's head in the rain.

"A mutant," she whispered. "The pollution . . ."

"No," said David. "I think he is as he was meant to be."

Swaddled in a blanket, bedded in a crate, Aesh slept.

Stella had sent Annabel to bed with sleeping pills; washed David as if he were the baby and propelled him into the common room; found the bottle of whisky inherited from some transient, pushed it into his hands with a glass. Wrapped Nadja's body in rubber sheeting and placed it in the storeroom. It was very light. Cleaned the infirmary with mop and bucket until the only blood that remained was left crusting on the tied-off stub of the child's umbilicus. Because she was going to sleep in here this night, with him. He mewled and snuffled a little, Aesh.

"The power line is cut," said David, tilting the glass. He was nowhere on the way to becoming drunk. "I wish I liked this stuff. The power line, the wireless . . . the others are gone or dead."

"Tomorrow we'll go down to the transformer."

"We'll try it . . . I wonder if we'll reach it."

"Why, David? Who will stop us?"

"Whoever, whatever cut the line. You'll realize when you see it."

"I'm not sure I understand what you're getting at." She was afraid she did.

"The power, the radio," he repeated. "The others—Clyde, Billy, and the rest—felt funny, and they left. Ephraim refused to feel funny—and he's gone. Nadja . . . isn't needed anymore. Is she? Could she bring up? that? child?"

"David, I think you're getting—"

"I wish I could. Oh God. But there was nothing. Even if we could have taken her south. Not with that. But we were kept here. The ones who were kept here were the ones necessary to make sure that child got born alive. In good health. That six-month full-term child." He looked at her as he had looked when she told him of her terrible fear. "It didn't all come into my head this minute. There were wisps of it before. I wouldn't let it come together and now I can't stop it. The ones who were needed were you and me and Annabel."

"And Mandros."

"Him."

"But—what is he? He's not—not like that child."

"Maybe he is, under a mask. I don't know."

"A . . ." she pushed the word out. "Procyon?" —*horrible fear that I was—oh it's so goddam silly, so irrational—because I can't remember—that the Procyons had, had made me and put me here for—* David, you don't think— "That he's the construct, what I was so afraid I was . . . but why?"

"Maybe I am drunk," said David. He capped the bottle and heaved himself up. "We have things to do, in the morning."

There were not many places in the rocky land where the earth lay deep enough for burial, but Mandros found one, and before the sun rose he had dragged Ephraim's body back on a travois. Annabel bandaged it and dressed it in the old fur-lined parka Ephraim's father had made for him; he and Nadja, having had nothing in common in life, shared a grave.

David watched. His cheeks sagged, his eyes were red behind the glasses. By the time the last shovel was tamped the sun was half-up, and the baby began to wail in a treble piping like the squeak of a bat.

Mandros swung the spade up so that its handle rested on his shoulder. "He wants feeding, that one."

"Babies don't get fed the first day," said David.

"That one does," said Mandros.

Without a word David went indoors to instruct Stella and Annabel in mixing boiled water with sugar and powdered milk.

"You don't know if it will take this," Stella said.

"It's all we've got." From the stores where everything was saved to be reused he had gathered small bottles and was putting them to boil in a pot of water. "Cut off the fingertips of some of my surgical gloves for nipples. They won't hold up well—" he bent over the shrilling, whimpering child, set in his crate-cradle by the stove for warmth, and ran his thumb over the red parted gums, "—but this one looks as if he'll be wanting solid food very soon."

"David—if we're closed in, as you say, line cut, no radio— where will we get it?"

"I don't know that either." He lifted a tiny wrist, noting that the fingers did not curl into a fist but clenched back on

themselves so that the claws did not dig into the palm. "Those
will bite, these will scratch, can't be cut because of the blood
vessels . . . webbing here—vestigial wing?—don't think he'll
fly with that . . . wonder what his insides are like."

Annabel looked down at the baby and away; her tearless
eyes were dull. "Spirit-child," she muttered. "Witch-child."

The rising sun caught two shining spots on the small tight
belly, and David bent closer. On each of the tiny crinkled
nipples a white drop had risen. "He's got witch's milk," said
David, "but that's a human phenomenon. Whatever else he is,
Aesh-in-our-language is half-human." He put on his jacket
again and paused in the doorway. "Mind the claws when you
feed him."

The earth outside was like a soaked rug: water pressed out
of it at each step. Too shallow to allow water to drain, it
would pool into sickly marshes in summer.

David followed the line, squelching in rotten leaves and
soggy twigs. The sky was grey-blue, the sun smoky; he de-
toured around the break. The baby's cry seemed to be within
him, a ceaseless mourning for Ephraim, that joyful friend,
and Nadja . . . because I kept letting it go when she should
have been sent away . . . and oh God, Ephraim and Annabel,
why didn't you leave? It would have hurt so if they left—and
now it hurts so much more.

He walked and walked. The sun rose.

It seemed so clear last night. Now it's broken into a kaleido-
scope. . . . Mutation? Procyons? Why did I say that? Because
Stella was so afraid of . . . *Mandros is the construct*. . . .

He trudged on, head down. The sun rose.

What is a construct? A made-up thing. Why that term?
Under a mask. I said it. What did I mean?

He glanced at his watch, at the sun, and stopped. He had
been walking for two hours, in soaked earth, through gullies,
over swelling rockfaces. The transformer was across the valley
on the hilltop. Or should have been. There was no transformer.

He felt as if he had the kind of disturbance of the ear that
creates dizziness with every head movement. Trees and rock
were ahead, and the line dipped into a hollow and disappeared. The familiar terrain warped around him, and he

closed his eyes, turned carefully to mark his progress by some landmark on the way he had come.

He opened his eyes and found it. The tortured snake-ends of the broken line rose with their splayed wires forty meters back. He had walked half a kilometer in two hours.

He bit hard on the gloved knuckle of his forefinger and refused to tell himself that he was crazy. He wheeled about and pushed foot before foot, holding hard to the central crystal of his being while the thoughts around it fragmented into wild patterns and the ground seemed to run under his feet like a treadmill. After a couple of dozen steps he gave up and turned back.

As soon as he took the first step toward the dome his mind started to clear and arrange itself into the well-known lattice of his personality.

And, again, he was not surprised.

He stopped for a moment. The sun shone, the sky was hazy and grey on the horizon. The earth accepted the weight of his step, the rock was solid.

"We are in quarantine," he said aloud. The squawk of a crow answered.

"You too," he said. He giggled. "Rabbits, foxes, worms, you—and us."

Shut up, you fool, and hold onto your head!

A bit dizzy still.

Think! reason! *cogite!*

Leona Cress, Tom Arcand and the rest will want to know why. What happened to Ephraim and his skins. Ephraim's gone, he won't be back . . . there's his skins, lying beside the burnt patch, soaked.

No, they won't. They won't ask. Here or down south. Dome NE73, last on the northeast roster, has disappeared from register, record, memory. Leaving seventy-two. Much nicer number, 72, even, neat, divisible by 2, 3, 4, 6, 8, 9 . . .

Ask Mandros.

But he would not. Ask that. Thing? So many things they had not asked, all these months, of anyone. They had gotten into the habit of not asking.

Tell me, hey, Mandros?

I know.

This is a crèche. They chose it, unspeakable T,H,E,Y,

chose this foul ungiving place, for him to be born in.

Stella was on her knees inside the doorway, slitting cords
from one of several bales. The same kind they had always
received, but without markings. From the packing she was
pulling bottles, blankets, clothes, food.

"How did that come here?"

"I don't know—it was just there. Outside."

"Ah. We are being provided for." He stopped himself from
giggling.

Aesh screamed for three solid weeks. The shrill whine
echoed through the empty spaces of the dome and killed sleep.
Stella and Annabel took turns massaging his belly, David
changed the formula a dozen times.

"What in God's name does he want?" Stella held the jerk-
ing, twisting child at arm's-length; her face and neck were
crisscrossed with scratches.

"To hazard a guess, meat," said David. He growled,
"Maybe blood." Haggard, he stumped off to tell Mandros the
goddam powers-that-be had better send lactic acid. He got it.

The thick curdy stuff silenced the child for an hour or two
after feeding. "Why in hell should we have to ask? You'd
think they'd know what to feed the brat."

"Maybe . . . maybe it's an experiment they haven't tried
before," said Stella.

It was cold in early May. The knobby buds pushed out of
the trees, but did not open. Aesh discovered the power of his
nails, shredded his blankets and clawed splinters of wood
from his crate. David coated them with the plastic used for
temporary tooth-fillings and while it was still wet bandaged
them.

The mittened hands, unexpectedly, did not make Aesh
scream. Surly-faced, he gnawed at them with his toothless
gums.

"Keep him busy," David said, "till the teeth grow in."

Stella picked him up and held him close, though he fought
like a bobcat.

"What do you want to do that for? Think he'll be grateful?'' The goblin face snarled.

"I don't know. I think somebody should." She patted his cheek and he tried to bite her. "Aren't there mothers for this kind of child, somewhere?"

David shuddered. "I hate to think."

Aesh would not tolerate clothes. Stella wound him in a blanket and carried him outside with her blue coat wrapped around him. Sunlight made him whimper and he turned his face against her neck.

"Better learn to like it, Aesh. It's your sun now."

She glimpsed a movement from the corner of her eye. Mandros, standing by the burial mound, had turned to face her. He was holding something unrecognizable in his hands, and she moved closer to see what it was.

A wood carving, or a natural growth of roots and branches twisting in and among each other in knots; he parted his fingers and held it in cupped hands for a moment, a convoluted flower of wood. It was attached to a pointed stake, and he bent and pushed it into the earth at the head of the grave. A marker. As he stood again he raised his face to the sky, hazed over and thick at the horizon; a few dewdrops sparkled on the branches.

Stella watched, though the child squirmed and water was seeping into her moccasins. The idiot face was expressionless.

"This, here, is a paradise," he said.

This here. This, here? A world of difference in a catch of breath.

"Paradise, he said."

"Paradise! What does that mean? They've got a world, dying even faster than ours. . . . They think they'll people it, with more of Aesh. I guess it's the only place they've found compatible."

"But why would they pick Nadja, when there were Anne-Marie, Jenny, so many other healthier ones?"

"Perhaps something in her genetic makeup. They'd probably find enough like that. There may be more—of these babies—in the world."

"I don't think so. . . ."

"Why?"

"I just don't."

"You surely have odd ideas, Stella."

"No odder than what's happening."

"One of a kind—who would he find to mate with?"

"It may not matter, just so they can be bred."

The child's demanding cry rose again. David tipped the last of the whisky into the glass. "My short career as a drunkard. No radio. If there's a radio here it's probably embedded in Mandros somewhere, unless he's a telepath. If we tried to attack him or the kid they'd be down on us like—like that lightning."

"Have you thought of it, David?"

"What?"

"What you said about attacking. I don't think they mean to keep us alive if they succeed."

"Ha." He shrugged. "I'm a coward."

"You may be a bit of a liar. You're not a coward."

"No? Well . . . if I'd have known what it would be I'd have aborted . . . and if she'd miscarried, okay. . . ." He turned his face into his shoulder in the odd gesture he always made when he was about to give something of himself away. "I'm on the earth to save lives and I'm willing to die doing it."

"That's probably why they chose us, then."

Always asking why. Why it happened. Why they chose. Why—*you surely have odd ideas, Stella*—why I think there's only one, plus Mandros. I don't know. Why Procyons?

"One is enough of you, Aesh." She held the clawed hands down across the tight belly. Thin dark lips drew back from the gums. At one month the eyeeth had come in, tiny pointed things like the claws.

"Fangs, for God's sake," said David. "I wonder what it's going to be when it grows up."

"I wonder how old it will be when it's grown." The bandages had been removed from the claws. "Aesh, you do not scratch people. You keep your hands to yourself and hold things with them." He kicked out with his feet. She grabbed them and knelt over him, hands grasped in one of hers and feet in the other. He shrilled. "I'm still stronger than you, Aesh."

"You mean," said David, "how long we have."

"Yes, and how much of the place they want, and what we can do." Aesh squirmed and shrilled in the double grasp.

"He needs a new crate. Or a cage."

She pulled her hands away quickly, and Aesh, finding his limbs free, waved them aimlessly and stared at them in silence. "Annabel . . ."

"Not so good. I know."

"She doesn't answer when I speak to her. This morning she put salt in her coffee and didn't notice when she drank it."

"Yeah. Another one."

Annabel had aged immensely. Her hair remained black, but her face thinned into harsh lines and her eyes were dull. She slept long and she did not knit or sew. Stella took over the cooking and cleaning. The Procyons were generous. Food and fuel appeared at the door as it was needed, and there was no more hunting or woodcutting to be done. Stella and David were left between the silences of Mandros and Annabel, amid the turbulence of Aesh, without hope to find whatever strength they could.

At six months Aesh crawled, and at eight he walked. His nails scraped the floor, and David made him clogs of wood covered with leather and deeply scored with grooves to accommodate the claws. "Stell-la!" he shrilled. "Da-veed!"

He hardly spoke to Mandros at all, but it was Mandros who caught him as he fell, or pulled him down from shelf or mantel when he climbed. His clogs racketed, his shrill cry echoed in the spaces.

As winter closed down David and Mandros cleared pieces of old furniture from the annex adjacent to the common room, moved the bunks there, and partitioned off some of the unused areas of the dome. Annabel whimpered when her bed was moved, and again when she saw Ephraim's tackle heaped on a pile of useless stuff in the storeroom. She walked ceaselessly among the echoes, her hair uncombed, her hands

clasped before her. The stillness of hands once so busy
wrenched at Stella, and when she sat the old woman down and
combed and braided her hair, the submissiveness of the bent
shoulders drove her to a fury at the universe. But she had no
claws, and no one to scratch.

What we can do. . . .

The snow fell heavily, the tree branches cracked in the driving wind.

One blue morning, Annabel combed and braided her own
hair, bound the braids in blue and red strands of wool; she put
on parka, boots and mittens, and stood before the doorway of
the dome, hands clasped.

Stella, Aesh clattering behind her and grabbing at her shirt-
tail, found her there. She stopped. "Annabel," she whispered.

Annabel stared at the wind-drifted snow.

"Annabel—"

"I'm going into the north." There was no inflection in her
voice.

"There is no place to go."

Annabel turned her head and looked at Stella. I know, her
eyes said.

Stella dragged Aesh into the common room and sat down.
The door slid open and thudded closed.

She covered her face with her hands. "Stell-la! Stell-la!" the
child whined.

Some feeling made her raise her eyes to the light. Annabel,
already half-whitened by driven snow, had stopped and was
looking in at her. She smiled once, her face crinkled in the old
way, and went on.

Go, Annabel, go and be free. The snow is full of peace. Go
on, God forgive me, I love you, Annabel, go on. . . .

"David, what can we do?"

"Nothing, sweetheart."

"There is peace—somewhere."

"Not for us yet."

"Hold me, I'm so cold . . . you're good and warm, like a
great old bearskin. So good."

"Ha. I always knew you wanted me for my body."

• • •

Two rows of small pointed teeth filled the spaces in Aesh's gums, and he ate meat, first cooked and then raw; sometimes a little cereal; drank water, sucking with his lips as if it were flower nectar. He slept deepest toward morning and napped for an hour at noon; if allowed, he would have been nocturnal, but shamelessly David drugged him every night. No retribution struck.

He spewed urine and feces unreservedly on carpet and floor. Stella and David battled him up and down the days, and bleeding from scratches wrestled him to the toilet bowl. After months he gave in. In revenge he screamed his fury every time he used it. Mandros watched. Sometimes, it seemed, in wry amusement.

He grew, hardly changing the shape he was born in, bent stick limbs and tight round belly; snarling face with sharp teeth, small hairy ears, black malevolent eyes: he hated light and his ears were so sensitive he went into fits of trembling at the sound of raindrops or scraping branches on the glass. He was ugly. The long shining hairs on his red-brown skin thickened and he would not accept the touch of clothes. When he went outside he allowed David to tape slit-eyed snow goggles to his head.

It became apparent early that his function was to break. From outside he threw stones at the glass; when it would not give he set about breaking all the branches he could reach. One time David pulled him inside and he tore the carpet with his teeth and nails.

Stella sat on him.

"Maan-dros!" he wailed.

"Shut up, you little bastard! He knows I'm not going to hurt you! You've done too much damage to the things made by people I cared for and you're going to stop if I have to sit on you twenty days and nights!"

Released, he jumped to the mantel and tried to wrench it from the wall. That was too much for him; he dropped to the floor and slept. Stella watched him. The fluttering of his bird-like heart raised the hairs on his chest a hundred and twenty times a minute. Little beast.

Mandros kept him from harming himself and was rewarded

with arrogance and contempt. He allowed David to treat his
scratches and bites, to release a foot caught between stones, to
pick out burrs so that they did not tear his skin, but he hated
being touched. Toward Stella he was violently contradictory.
Sometimes he cursed every word she addressed to him, for he
had learned to speak well, had gathered David's and Stella's
curses and even seemed to pick some out of the air. Other
times he ran after her plucking at sleeve or hem, whimpering,
"Stell-la!" as he had done when he was a baby.

"What do you want, Aesh?"

"I don't know."

She reached out a finger to touch his cheek, gently. He
pulled back shrilling, and ran.

Stella thought of the ones who had left and the ones who
had died, watched David's worn face, considered her own im-
prisonment, and cursed.

Years passed.

Stella stood in the church doorway. "Do you know how
years pass?" she asked the Procyons. "Like weeks. All the
years I can't remember are lost, I don't know how many, and
God damn you, you've taken away the rest."

She pushed and pushed at the wall in her mind, tortuously
following the pathway back, to salvage some area of hope and
freedom, and always the track stopped short one grey morning
before the dome.

David grew somewhat thinner and white streaks ran down
his beard. Stella hardly glanced at herself in the mirror and
could not tell whether she seemed older. Mandros did not
change at all.

Near ten Aesh was the size of a boy of seven or eight; his
limbs thickened and his belly drew in; he had powerful
shoulders and walked straight-legged instead of scuttling like a
lizard. But he would not sit still long enough to learn anything,
and on dull days that were not too cold he moved ceaselessly in
the confines of the force-field, climbing trees, squirming
among bushes and rocks, rolling in the mud of stagnant pools
undeterred by mosquitoes and blackflies.

● ● ●

In the August heat Mandros sat outside on a stone with his hands folded, staring at nothing. Aesh was rampaging nearby.

Stella squatted on a hummock in front of Mandros; she knew that he was the agent of her death, but she did not yet see death before her, and she was no longer repelled by his dark oily skin, scraggy hair, loose mouth that opened on stained yellow teeth.

"Mandros, you are from Procyon, I don't have to ask. What is your planet?"

"The fourth." He did not look at her.

"What are your people called?"

"Shar. In your language."

"But you were made to look like us—"

"That is true."

"And Aesh looks like other Shar."

"Not completely. He looks somewhat like his mother."

She said faintly, "I hadn't noticed."

"His legs are abnormally long and his face is narrow."

"Your men and women, do they have the differences we have?"

"Of course not. The women are only womb-casings, without head or limbs."

She swallowed to avoid retching. "Then no child can love its mother, or be loved."

"Why should it? It is not necessary. We worship."

"Dear Lord," she murmured, "fruit of the womb. Mandros! You say this is paradise, but we are infertile and the world is dying."

"Not so fast as ours."

"For the same reasons?"

"I know what I am told: the wombs are scarce and sterile; the world is barren. Perhaps we are cursed."

He made a quarter turn away from her, and she fell silent.

Aesh appeared before them, eyes slitted against the sun, the claws of his feet pressing into damp earth. "Why are you talking to this thing?"

Stella said, "I was speaking to Mandros because I wanted to learn about your people."

"This has nothing to teach you. Thing!" He flicked a claw near Mandros's eye. Mandros did not blink or flinch.

"Stop that!"

The claw paused in midair. He was looking at her strangely.

"Mandros is here to take care of you in this place and you will have to answer to your people if you hurt him."

Aesh's laughter could crush bones. "I don't have to answer to anyone because my father is the Emperor. Do you think this thing can be hurt?" He dug claws into Mandros's forehead and began to pull down.

"No!" Stella grabbed his arm. She was not stronger than Aesh anymore, but she was a good match. She caught the other hand aiming for her eyes, hooked his feet from under him with her heel, they went down, rolling in the mud. Mandros sat unmoving on the rock.

They fought over rocks and brambles and splashed in pools, scattering clouds of insects; Stella protected her eyes with an arm and he bit, she grasped one of his and held it with her teeth, his feet clawed her legs, his shrilling made the air tremble, his nails hooked in and pulled out in a hundred places, reached again and again for her eyes, her sleeves shredded protecting them, his teeth tore at her ear, he ripped out a handful of her hair, and finally butted her belly with his head, left her flat on the ground and breathless, stood over her laughing for a moment, then climbed the framework of the dome, leaned against the tower with his arms crossed and laughed.

Mandros moved, then. He stood up and called, "Aesh! Come down, you will hurt yourself!"

Stella sat up, gasping, pulled herself first to her knees, then to her feet, pushed the hair out of her eyes. She panted. "Sonofabitch! Him hurt!" She was bleeding from dozens of punctures and scratches. David, on a distant rise holding a basket of berries, was standing in a shocked stillness like a tiny figure in a great painting.

Aesh scrambled down the dome, laughing, and ran up the path to the church.

Her church. Stella followed, stumbling. A cloud had covered the sun and the sky was thickening. She was dizzy, held her head to steady it.

Mandros came after, caught hold of her arm, and pulled her back a few steps.

"You idiot!" she snarled. "I'm not going to hurt hi—"

A bolt of lightning struck a meter before her.

She screamed in fury, wrenched away and leaped over the charred ground toward the path.

In the church Aesh had his legs hooked round a rafter and was swinging from it. He shrilled and laughed and shrilled.

"Get out of here!"

He laughed, caught the next beam with his hands, and grasped it with his legs.

Stella let her breath loose and lowered her voice. "Get out of my church. I'm not going to hurt you."

"Hurt me?" He laughed and swung.

"Come down!"

He sang, swinging, chorused by echoes:

"Damn the poor, for they shall be trampled!
 Damn the mourners, they shall have more to mourn!
 Damn the meek, they shall be driven from Earth!"

"Come down!"
 He swung to the next beam, and sang:

"Damn the peacemakers, they shall be wartorn!
 Damn the merciful, they shall be—"

"Aesh!" David's voice. "Stella, for God's sake—"

Lightning struck and shivered a beam above her head. She jumped forward and the timbers missed her. Aesh screamed.

The fearful noise had sent his arms and legs flying out convulsively.

As he fell, Stella, without thought, leaped once more. When he hit, she blacked out.

She opened her eyes. David was rubbing ointment into her wounds.

Headache. Head-quake, maybe. About seven points on the Richter scale, she thought. "What's the damage?"

"There's a hole in the church roof."

"There's a few in me."

"I gave you a shot of antitet."

"Maybe it should be antirabies."

He looked at her wisely. "Mild concussion. Likely your backside aches too. That was where his head hit, and it drove your head onto the floor. Otherwise his skull would have cracked. He broke a humerus and three claws; he bled more than you did."

"Too bad. Oh well. I guess I should have let him take it out on Mandros. It was just the funny look he gave me before he did it. As if he was daring me to intervene."

"He was testing. To see how far he could go. All kids do that."

"I should have known after all these years. I just haven't had a wide experience."

"I had a kid once," he said.

Don't ask, Stella!

Okay, I won't.

"Mandros saved me. They were trying to kill me with one of their bloody lightning bolts. He pulled me back."

"I saw. I wonder whose rules he's playing by."

"I don't think I'll ask. I'm alive. I wonder for how long. . . ."

"The second one missed."

"Did it? Who do you think it was meant for—me or him?"

"Mandros?"

"No. Aesh."

His brow puckered. "Him, Stella? Why?"

"I don't know. I get these feelings. . . ." She began to pull herself up.

"Hey, you better not do that! You've got to rest."

"David, I don't think it matters at this point." She lowered her feet to the floor. He was right. Her backside ached. Her head roared; her teeth felt loose, probably they had cracked together when her head hit.

"Where are you going?"

She staggered drunkenly to the door. "To see him."

Aesh had three expressions: rage, sulks, and unholy glee. He was sulking. His arm was in wired splints, his nails had been cemented.

She looked down at him in the bed where he had been born out of Nadja's screams and blood.

He looked away first, and then at her. "You saved me."
Probably he would never forgive her for it.

"Mandros saved me. One good turn."

"You wouldn't let me hurt him."

"And he wouldn't let me hurt you. That's the house that
Jack built."

"That is nonsense talk. You would never have hurt me."

"No, I wouldn't." His eye membrances were red and so
were his lids. She had never seen him cry. "Did David give you
something to take away the pain?"

"Yes." His left arm twitched in its sling.

"Do you read books?"

"No. That is nonsense too. Why do you ask?"

"I was wondering where you got the anti-Beatitudes."

"I don't know what that is."

"Damn the meek and damn the merciful. That's much
something written in a book of ours. Did you make it up?"

He shook his head impatiently. "Why are you bothering
with that? I don't know. Perhaps someone told it to me."

"Maybe," she said. "But in our book we bless them."

She turned to go, but he grabbed at her nightgown. "
la!" he wailed.

She faced him again.

What do you want, Aesh?

I don't know.

Something new in his eyes, now, a little like fear.

"What is it?"

"Stell-la! Do you love me?"

Her mind went blank.

Love?

Aesh?

That is nonsense talk.

Stell-la! a cry . . .

The pain roared in her head. Her mouth worke
friends died so you could be born. I took care of you–

He was trembling.

"—when I knew that I would die for it, a
too. . . ." And the rest of world. I am the agent o
tion.

His eyes begged.

"They could have cared for you, couldn't they? I

not. You were half born of this world, a different chemistry, a different mind. . . .''

"You are not saying!''

"I swear I don't know why I did it. You were a newborn baby, and a child. You needed care. I gave it.''

"But that *is* love, Stell-la! Da-veed said it is love!''

"All right.'' She nodded. "David's a truthful man, and if he said it, it's so. I love you, Aesh.''

"Good,'' he said. "I will sleep now.'' And closed his eyes.

She stood before the blasted church, reeling.

"Shar!'' she screamed. "Damn you! No,'' she lowered her burning head and crouched on the rock, "forget I said that. I take it back. There's been too much damnation.''

A hand touched her arm. She was beyond flinching.

"You must go in and lie down,'' said Mandros.

"I won't damn you either,'' she said thickly. The insects hummed in the shimmering air, and in her head. "Mandros, why did you save me?''

Inside the church a charred beam cracked and fell, splinters bounced on the floor.

"So that you could save him.''

She saw him double. Her voice was so slurred her ears hardly registered it. "They fight among themselves, then, those Shar of yours?''

"Who does not? More than one would wish to be Emperor.''

"What do you mean?'' A wind rose and chilled her sweat.

"The Emperor died . . . a few hours ago, by your time.''

She lay on the bed and dreamed. Sometimes David washed her face, and occasionally tested her reflexes; she felt his thumbs raising her eyelids. In those seconds of vision she saw Mandros standing at the foot of the bed, or thought she saw him.

In her dream she got up and walked out of the door. David sat on tending the body on the bed, but Mandros followed her with his eyes.

The sky was lead. The trees straightened and turned to iron, with burning sconces in their centers. The shadow of each was clear, squat and crook-legged. Their eyes were like pome-

granate seeds, black pips in red membrane. Crepy skin hung
from their armpits in folds, vestiges of a once-winged people.
The swampy pools became basins where females, dark hairy
lumps of flesh, lay in nutrient baths: unwomen with recep-
tacles into which men might empty their seed without joy;
black crinkled teats to be mindlessly sucked by their infants.

Mandros, when will they come?

In twelve days, when the child is healed. Shar heal fast.

And kill us then?

*They will take him to the ships. The Emperor Aesh will lead
them.*

The Shar came forward with hands cupped. In every cup of
hands lay a stone, a flat pebble washed endlessly by rain and
sea.

Her feet were in wet earth, the wind raised her hair; the air,
as always, stank of sulphur.

The cupped hands waited. She picked up a stone: *when the
planet was in eccentric orbit, half the time in a void so deep it
deadened the soul*

The black pips swam in the red membrane, glittering with
fire.

She picked a stone: *and men learned to shift it in its course,
to bring it toward the sun*

A stone: *but had not waited long enough to learn to do it
well*

:and the world drifted into the orbit of the void they hated
Stone.

:and the hatred perverted itself and became pride

*:for what they had not done except build towers of iron and
stone*

Beyond the arches she saw the walls of the towers, iron and
stone, glittering with flame and carved with warped and tortured flowers.

*:so that they hated themselves and each other, in treachery,
deceit, torment, murder; often out of spite they would not
beget and when they did found over the millennia*

The last stone: *that their seed, which not only contained
sperm, but gave the ovum its female fertility as well, was losing its quality because it too needed light*

Her hands were full of pebbles; she skimmed them in a
sulphur sea.

And all the other planets of Procyon?
:burning gas or thin crusts over fire
Mandros, why are you telling me all this?
:because—

"Christ, I thought you'd never come out of it!" David was gripping her hand.

"What have I done now?"

"Caught a fever from running around outside, on top of everything. For God's sake, don't do that again, eh?"

She scratched the scab on her ear where Aesh had bitten it. "How long?"

"Four days. Mandros and I have been switching between you and Aesh the whole time. It would be nice to have both of you in good health."

Eight days more. "David, will you send Mandros here?"

"Stella! What—"

"No, no, David! I'm not going to conceive another one. Bring Mandros here and stay. There are a lot of questions I have to ask."

Mandros stood at the foot of the bed.

"When I was delirious it seemed to me that you were telling me many things about the Shar. Was it only my fever or were you really telling me those things?"

"I was. Your brain was more receptive when it was feverish."

"Now I'm well. I think." She sat up. "But I remember. You were going to explain why you had told me."

"Because I was made to serve the Emperor and no one else."

"That's not an answer." He was silent. "I suppose I'm to pull an answer from that?" She sighed. "The Emperor is dead, the Shar will be here in eight days to claim their new one and then decide whether to claim this world. How long will that take?"

"I don't know."

"But he's a child," said David.

"It doesn't seem to matter to them. The Shar . . . they want to exchange one dying world for another, and I suppose they will kill us all if they take it. That's pitiful as well as horrible. But Shar are horrible—'' Mandros did not blink, ''—and I used to think you were too, Mandros. All those hundreds of people in the starships were killed, over fifteen years ago. But . . . after Nadja conceived, Billy and Clyde, Anne-Marie and the rest were sent away. Was Ephraim killed on purpose?''

"Oh no," Mandros said. "He happened to be at the place where they broke the line. That was unfortunate."

David growled, "And I suppose Nadja was unfortunate too, hah?"

"No. That was." He was silent for the moment it took him to find the word. "Shameful. Of Ephraim I said I was sorry, and I am still. I am not a true Shar. I have been made like a man and like a man I can be sorry."

"And a few *were* saved," Stella said. "The world is dying, but it might be possible to make it live and grow again. If the Shar leave us alone perhaps people will have new hope—but they must have searched a long time among their nearer stars before they came here, and they won't be willing to go back. Still, there are other places in this system beside the paradise they think they want—planets, moons they could make livable with their technology. Bargains, Mandros. We could make bargains. And they would have their light."

"Their minds are very dark," said Mandros.

"*Theirs?* Clyde and the others were freed. You saved me. Aesh demands love. . . . I think, Mandros, that you and Aesh . . . and . . . and even perhaps the old Emperor, if he was watching . . . have been corrupted by our paradise. By our light.'' She added, "In your language."

Mandros stood without a word. His eyes were blank.

Across the hall, Aesh began to cry. "Maan-dros!" He turned and left them.

"Eight days, Stella? Traveling out beyond Pluto? He won't be well by then."

"Mandros says he will."

"Emperor! My God, even for a quick-growing Shar he's young for that."

"He'll have advisors."

"Yes, and I can guess what they'll advise, if they don't kill him first. Mandros isn't all that effective a guardian. I still don't understand why he told you."

"I don't either. All I know is—David!" She took his face in her hands and drew it to hers. "There *is* very little time!"

His arms went round her. "You're not well," he whispered.

"Oh, I am now—but does it matter?"

Aesh the Emperor gave no orders, climbed no walls. He kneeled on a settee made from a church pew and stared out through the triangles at the rain, the sun, the blowing trees. He let David coat his claws with the plastic filling so he could not scratch his splinted arm. At night he walked the spaces of the dome; his noisy clogs echoed and no one reproved him.

Stella, David and Mandros went through the motions of life, and did not speak much. Mandros became again the automaton he had been in the old days. Stella mopped and swept, paused to finger the rugs she had braided with Annabel and the others, refolded shawls and sweaters. They were torn and raveling.

She felt, not quite fear, but something she could not name. A heaviness in her belly, as if she were about to give birth, or else a pressure at the top of her head as if she were a fetus butting at the amniotic membrane, about to be born. At times she thought she must be going back into her old neurosis, or still suffering from concussion, because the weight shaped itself into WHY DID HE SAVE THEM? and the pressure into WHY DID HE TELL ME? Then she felt a stab of fear. She pushed it away, and made love with David in quiet and powerful tenderness.

On the eighth day the sky was dark, and they moved like sleepwalkers.

"You haven't eaten," said David.

"I'm not hungry." She went into the common room to have a smoke and found Mandros standing in front of the fireplace.

He was holding something, and staring at her.

"What is that?" she asked dully.

He held it out to her.

She had thought at first that it might be a wooden flower,

like the one with which he had marked the grave, but it was a stone sphere.

It was heavy, she had to grip tightly to keep from dropping it.

Black stone, with a few bright crystals embedded in it like stars; marked off in triangles and hexagons, in each a small perfect carving. A sun and the eccentric orbit of its planet, a Shar with crooked body and pitted eyes, a warped and tormented flower . . .

"The Emperor's seal," he said.

"But why give it to—Mandros!"

He had sat down on the floor and was taking off his boots. Then he crossed his legs, rested his hands on his knees.

"It *is* time," he said. His face was pale, but his eyes were clear and alive, there might have been a glint of humor in them at the expression on her face.

"For what?"

"To destruct. Please don't be offended. It is not ugly. Though," he cocked his head, "I am glad I was not made more beautiful or I might not be willing to go."

"Destruct!"

"Yes." He was becoming translucent. He said gently, explaining to a child, "To dissolve and—go."

She saw the shadows of skull and bones. "But Aesh—"

"I was made to last until the son of the Emperor could be delivered. I had the honor of helping to prepare the Emperor himself."

"You can't! You—"

His flesh was a skin of water around the bone. But he was right. His dissolution was not ugly, but had the beauty of a fine anatomical drawing. "I have no choice. I was timed for this." She bowed her head to the sphere. "I was the seed-capsule of the Emperor. I did what was required. But I had feelings, once, and I was a man." She closed her eyes. "Listen!"

She raised her head. The bone hands lifted and turned up, in offering. The skull said, "I did not want them to die, and that is the truth, I swear. . . ."

A dwindling, a crumbling into whiteness.

A few scattered crystals among the clothes.

• • •

David's hands came round her shoulders. "What did he give you?"

"A stone."

From behind them came a whimper. Aesh was standing in fearful loneliness.

David removed the metal splint and sealed the small wounds it had made. Aesh flexed his arm. "That will be stiff for a while," David said. His hands, once they had finished their work, began to shake.

Aesh knelt on the window seat and looked out. The sky was clearing.

Stella, still gripping the sphere, was looking down at Mandros's bunk. The bedding had been stripped and piled, neatly folded, in its center. Except for his clothing, Mandros had owned no object. His place was bare.

Aesh too had owned no toy or keepsake, and Stella herself was holding the only thing that was due to him. She held it to her forehead, and once again it told its story.

Why did you save?
Why did you tell?
Why did you give?

I suppose I'm to answer....
Her head butted against the membrane, and forced.

The sun was westering.

"Maybe they won't come today," David said.

"I think they will."

There was a roaring in the sky. Aesh trembled. He was holding the seal.

Stella took her coat from the hook. It would be a cool evening. The blue coat was very old, very worn. She had given up her vanity, the cornmeal, and the nap was worn down, the edges grimy, the fur matted. Only Ephraim's stitching remained sound and beautiful. It had been the color the sky should have been, and become the color the sky was. She held the coat and listened to the roar. Her body felt like phosphorus, pale and burning.

"Stella?"

She turned.

"You can't go out now, it's dangerous! Did you think you could take him to the—"

"I'm going with him."

"With him!" The implication struck. He stood up, his face darkened and burst into sweat. "No," he whispered.

"If Aesh wants."

She looked at the Emperor. His lips were quivering. He pressed the seal against them and nodded.

"Why, in God's name, why, Stella?"

She moved close and met his eyes.

"Stella . . . good Lord, *what are you?*"

Her breath caught on a sob. "Don't look at me like that!"

"I can't help it!" He palmed the sweat from his face. "You're not—you're not—"

"I'm not a Procyon, David! I'm not!"

"No . . ." He seemed to be speaking without breath. "And you're not Stella either."

Her voice shook. "I'm as much Stella as I ever was."

He stood with head bowed, arms hanging. "Bargains. You really believe . . ."

"David! Are you sorry you loved me?"

His head and arms rose, she dropped the coat and flung herself against him, his fists knotted behind her back, she could not tell whether the burning tears between their faces were his or her own.

The noise stopped.

She turned once for the last sight of David before the dome. His glasses flashed stars from the setting sun.

Aesh, gripping his seal, huddled against her body beneath the coat, and their faintly luminous shape moved over earth darkened with broken twigs, moldering leaves, and the shadow of night. She followed the path she had taken so many times and remembered the steps she had retraced endlessly toward the past, when in truth her life had begun at the farthest step to bring her here.

"Are you afraid?" Aesh whispered.

"No." She was full of sorrow, and if she had looked at David one more time or one moment longer she would have been in torment.

The shuttle, a sphere, had landed on the rock; its fires had exploded the church into blackened fragments, a final obscenity.

Aesh moved away from her, kicking off his clogs, and she waited. She felt the dampness of the soil through her moccasins; the wind lifted her hair, for once swept away the drench of sulphur and brought the sweetness of the earth.

A lock door opened, a ladder descended. Three Shar stood in the shadow of the opening, and though their mouths and noses were masked in the alien atmosphere she could see their eyes, like pomegranate seeds, catching a flicker of red sunset, and the dark drape of the folded skin in their armpits. Their bodies were thick and crook-legged, and Aesh's arrow-slender body seemed very vulnerable facing them. He climbed the rungs lightly, and she did not hear, but understood the word that greeted him.

Majesty.

It was heavy with irony.

Aesh, on the threshold, nodded, and with deliberation turned his back on them. On the fingers of one hand he balanced the seal lightly as a bubble, and with the other beckoned to Stella. Whatever his back may have told them, his face, in the last light, was filled with unholy joy.

He was after all not alone.

Stella placed a foot on the first rung, and the three voices struck like brass bells in her head:

Who/who are/are/you?

Why are/what for/are you/are/here?

She climbed the second rung. "I am . . ." She paused for the word of the maker, the bargainer, the most delicate word in the world.

messenger

"I am a messenger of the Adversary," she said.

— The Military Hospital —

The helicopter moved through the city in the airlane between skyscrapers. It was on autopilot, preset course, and there was no one to squint down the canyons of the streets where the life-mass seethed. Children looked up at it with dull eyes; if it had come lower they would have stoned or shot at it. The armored cars that burrowed among them were scratched and pocked from their attacks.

Fresh and smooth, dressed in crisp white, DeLazzari came into the Control Room at the top of the Hospital. He had had a week off, he was on for three; he ran the Hospital, supervised nurse-patient relationships, directed the sweepers in the maintenance of sterility, and monitored the pile. He took over this function wherever he was told to go, but he particularly liked the Military Hospital because it was clean, roomy, and had very few patients. He was a stocky man with thick black hair, broad wings of mustache, and skin the color of baked earth; he had the blood of all nations in him. "The bad blood of all nations," he would add with a laugh if he felt like impressing one of the trots Mama Rakosy sent up to the apartment, though it was rare he felt like impressing anyone. He was sworn to forego women, drugs and liquor for three weeks, so he switched on the big external screen and dumped out of his bag the cigars, candy and gum that would sustain him, while he watched the course of the helicopter over the city.

A trasher's bomb went off in one of the buildings; daggers
of glass blew out singing, and sliced at the scalps and shoulders of a knot of demonstrators clumped at its base; a fragment of concrete hurled outward and grazed the helicopter,
then fell to dent a fiberglass helmet and concuss the bike-rider
who fell from his machine and lay unconscious under the
bruising feet; the wounded demonstrators scattered or
crawled, leaving their placards, and others took their places,
raising neon-colored cold-light standards of complicated symbols; they camped in the table-sized space, oblivious to bloody
glass, hardhats with crossbows, skinheads with slingshots,
longhairs, freaks, mohicans, children, and above all the
whoop and howl of police sirens coming up.

The helicopter moved north and away; the armored cars
butted their way through, into less crowded streets where merchants did business across wickets in iron cages in which one
touch of a floor button dropped steel shutters and made a
place impregnable fast enough to cut a slice off anyone who
got in the way. Farther north the City Hospital and the Central Police Depot formed two wings of a great moth-shaped
complex webbed about by stalled paddy wagons and am-
bulances.

DeLazzari grinned. In City Hospital twelve Directors
manned the Control Room, endlessly profane and harried.
Shop was always depleted: the sweepers rusted and ground
down from lack of parts and the nurses were obsolete and inefficient. Only the Doctors moved at great speed and in Olym-
pian calm.

He switched on his own O.R. screen. Doctors were already
closing around the operating table, waiting. They were silver,
slab-shaped, featureless. They drew power from a remote
source, and nobody he knew had any idea where it was. They
had orders and carried them out—or perhaps they simply did
what they chose. He had never been in their physical presence,
nor wanted to be.

The helicopter was passing between blank-walled buildings
where the dead were stored in very small vaults, tier upon tier
upon tier; at street level the niches reserved for floral tributes
were empty except for wire frames to which a few dried leaves

and petals clung trembling in the down draft from the rotors. North beyond that in the concrete plaza the racers were heating up for the evening, a horde endlessly circling.

But the city had to end in the north at the great circle enclosing the Military Hospital. It had no wall, no road, no entrance at ground level. What it had was a force-field the helicopter had to rise steeply to surmount. Within, for a wall it had a thicket of greenery half a mile deep going all the way round; outside the field there was a circuit of tumbled masonry pieces, stones, burnt sticks, as if many ragged armies had tried to storm it and retreated, disgusted and weary.

Inside there was no great mystery. The Military Hospital healed broken soldiers from distant and ancient wars; the big circular building had taken no architectural prizes, and on its rolling greens two or three stumbling patients were being supported on their rounds by nurses. Like all Directors DeLazzari tended to make himself out a minor Dracula; like all the rest his power lay in the modicum of choice he had among the buttons he pushed.

The helicopter landed on its field and discharged its cell, a Life Unit in which a dying soldier lay enmeshed; it took on another cell, containing another soldier who had been pronounced cured and would be discharged germ-free into his theater of war; it was also boarded by the previous Director, pocket full of credits and head full of plans for a good week.

The Hospital doors opened, the cell rolled through them down a hall into an anteroom where it split; a wagon emerged from it carrying the patient and his humming, flickering life-system, the anteroom sealed itself, flooded with aseptic sprays and drained, washing away blood-traces; the O.R. sweeper removed the wet packs from the ruined flesh and dropped them on the floor, which dissolved them. In the operating room the i.v. system was pumping, the monitors pulsed, the Doctors activated their autoclaves in one incandescent flash and then extruded a hundred tentacles, probes, knives, sensors, and flexed them; their glitter and flash was almost blinding in the harsh light. DeLazzari was obliged to watch them; he hated it, and they needed no light. It was provided on demand of the Supervisors' and Directors' Union, though if machines chose to go renegade there was very little the Supervisors and Directors could say or do.

Doctors had never gone renegade. Neither had sweepers or nurses; it was a delicious myth citizens loved to terrify themselves with, perhaps because they resented the fact that madness should be reserved for people. DeLazzari thought that was pretty funny and he was scared too.

The O.R. sweeper sprayed himself (DeLazzari thought of it as delousing), the doors opened, the sweeper pushed in the body, still housing its low flicker of life, removed the attachments and set it on the table. The Doctors reattached what was needed; the sweeper backed into a corner and turned his own power down. DeLazzari flicked a glance at the indicator and found it correct.

One Doctor swabbed the body with a personal nozzle and began to remove steel fragments from belly and groin, another slit the chest and reached in to remove bone slivers from the left lung, a third trimmed the stump of the right forefinger and fitted a new one from the Parts Bank, a fourth tied off and removed torn veins from the thighs, all without bumping head, shoulders, or elbows because they had none, a fifth kept the throat clear, a sixth gave heart massage, the first opened the belly and cut out a gangrened bowel section, the third sewed and sealed the new right forefinger and as an afterthought trimmed the nail, the fifth, still watching every breath, peeled back sections of the scalp and drilled holes in the skull. All in silence except for the soft clash and ringing of sensors, knives, and probes. Blood splashed; their body surfaces repelled it in a mist of droplets and the floor washed it away.

The sweeper turned his power up on some silent order and fetched a strange small cage of silver wires. The fifth Doctor took it, placed it over the soldier's head, and studied its nodes as coordinates in relation to the skull. Then he spoke at last. "Awaken," he said.

DeLazzari gave a hoarse nervous laugh and whispered, "*Let there be light.*" The boy's eyelids flickered and opened. The eyes were deep blue; the enlarged pupils contracted promptly and at an equal rate. DeLazzari wondered, as always, if he were conscious enough to be afraid he was lying in an old cemetery among the gravestones. Silver graves.

● ● ●

"Are you awake?" The voice was deep, God-the-Father-All-Powerful. The Doctor checked the nose tube and cleared the throat. "Max, are you awake?"

"Yes . . . yes . . . yes. . . ."

"Can you answer questions?"

"Yes."

"Recording for psychiatric report." He extruded a fine probe and inserted it into the brain. "What do you see? Tell me what you see."

"I see . . . from the top of the Ferris wheel I can see all the boats in the harbor, and when I come down in a swoop all the people looking up. . . ."

The probe withdrew and reentered. "What do you see now, Max?"

"My father says they're not sweet peas but a wildflower, like a wild cousin of the sweet pea, toadflax, some people call them butter-and-eggs. . . . 'Scrophulariaceae Linaria vulgaris is the big name for them, Max, and that vulgaris means common, but they're not so common anymore. . . .' "

Probe.

". . . something like the fireworks I used to watch when I was a kid, but they're not fireworks, they're the real thing, and they turn the sky on fire. . . ."

"Area established."

Probe.

"One eye a black hole and the kid lying across her with its skull, with its skull, with its skull, I said Chrissake, Yvon, why'd you have to? Yvon? why'd you have to? why? he said ohmigod Max how was I to know whether they were? Max? how was I to know whether?"

The probe tip burned, briefly.

"Yes, Max? He said: 'how was I to know whether' what?"

"Know what? Who's he? I don't know what you're talking about."

DeLazzari watched the probes insinuate the cortex and withdraw. The Doctors pulled at the associations, unraveling a tangled skein; they didn't try to undo all the knots, only the most complicated and disturbing. Was the act, he wondered, a healing beneficence or a removal of guilt associated with killing?

After four or five burns the cage was removed and the scalp repaired. Surprised, Delazzari punched O.R. Procedures, Psych Division, and typed:

WHY SURGEONS OMIT DEEP MIL. INDOCTRINATION?

NEW RULING ONE WEEK PREVIOUS, the computer said.

WHOSE AUTHORITY?

BOARD OF SUPERVISORS.

And who ordered them around? He switched off and turned back to the Doctors.

After their duties had been completed they followed some mysteriously developed ritual that looked like a laying on of hands. All probes and sensors extended, they would go over a body like a fine-tooth comb, slicing off a wart, excising a precancerous mole, straightening a twisted septum. DeLazzari switched off and lit a cigar. There were no emergencies to be expected in the next ten minutes. He blinked idly at a small screen recording the flat encephalogram of a dead brain whose body was being maintained for Parts.

The Doctors had other customs that both annoyed and amused him by their irrationality. Tonight they had been quiet, but sometimes one of them, sectioning a bowel, might start a running blue streak of chatter like a Las Vegas comic while another, probing the forebrain, would burst out in a mighty organ baritone, "Nearer My God to Thee." On the rare but inevitable occasions when an irreparable patient died with finality they acted as one to shut down the life-system and retract their instruments; then stood for five minutes in a guardian circle of quietness, like the great slabs of Stonehenge, around the body before they would allow the sweeper to take it away.

The big external screen was still on and DeLazzari looked down into the city, where a torchlight procession was pushing its flaming way up the avenue and the walls to either side wavered with unearthly shadows. He shut off and called Shop. He peered at the fax sheet on Max Vingo clipped to his noticeboard and typed:

YOU GOT A CAUCASIAN TYPE NURSE APPROX FIVE-SEVEN FAIR HAIR QUIET VOICE NOT PUSHY MILD-TO-WARM AND FIRST RATE?

2482 BEST QUALITY CHECKED OUT LIGHT BROWN WE CAN MAKE IT FAIR HAIR.

LIGHT BROWN OK HEALING UNIT 35.

He yawned. Nothing more for the moment. He dialed supper, surveyed the sleeping-alcove and bathroom, all his own, with satisfaction, checked the pill dispenser which allowed him two headache tablets on request, one sleeping pill at 11:00 P.M. and one laxative at 7:30 A.M. if required. He was perfectly content.

All nurses looked about twenty-five years old, unutterably competent but not intimidating unless some little-boy type needed a mother. 2482 was there when Max Vingo first opened his eyes and stirred weakly in his mummy-wrappings.

"Hello," she said quietly.

He swallowed; his throat was still sore from the respirator. "I'm alive."

"Yes, you are, and we're glad to have you."

"This is a hospital."

"It is, and I'm your nurse, 2482."

He stared at her. "You're a—a mechanical—I've heard about you—you're a mechanical—"

"I'm a Robonurse," she said.

"Huh . . . it sounds like some kind of a tank."

"That's a joke, baby—God help us," said DeLazzari, and turned her dial up half a point.

She smiled. "I'm not at all like a tank."

"No." He gave it a small interval of thought. "No, not at all."

It was the third day. DeLazzari never bothered to shave or wash on duty where he didn't see another human being; his face was covered with grey-flecked stubble. Outside he was vain, but here he never glanced into a mirror. The place was quiet; no new patients had come in, no alarms had sounded, the walking wounded were walking by themselves. Besides 2482 there were only two other nurses on duty, one with a nephritis and another tending the body soon to be frozen for Parts. Still, he did have 2482 to control and he watched with weary amusement as she warmed up under the turn of his dial.

"You're getting better already." She touched Max Vingo's forehead, a nonmedical gesture since the thermocouple already registered his temperature. Her fingers were as warm as his skin. "You need more rest. Sleep now." Narcotic opened into his bloodstream from an embedded tube, and he slept.

On the fifth day the people of the city rose up against their government and it fell before them. Officers elected themselves, curfews were established, the torchlight parades and demonstrations stopped; occasionally a stray bomb exploded in a callbox. Packs of dogs swarmed up the avenue, pausing to sniff at places where the blood had lain in puddles; sometimes they met a congregation of cats and there were snarling yelping skirmishes. DeLazzari eyed them on his screen, devoutly thankful that he was not stationed in City Hospital. He filled City's requests for blood, plasma and parts as far as regulations required and didn't try to contact their Control Room.

At the Military Hospital the nephritis got up and walked out whole, the deadhead was cut up and frozen in Parts, an interesting new malaria mutation came in and was assigned a doctor to himself in Isolation. 2482 peeled away the bandages from Max Vingo's head and hand.

He asked for a mirror and when she held it before him he examined the scars visible on his forehead and scalp and said, "I feel like I'm made up of spare parts." He lifted his hand and flexed it. "That's not so funny." The forefinger was his own now, but it had once belonged to a black man and though most of the pigment had been chemically removed it still had an odd bluish tinge. "I guess it's better than being without one."

"You'll soon be your old handsome self."

"I bet you say that to all the formerly handsome guys."

"Of course. How would you get well otherwise?"

He laughed, and while she was wiping his face with a soft cloth he said, "2482, haven't you ever had a name?"

"I've never needed one."

"I guess if I get really familiar I can call you 2 for short."

"Hoo boy, this is a humorist." DeLazzari checked the dial and indicator and left them steady on for the while. The malaria case went into convulsions without notice and he turned his attention elsewhere.

• • •

She rubbed his scalp with a cream to quicken regrowth of hair.

"What does that do for a bald guy?"

"Nothing. His follicles no longer function."

He flexed his new finger again and rubbed the strange skin with the fingertips of his other hand. "I hope mine haven't died on me."

By day 7 DeLazzari was beginning to look like a debauched beachcomber. His hospital whites were grimy and his mustache ragged. However, he kept a clean desk, his sweeper cleared away the cigar stubs and the ventilators cleaned the air. Two badly scarred cases of yaws came in from a tropical battleground and two Doctors called for skin grafts and whetted their knives. In the city a curfew violator was shot and killed, and next morning the first of the new demonstrators appeared. One of the Doctors took the chance of visiting Max for the first time when he was awake.

The soldier wasn't dismayed; he answered questions readily enough, showed off his growing hair, and demonstrated his attempts to use the grafted finger, but he kept looking from the Doctor to 2482 and back in an unsettling way, and DeLazzari turned up the nurse's dial a point.

When the Doctor was gone she said, "Did he disturb you?"

"No." But his eyes were fixed on her.

She took his hand. "Does that feel good?"

"Yes," he said. "That feels good." And he put his other hand on top of hers.

DeLazzari ate and slept and monitored the screens and supervised the duties of nurses and sweepers. Sometimes he wiped his oily face with a tissue and briefly considered rationing his cigars, which he had been smoking excessively because of boredom. Then three cases of cholera came in from the east; one was dead on arrival and immediately incinerated, the other two occupied him. But he still had time to watch the cure of Max Vingo and by turns of the dial nourish his relationship with 2482. He thought they were a pretty couple.

Max got unhooked from his i.v., ate solid food with a good

appetite, and got up and walked stiffly on his scarred legs, now freed of their bandages. His hair grew in, black as De-Lazzari's but finer, and the marks on his skin were almost invisible. He played chess sometimes with 2482 and didn't make any comments when she let him win. But there was an odd sadness about him, more than DeLazzari might have guessed from his Psych report. Although the ugliest of his memories had been burned away, the constellations of emotion attached to them had remained and the Doctors would never be able to do anything about those during the short time he stayed in the Hospital.

So that often at night, even sometimes when he fell into a light doze, he had sourceless nightmares he couldn't describe, and when he flailed his arms in terrified frustration 2482 took his hands and held them in her own until he slept at peace.

DeLazzari watched the TV news, followed the courses of battles over the world and on Moonbase and Marsport, and made book with himself on where his next casualties would be coming from. Not from the planets, which had their own Hospitals, or from the usual Military Base establishments. His own Hospital (he liked to think of it as his own because he was so fond of its conveniences and so full of respect for its equipment) was one of the rare few that dealt with the unusual, the interesting, and the hopeless. Down in the city the fire marchers were out and the bombs were exploding again. He knew that soon once more the people of the city would rise against their government and it would fall before them, and he kept check of blood and parts and ordered repairs on old scuppered nurses.

Max Vingo dressed himself now and saw the scars fade on his newly exposed torso. Because he was so far away from it he didn't think of the battle he might be going into. It was when he had stood for a long time at the window looking out at the rain, at how much greener it made the grass, that 2482 said to him, "Max, is there something you're afraid of?"

"I don't know."

"Is it the fighting?"

"I don't even remember much of that."

"The Doctors took those memories away from you."

"Hey!" DeLazzari growled, hand poised over the control. "Who said you could say a thing like that?"

"I don't mind that," Max said.

DeLazzari relaxed.

"Don't you want to know why?"
"If you want to tell me."
"I'm not sure . . . but I think it was because the Doctors knew you were a gentle and loving man, and they didn't want for you to be changed."

He turned and faced her. "I'm the same. But I'm still a man who has to dress up like a soldier—and I don't know when that will ever change. Maybe that's why I'm frightened."

DeLazzari wondered for a moment what it would be like to be sick and helpless and taken care of by a loving machine in the shape of a beautiful woman. Then he laughed his hoarse derisive crow and went back to work. He had never been sick.

On the eighteenth day five poison cases came in from a bloodless coup in a banana republic; DeLazzari sent a dozen nurses with them into the Shock Room and watched every move. He was hot and itchy, red-eyed and out of cigars, and thinking he might as well have been in City Hospital. They were having their troubles over there, and once again he sent out the supplies. By the time he had leisure for a good look at Max Vingo, 2482's dial was all the way up and Max was cured and would be going out next day: day 21, his own discharge date. He listened to their conversation for a while and whistled through his teeth. "End of a beautiful interlude," he said.

That evening Max ate little and was listless and depressed. 2482 didn't press him to eat or speak, nor did DeLazzari worry. The behavior pattern was normal for situation and temperament.

Max went to sleep early but woke about eleven and lay in the darkness without calling or crying out, only stared toward the ceiling; sometimes for a moment he had a fit of trembling.

2482 came into the room softly, without turning on the light. "Max, you're disturbed."

"How do you know?" he said in an expressionless voice.

"I watch your heartbeat and your brainwaves. Are you feeling ill?"

"No."

"Then what is the matter? Do you have terrible thoughts?"

"It's the thoughts I can't think that bother me, what's behind everything that got burned away. Maybe they shouldn't have done that, maybe they should have let me become another person, maybe if I knew, really knew, really knew what it was like to hurt and kill and be hurt and be killed and live in filth for a lifetime and another lifetime, ten times over, I'd get to laugh at it and like it and say it was the way to be, the only way to be and the way I should have been. . . ."

"Oh no, Max. No, Max. I don't believe so."

Suddenly he folded his arms over his face and burst out weeping, in ugly tearing sobs.

"Don't, Max." She sat down beside him and pulled his arms away. "No, Max. Please don't." She pulled apart the fastenings of her blouse and clasped his head between her tender, pulsing and unfleshly breasts.

DeLazzari grinned lasciviously and watched them on the infrared scanner, chin propped on his hand. "Lovely, lovely, lovely," he whispered. Then he preset 2482's dial to move down three points during the next four hours, popped his pill, and went to bed.

The alarm woke him at four. "Now what in hell is that?" He staggered groggily over to the console to find the source. He switched on lights. The red warning signal was on over 2482's dial. Neither the dial nor the indicator had moved from UP position. He turned on Max Vingo's screen. She had lain down on the bed beside him and he was sleeping peacefully in her arms. DeLazzari snarled. "Circuit failure." The emergency panel checked out red in her number. He dialed Shop.

REROUTE CONTROL ON 2482.

CONTROL REROUTED, the machine typed back.

WHY DID YOU NOT REROUTE ON AUTO WHEN FAILURE REGISTERED?

REGULATION STATES DIRECTOR AUTONOMOUS IN ALL ASPECTS

NURSE-PATIENT RELATIONSHIP NOW ALSO INCLUDING ALTER-
NATE CIRCUITS.

WHY WAS I NOT TOLD THAT BEFORE?

THAT IS NEW REGULATION. WHY DO YOU NOT REQUEST LIST OF
NEW REGULATIONS DAILY UPDATED AND READILY AVAILABLE
ALL TIMES?

"At four o'clock in the morning?" DeLazzari punched off.
He noted that the indicator was falling now, and on the screen
he could see 2482 moving herself away from Max and smoothing the covers neatly over him.

DeLazzari woke early on the last day and checked out the
cholera, the yaws and the poison. The choleras were nearly
well; one of the yaws needed further work on palate defor-
mity; one of the poisons had died irrevocably, he sent it to
Autopsy; another was being maintained in Shock, the rest
recovering.

While he ate breakfast he watched the news of battle and
outrage; growing from his harshly uprooted childhood faith a
tendril of thought suggested that Satan was plunging poisoned
knives in the sores of the world. "DeLazzari the Metaphysi-
cian!" He laughed. "Go on, you bastards, fight! I need the
work." The city seemed to be doing his will, because it was as
it had been.

Max Vingo was bathing himself, depilating his own face,
dressing himself in a new uniform. A sweeper brought him
breakfast. DeLazzari, recording his Director's Report, noted
that he seemed calm and rested, and permitted himself a small
glow of satisfaction at a good job nearly finished.

When the breakfast tray was removed, Max stood up and
looked around the room as if there was something he might
take with him, but he had no possessions. 2482 came in and
stood by the door.

"I was waiting for you," he said.

"I've been occupied."

"I understand. It's time to go, I guess."

"Good luck."

"I've had that already." He picked up his cap and looked at
it. "2482—Nurse, may I kiss you?"

● ● ●

DeLazzari gave her the last downturn of the dial.

She stared at him and said firmly, "I'm a machine, sir. You wouldn't want to kiss a machine." She opened the top of her blouse, placed her hands on her chest at the base of her neck and pulled them apart, her skin opened like a seam. Inside she was the gold-and-silver gleam of a hundred metals threaded in loops, wound on spindles, flickering in minute gears and casings; her workings were almost fearsomely beautiful, but she was not a woman.

"Gets 'em every time." DeLazzari yawned and waited for the hurt shock, the outrage, the film of hardness coming down over the eyes like a third eyelid.

Max Vingo stood looking at her in her frozen posture of display. His eyelids twitched once, then he smiled. "I would have been very pleased and grateful to kiss a machine," he said and touched her arm lightly. "Good-bye, Nurse." He went out and down the hall toward his transportation cell.

DeLazzari's brows rose. "At least that's a change." 2482 was still standing there with her innards hanging out. "Close it up, woman. That's indecent." For a wild moment he wondered if there might be an expression trapped behind her eyes, and shook his head. He called down Shop and sent her for postpatient diagnostic with special attention to control system.

He cleaned up for the new man. That is, he evened up the pile of tape reels and ate the last piece of candy. Then he filched an ID plate belonging to one of the poison cases, put everything on AUTO, went down a couple of floors and used the ID to get into Patients' Autobath. For this experience of hot lather, stinging spray, perfume and powder he had been saving himself like a virgin.

When he came out in half an hour he was smooth, sweet-smelling, and crisply clothed. As the door locked behind him five Doctors rounded a corner and came down the corridor in single file. DeLazzari stood very still. Instead of passing him they turned with a soft whirr of their nylon castors and came near. He breathed faster. They formed a semicircle around

him; they were featureless and silver, and smelt faintly of
warm metal. He coughed.

"What do you want?"

They were silent.

"What do you want, hey? Why don't you say something?"

They came nearer and he shrank against the door, but there
were more machines on the other side.

"Get away from me! I'm not one of your stinking
zombies!"

The central Doctor extruded a sensor, a slender shining limb
with a small bright bulb on the end. It was harmless, he had
seen it used thousands of times from the Control Room, but
he went rigid and broke out into a sweat. The bulb touched
him very lightly on the forehead, lingered a moment, and
retracted. The Doctors, having been answered whatever question they had asked themselves, backed away, resumed their
file formation, and went on down the hall. DeLazzari burst
into hoarse laughter and scrubbed with his balled fist at the
place the thing had touched. He choked on his own spit,
sobered after a minute, and walked away very quickly in the
opposite direction, even though it was a long way around to
where he wanted to go. Much later he realized that they had
simply been curious and perplexed in the presence of an unfamiliar heartbeat.

He went out in the same helicopter as Max Vingo, though
the soldier in his sterile perimeter didn't know that. In the
Control Room the new Director, setting out his tooth-cleaner,
depilatory and changes of underwear, watched them on the
monitor. Two incoming helicopters passed them on the way;
the city teemed with fires and shouting and the children kicked
at the slow-moving cars. In the operating theater the silver
Doctors moved forward under the lights, among the machines, and stood motionless around the narrow tables.

– **Gingerbread Boy** –

Benno was sitting in the closet with the door closed. It was dark and stuffy, and the toe of a shoe was digging into the base of his spine, but he liked the closeness. He had been grown in a tank as narrow as this closet, in dark warm liquids. He had no true memory of that time, but he closed his eyes and imagined that he could remember the warmth, and the love and kindness that seemed to be around him then. . . .

There was a thump and a yell of laughter, and he blinked. Poppy and her ball. She had nothing to worry about. He had been playing with her a few minutes ago. He would throw the ball, and she would miss it and run after it, shrieking.

"Come on, Benno, throw it, Benno!" And Benno threw it, mouth drawn in the thin ironical line that served him for a smile.

Finally, running to catch it, she overreached herself and fell. She sat there a minute, lower lip shoved out and mouth drawn down at the corners into a deep inverted U before it opened into a howl.

"No, no, Poppy. Don't cry, lovey." Benno pulled her up as Mrs. Peretto came running into the room.

"Benno, what did you—" She bit off the words and grabbed the child. "What happened, sweetie?"

Benno said quietly, "Mrs. Peretto, why don't you ask Poppy *what I did to her*?"

The woman twisted to face him and he saw that she was shaking. She loosened her hold on the little girl and stood up.

"*Mrs. Peretto,* Benno? Not 'Mom'? Benno," her eyes filled, "I—I don't know what's got into you. . . ." She hurried out of the room.

But she had left the child behind—*afraid to let me know she doesn't trust me*—and Poppy, sorrow forgotten, trotted over to Benno and yanked at his trouser-leg. "C'mon, c'mon, Benno, let's play some more."

"No more for now, Poppy." Benno gently detached the sticky fingers. "Go find your mummy."

So he went and sat down in the closet with the door shut and brooded. He would have enjoyed one of Wenslow's cigars right now, but the closet was no place to smoke it. Anyway, the whole business was no good. But as he was about to get up he heard another sound: Mrs. Peretto dialing the intercom. He stayed still.

"Helen? Oh . . . fine, I guess . . . nothing really new, but I've been having a little bit of trouble, too . . . the thing is, I can't even say it's anything I haven't made up in my own mind. I'm just . . . just getting to be a little scared. . . ."

Benno waited till he was sure she had gone. If she knew he skulked in closets and listened to private conversations it wouldn't have helped at all. He always went into closets when he felt moody, but he didn't care to advertise it.

As he opened the door he saw himself in the full-length glass, the image of a broad stocky twelve-year-old boy.

But he was five years old, not twelve. He had been made in this shape and he would die in it: pseudomale and sterile, hairless except for the strong dark line of brow and the close-cropped head of hair so dark and wiry it looked artificial. Even the temper of his skin was dark and sullen.

He ran a hand over his face. He had been grown from a piece of Peretto's flesh, so the features were Peretto's; but Peretto was a man, and Benno a secondhand copy pretending to be his child.

He sneered at the image and slipped out of the house.

Peretto and Wenslow shared one of the shabby portables in Administration; it contained the lab where Benno had been born, and a small private office. When Benno reached it he was glad to find Peretto in and Wenslow out.

As he closed the door behind him, Peretto looked up. "What's eating you, Benno?"

"Not me," said Benno. "You."

"I don't think I'm giving you any trouble. What is it?"

"Mrs. Peretto thinks I've got it in for Poppy, or something. She thought I hurt her when she fell today."

Peretto shrugged. "Parents always worry about jealousy problems between older and younger children."

Benno helped himself in Wenslow's humidor and lit up.

"She's not worried. She's frightened. I heard her saying so to Mrs. Metzner on the phone. She's scared of me."

Peretto said hesitantly, "That's not so, Benno. . . . I think she's feeling a little guilty . . . like a lot of the rest of us."

"Because it's hard to keep loving made-up things like us when you've got real kids of your own."

"We put a lot of love into you—"

"But that was different. That was when you thought you couldn't have any kids."

"Earth was pretty hot when we left. We couldn't be sure we wouldn't be sterile forever. We had to have something, Benno."

"So now you've got something and you're stuck with it." Benno looked out of the window where the yellow sun of Skander V was shining on experimental plots and groves of trees, on Residential, on the dunes and the salt lake and the rest of the Colony beyond. "And it makes you sick to look at us and think you wanted and loved us."

"Benno!"

"But it's true. Dickon told me Wenslow said that to him."

"Oh, Wenslow!"

"Well, maybe you don't like him so much either. But you and he are on the same side."

"Do we have to pick sides?"

"We can't help it. A lot of the guys are talking funny, too."

Peretto waited. The androids were unable to lie and he did not want to make Benno compromise himself.

Benno said uncomfortably, "About Bimbo Harrington."

"But you know he drowned. We couldn't do anything for him."

"Nobody ever saw his body."

"It wasn't a thing to see. He—the android body decomposes so—we can't do anything about . . ."

"Well, they think—" Benno began, but the door opened. Wenslow came in.

His pale eyes flashed and his thin nostrils twitched at the smoke in the air. "At the cigars again, I see, Benno," he said pleasantly.

Benno blew a mouthful of smoke into his face and walked out.

He heard the voices through the closed door.

"I swear to God if that thing belonged to me—"

Peretto interrupted wearily, "You leave cigars around because you get a good snide laugh out of seeing him smoke them. If he manages to do it without amusing you, too bad for you. Now let's quit niggling and get to work."

"And then she said, 'I don't know what's got into you, you always called me Mom until—' "

"And if you tried it, she'd twist your ears off for you, the bitch!"

Benno watched the bitter face across the campfire and realized that Dickon had probably paid very heavily for his own enjoyment in blowing smoke at Wenslow. He would have to be more careful of his pleasures in the future.

He said, trying to keep peace, "The Perettos aren't bad, Dickon. You have to be fair to them."

The shadows in Dickon's eyes were as deep as the humps of the dunes against the night sky. "You can say that, smoking cigars and turning yourself into a clown to suck up to them."

"If I did that, I'd be selling my soul," said Benno. "But if I left off smoking when I like it just for fear of anything they might do, I'd be selling it twice over."

"Soul! I'd like to see you show me where you've got a soul!"

"Nothing *you* could see! Oh hell, I guess if I had to live with the Wenslows I'd be as big a bastard as you are." Dickon answered him in kind, and he waited for a slackening. "But don't you see? They loved us and made us love them, so they think we've got immortal souls. That's the only thing that's keeping them from wiping us out."

"What makes you think they haven't started wiping us out

already?'' Rudi Metzner asked. ''What about Bimbo?''

''I asked Peretto about that today,'' Benno said slowly. ''He said he'd drowned.''

''And you believed him? Sure he drowned. But it was in one of those tanks, you can bet. Did you know they'd started up the tanks again? What's your guess about what they're doing?''

''I don't get you.''

''Take a look in one of those tanks,'' said Dickon. ''Try it in the middle of the night, sneak around the back where the guard won't see you. You'll see they've got a thing in there, something new they're making, and I'll bet they started it with Bimbo. Maybe Peretto and Wenslow wouldn't bloody their hands on us, but that don't stop them from making a new kind of android to do their work, a killer that's not so scared of souls! Take a look and see.''

''I'll promise this,'' said Benno. ''You try messing around with the Perettos and I'll kill you dead, Dickon, because *you* haven't got the soul of a flea!''

The stars were dim beyond the two moons that made the shadows shift and fall; rustling trees covered his footsteps in the grass.

He cursed them, he didn't believe them, he had sworn he wouldn't go. But here he was. He had wakened in the night as if he had planned it, and dressed and crept out. He paused; if his world broke now he would never be able to love the Perettos again, and there was nothing else. He went on.

At the back of the fence he had the whole building between himself and the guard. He climbed the chicken-wire and dropped down silently. He knew that the lock of the tank-room window was broken. No one was worried about theft; the guard was there only to prevent the disturbance of delicate adjustments in the equipment.

He pushed at the window; it creaked but the wind covered the noise.

Inside it was very dark, but he knew the room well. Two steps and he found the bank of switches on the first tank. One dim light was all he dared. The glimmer inside, faint as it was, showed that one was empty. He pressed back the toggle and moved on to the peephole of the next. That one was empty, too, and he began to hope. The third—

He was afraid to turn on more than one light, and the liquid was cloudy, but there was definitely a creature there.

In a second it became sensitive to the light and began turning and threshing. The cloudiness enveloped it again but he had seen it. Sickened, he turned the light out and groped for the window.

He dropped down and climbed the wire without caring where he went or whether he was caught.

A few steps away from the fence a group of figures emerged from the bushes and surrounded him.

"Couldn't resist, eh, Benno?"

"What do you want?" he whispered.

"We had a bet on you," said Dickon, grinning. "Go ahead, tell us what you saw there."

After a moment, he said, "All right. I saw something there —but not clearly enough to tell what it was."

"But we told you what it was and you know. Go on, don't you?"

"Yes," said Benno.

"Not feelin' so snotty now, are you, Benno?"

Hurrah for our side. He would have hit out at them, but there were too many. He turned to find the weak point in the circle, but they were his equals.

"Let me go," he said.

"Okay, for now. But remember, we'll be calling on you one day. You'll come."

He ran, and their laughter followed him.

It was afternoon; with Poppy swinging on his hand Benno tramped along the stretch of sand that threaded through the tufted dunes and separated the back gardens of Residential from the lake. The sun was shining, but not for Benno.

He tried to tell himself that he had no proof of anything, but he felt weak inside in the face of Dickon's hatred of the humans.

"Let's dig here," said Poppy, "and we'll find the treasure." Benno sat down while she went to work. Her presence was Mrs. Peretto's way of saying: I was a fool yesterday and didn't mean what I said. If that was the case, he had nothing to fear there. He looked around. The beach was quiet, the waters rippled sluggishly.

A few houses down, a woman came through the back gate and out onto the sand, a naked baby tucked under one arm and a flannel blanket under the other. Mrs. Harrington. She was wearing brief red shorts and a fluffy blouse; a black ponytail bobbed on her tanned neck.

She trotted down to one of the sundecks near the water and sat there, sloshing her feet while the baby kicked on the blanket beside her, gurgling.

Then Harrington, out from work, swung down the garden, leaped over the gate, and ran across the sands. He grabbed the ponytail, pulled his wife's head back, and kissed her upside-down face. He whispered in her ear, gesturing back toward the house. She shushed him, glancing at Benno and Poppy. He cajoled; she resisted. Finally she shrugged, tucked up the baby, and followed him back to the house. Benno could hear them giggling as they went.

"When I get big I'm going to be a mummy," said Poppy. "And you can be the daddy, Benno."

"Yeh," said Benno.

He crouched, trapped in the amber of twelve-year-old boyhood on Skander V. Peretto had said, "We would have made you—complete, if we could. We just don't know enough. . . ."

Benno, watching the Harringtons, knew well enough what he would never be.

Poppy put aside her pail and shovel and came over to him, bracing herself between his knees and resting her forehead against his. Her breath was like apples; she scratched his face gently and he kissed her, rich with the pleasure of feeling a living being against him. *This is all I'm good for.* He hugged her as she giggled, and ruffled his hair in her neck, grunting like the wild pigs the colonists hunted for sport.

Someone shrieked behind him: "You filthy beast! Let go of that child at once, do you hear?"

He was so taken with surprise that he fell back in the sand, pulling Poppy on top of him. Mrs. Wenslow was standing over him, fists tight, face contorted.

"Dirty, dirty thing! Wait till they hear about this! Peretto's darling! I'll tell them different, you filthy—"

Benno righted himself and ran, leaving Poppy howling behind him. The woman knew he wasn't, he couldn't—! But there was no arguing with that— He ran.

In the hills there were caves hidden behind thickets of low gnarled trees. . . .

He squatted, nursing his hurt as the sun sank and the moons swung by. He thought and thought till his mind turned sickly and his head ached. Was he as innocent as he had always believed? He was afraid to search the unexplored reaches of his mind, but he knew for sure that his loins were empty and he cursed himself and his makers.

Exhausted at last, he groped in his pocket for one of the cigars he had filched the day before. He stared at it, shrugged, and lit it.

He sat smoking and watching the stars as they filtered in and out of the leaves. He didn't know what he was waiting for.

"Put that out, you nut! You want to get caught?"

Benno peered out; he saw nothing but stars and branches. "Dickon?" He called tentatively.

Pushing aside the boughs, Dickon slipped in and sat beside him. "Go on, put it out. They'll see us a mile off."

"I don't care."

"I do, God damn it, the thing's suffocating me."

Benno mashed it out. "You wouldn't have found me without it."

"Now they're not going to find *us,*" said Dickon. "What happened? I was out hunting and they rounded us up and sent us to bring you in. Huh!"

"I was playing with Poppy, horsing around. Somebody thought it was something dirty."

"Boy, I love you for that!" Dickon thumped him on the back. "It's what I've been waiting for—but I never thought you'd be the one. Who was it? Not Peretto?"

"No. It was Mrs. Wenslow."

Benno was shocked by the silence. No sneers, no laughter. He turned to look for Dickon's face in the dark, and thought suddenly: *he loves them.*

Dickon said in a low voice, "Nobody'd play with that

scrawny kid of theirs. They got him so he's scared to let out a peep."

"I'm sorry, Dickon."

"What for, you bloody fool? What do you mean?"

"Nothing," said Benno.

Dickon raised his head. "Listen, there they are! Halloo! Halloo!" he called softly down the hill.

"Who?"

"The rest of us! I've got twenty-five down there, only ten missing." He divided the branches and called, "Come on up, you guys, I found him!"

"But what—" Benno began, but Dickon was waving the others in.

"Hi!" they cried. "What was all the business about?"

Dickon guffawed. "He was horsing with the Peretto brat and they thought—" He elaborated to an extent that made Benno glad the darkness hid his flushed face. Their eyes glittered in the dimness: they were staring at him with respect.

"Gee, lemme touch you! You been holding out on us, Benno? Maybe you got—"

"Shut up, shut up for God's sake!" Benno snarled. "He's feeding you a line. I'm just the same as you are, dammit!" His people!

Dickon laughed again, nastily. "All right, forget it for now. We've got to get the others together and we can start out."

"Start out for what?" Benno felt the incredulous stares around him.

"You all there? What d'you think we got these guns for? We're all set to knock the lot of them off the planet!"

Benno caught his breath. "Just on account of this thing with me?"

"Who else? Think we're gonna let 'em get away with it?"

Benno gaped at their set faces in the dusk. "But they're not mad at you, you damn fools!"

"What do you mean? Think you're going to back out after getting us all up here?"

"I didn't. You came after me." He tried to keep his voice level. "They got nothing against you. I just came up here to think for a while. Let me go back and take my lumps and we'll forget the whole business."

"Forget it!" Dickon swung up the rifle. "You're coming down with us right now! I'm giving the orders and you're gonna do it!"

"Yeah? You want to fight, okay. But you don't pin it on me." Benno grasped the rifle barrel and pulled it to his chest. "Go on. Kill me."

Dickon stood indecisive. Everyone knew that if Benno were dead the whole affair would collapse. Then he pulled the rifle out of Benno's hands and set it aside. "The kid wants to take his lumps," he sneered. "Okay . . . put the guns away and give him what he wants!"

Words rattled at him: ". . . betbetbetterterter i-i-ide-de-dea . . ." He shook his head and the words rolled around inside it as he pulled himself out of his sleep or coma, he never knew which.

Mist was pushing into the cave. The trees outside seemed clotted with cobwebs. His lids were heavy and crusted, his body felt flayed to the bone, sore in every joint, muscle, nerve. His tongue pulled away from his palate with a wrench and his arms flopped like dying fishes. He looked at them and saw that the wrists were bound.

". . . don't know why I never thought of it before . . ." Benno moved his head again and nearly groaned. There was no comfort in the sickly early dawn rolling by in wet drifts of fog.

". . . much better idea," Dickon was saying. "We can't just run down there waving guns. They'd knock us off in an hour. But if we pick up one of their brats they'll come after us. They'll never know where to find us in all these holes and we can do what we like with them."

Benno pulled himself up till he sat hunched over his knees. He didn't dare touch his face, even to rub his eyes.

"All we have to decide is whose kid," said one of the others.

"The creep's up," said Dickon. "Knock him on the head, somebody."

"Leave him alone, Dickon, he never hurt you." Dickon cocked an eyebrow at the speaker and went back to his plan.

"Whose! Think anybody'd miss Wenslow's brat? We want Peretto's. They'll put it on Benno, and if he gets killed, nobody'll worry."

Benno stared at Dickon with horror and pity. His personality had degenerated like a child's in a tantrum, leaving only an idiot rage. The other androids were shifting about, looking at each other.

Finally, Rudi said, "We didn't figure on anybody getting killed in this, Dickon."

Dickon turned on him. "What did you think, you were playing tiddleywinks?"

"We wanted to get even a bit, get them under our thumb and give them a scare—"

"Yeah, and end up with love and kisses and an all-day sucker!"

Benno said, "Isn't that what *you* want, Dickon?"

"You shut up! Keep your mouth out of this!" He was almost sobbing. "I could kill you, I could kill you now so —damn—easy—"

"No you couldn't, Dickon," Rudi said quietly.

"Jesus, a bunch of cupcakes! I used to think you wanted to be men! I'll do it, I'll do it myself, damn you, and I'll pull you in with me! Watch, you'll see! I'll split the whole damn planet in two!"

He leaped out and flung himself down the slope with a crash of branches and was lost in the mist.

"Oh, God," Rudi said. He was about to follow, but Benno cried out, "Don't do it! It's too thick to find him in that."

"But if he hurts the kid they'll wipe us all out!"

"Undo my hands." They freed him.

"What do you think you can do?"

"I shouldn't have run off in the first place." Benno peered into the mist; it was settling slowly like water down a clogged drain. "He won't get much of a head start in that. If I can reach Peretto he'll listen to me."

"But you're a mess."

Benno rubbed his wrists. "We'll all be pretty messy if I don't go."

Rudi said, "We've got the guns—"

"We'd end up killing somebody. Besides . . . this is between the Wenslows and me, and that's how it'll have to be settled."

"What do you want us to do?"

"Oh, wait around here half an hour, and when you get back tell them I got away. That way your tongue won't tie up on you. It's true as far as it goes."

"But hell, they'll know there's something fishy there!"

"Sure, but they won't do anything about it." Benno rubbed his sore head. "They might even respect you for sticking up for me."

Rudi said awkwardly, "Don't rub it in, Benno. Here, take a gun anyway."

"Nuts. I don't want to shoot anybody. Or give them an excuse to shoot me."

He scrambled down, aching at every move, catching drunkenly at the dripping branches. At the bottom he stopped to get his breath and pull his ripped clothes together.

How would Dickon go about stealing a child from the midst of Residential?

The children usually played outside after breakfast when the mist had cleared and the grass dried off a little. Sometimes the androids took care of them after their work in the fields and vegetable gardens. Today there would be no androids, and perhaps the children would not be trusted outdoors. Would the humans be expecting an attack? Dickon wouldn't care; he was set for any risk.

Benno cut over toward the lakeshore and the dunes, in spite of the possibility of ambush. There weren't enough men to hide behind every dune. As the sun came out he climbed a rise and checked his direction. The quarry might have changed plans a hundred times already, but with Dickon's anger, and the rifle under his arm, Benno thought the chance was small.

He dipped in and out among the dunes. He couldn't see anyone else on the sands, but he knew his dark moving figure would be eminently noticeable. Scrambling along, he glanced uneasily at the buildings as he passed them. If Dickon had headed for Administration in an attempt to attack Wenslow there would have been some noise and running about. There was only a waiting quiet. He had to assume that Dickon, like himself, was still skulking. But there was very little time.

Here, now, was the place where he and Poppy had been—
yesterday? And where Mrs. Wenslow—he closed his mind . . .
but where, also, he had watched the Harringtons with lewd
eyes as they whispered . . .

—*don't start on me here, Bob, for God's sake. There's
Benno and Poppy over there watching us.*

A kid and an android? What's it got to do with them?

I don't know . . . some of those androids . . .

Some of those androids lie awake at night, listening for
sounds of love.

Benno lay on the grass-tufted dune, the sun had risen. The
throbbing aches in his body washed away, he was comfortable. The warmth of the sun told him this was all he could
ever want. Men were hateful, he did not need them, but the
warmth and the sun . . .

Dickon! Where was Dickon? He leaped up, afraid that he
had slept an hour, and what Dickon could have done in that
time—but the sun hadn't moved; his drowsiness had only
stretched the moment. But the danger of sleep was real. He
shook his head and rubbed his eyes.

Then he saw his first man, back down where the sundecks
began. It was too far to tell whether he was armed, but he was
moving east and heading for Benno. Benno scrambled for the
next hillock. The man speeded up. *That's done it.* He'd never
make the last half-kilometer at this rate. He gave up and began
to run.

". . . or I'll shoot!" came the end of a yell. Benno thought
he was a liar. The noise of the shot knocked him off his feet
with fright. He scurried on, glancing back once to see the pur-
suer running, not stopping to aim. *Because I'm not armed.* He
had no idea how to stop Dickon without a gun, but if he had
brought one he would have been dead by now. He looked back
again. Now there were two of them. Good, let's have a race!

He cut north, straight through the trees, and made a beeline
across the central green, gathering pursuers and frightening
children with his torn clothes and beaten face.

Then he heard a shriek from back of the Perettos'.

In the yard he found Dickon, Poppy screaming under one
arm, rifle in the other hand, Mrs. Peretto at bay. Benno pulled

up, stopped by the look on Dickon's face. As if he had evolved from some other feral animal, and were now reverting to it.

Benno screamed, "Dickon! Dickon!" and without thinking tore up a lump of sod from the border edge and threw it. It struck Dickon in the face, but almost before it struck Benno heard the sound of a rifle, and Dickon fell, shot through the heart.

Behind them, Wenslow lowered the rifle.

Dickon sprawled grotesquely, his face tamed at last and his mouth full of dirt.

I didn't have to do that to him. . . . He looked up at Wenslow's savage face, Dickon's counterpart. *I'm the only one who's sorry.* . . . He was cold and sick.

Poppy flung herself against him; she had wet her pants in fright and her hands grabbed his hair like balls of sticky resin, but his arms went tightly around her. Peretto's hand was on his shoulder. Mrs. Peretto crowding at his side. . . .

Peretto said, half-teasing, half-rueful, "You love him more than us, hey, Poppy?"

Wenslow snarled. "He has perverted her!"

Benno was packing. Since nearly all he owned had been given him by humans, he was too proud to take everything he wanted. But he had a knife, the clothes he wore, a few things he had made himself . . . He left off a moment, went over to the window and looked out.

Below, the children were playing, and he watched their wheeling patterns on the grass; their cries were like birdcalls in the misty verge of evening. . . .

When I grow up I'm going to be a mummy. And—

The door opened. Peretto came in and closed it behind him. His eyes took in the colored handkerchief in the best tradition spread out with Benno's possessions.

"You need an icebag for that face," he said. "I brought it."

"I don't want it." But he took it and held it to his swollen jaw.

Peretto drew in on his cigarette and let the coil of smoke drift away on his words. "Why are you running away?"

"You saw what he did. You heard what he said."

"Do you know anyone who agrees with him?"

Benno looked away. "They're all afraid of us."

"You've shown them not to be. The rest are back and there won't be any more trouble . . . you know, you didn't have to go running off yesterday, nobody believed that woman."

"I—I'm not going because of her."

"You're running away so you can be by yourself and pretend to be a man."

"That's a lousy thing to say!"

"You're an android, Benno," Peretto said gently. "You can only be a man between the ears."

"I'm nothing." They stared at each other, two cloudy images beyond the looking glass.

"The men and women who have androids love them—"

"They ruin them and kill them!"

Peretto sighed. "There were some wild stories flying around about what was in the tank, weren't there? Dickon started most of them."

"What of it?"

"Only that the Harringtons wanted another android. Another Bimbo."

"Oh . . ." said Benno. Then he sneered. "So he can mind the baby while they—" He clapped his hand over his mouth and sat down on the bed, trembling.

Peretto's voice was almost a whisper. "You sounded exactly like Wenslow when you said that. You even looked like him."

Benno saw a black gulf falling away before him, the goal he had been running for, a cave in the hills where he would eat hate till his soul was consumed, his humanity gone, and he had become the animal looking out of Dickon's eyes when he died.

"What am I to do?" He clasped his aching head in his hands.

"Dammit, Benno, what can I tell you? You have to do the best you can to live without envy or hate. . . ."

When he looked up Peretto was gone. The dark was rising to blend him with the room, the house, the Colony. There was nothing else. All he could ever have was here.

He sat there while the moons rose and swung in their eccentric orbits. When he stood up he did not unpack his bundle. Not yet. But he left it behind him on the table and went down to the Perettos.

— Blue Apes —

A man sat on a rock outcropping in a valley, weeping. His clothes were torn, his body bruised. His hands trembled on his knees; tears watered the blood of cuts on his face and neck, stinging.

The sun shone brightly, the air was fresh and crisp. Wind ruffled the green and yellow trees, blowing down yellow leaves even as green buds sprang on the branches. Blue-furred animals giggled and chattered among them; once in a while one would pause and stare with pink eyes down at the seated figure, sometimes break off a twig and throw it at him. They were not hostile; mildly, they discouraged intruders.

The man plucked a twig from his hair and let it fall. He did not listen to the blue apes. The wind was singing him a song.

König moved quietly from the hypnoformed shuttle. It blended with the bedding of yellow leaves in the dip of the forest floor. The air was cold. He stood for a moment. There was no moon in the dark sky, the stars were unfamiliar. The wind rustled the leaves of great-branched trees, whistled thinly among conifers. He pulled up the hood of his robe and tied the string. The rough brown hopsacking did not keep out the wind but his hair and beard were thick, close-curled, and he was wearing a quilted suit underneath. He took one tentative step, crunching the leaves, and heard a *chirr* in the branch above his head. His hand slipped into the knapsack and found the stunner between the knife and the breadcrust. He went on slowly without looking up; the branch shook, a few dead leaves fell on his shoulders. He stopped rigid: his imagination, like an ancient memory, felt the weight of the animal on his neck, the bite, his own scream, the vomiting bowel-loosening death.

The animal jeered. The leaves fell. He shuffled gently through the leaf-layer, away from the tree, between two blue-black conifers. Another animal woke, whistling, the two muttered for a moment, became quiet, slept. Some flying creature in the conifers whooped, swept up and sheared by him with long wings, found another tree. The forest slept again.

Beyond the conifers the woods ended in a low thicket and the land fell in a short steep cliff toward a stream that frothed over stones. König pushed through the scrub; it tore at his robe and scratched his hand. The wind quickened, smoothing away his leaf-spoor. The cliffside was covered with woody vines. He dropped the stunner in his pocket and climbed down, pausing at each creak of a stem.

He stood on the stony bank, unseen by the forest, and licked at his hand. Dipped into the pack again and pulled out a film bag, rummaged until he found a vial with capsules and took one: it was a powerful antibiotic, but it did not protect against the bite of the blue ape. He returned the vial, took out and unwrapped a bundle of three rod-shaped instruments. With the first, an infrared scanner, he found no significant heat-source in any direction. The second was a penlight, and he hunkered against the cliff, spread the wrapping on his knees and studied it: it was a survey map. Presently he rose, dropped light, map and scanner into bag and pack, pulled out the knob on the end of the third piece, uncoiling a length of fine wire, and set the knob in his ear. The illuminated dial on his wrist gave him two hours to dawn. He felt his way along the cliff; his thick rawhide boots hardly crunched the stones. Fifty meters of cliffside told him nothing until the earpiece began to hum, and the pointing rod, a metal detector, gave him destination. He backed one step, pushed a button on his wrist chronometer, and a section of cliffside rose, wrenching away roots where a few vine-ends had taken hold. He did not like the shriek of rusty metal and allowed the hidden door to rise only enough to let him roll under into the cavern; with the penlight he found the switch.

The light inside was very dim, and he was glad of that. He could see clearly enough the skeleton of a shuttle, and the skeleton of a Solthree human.

The shuttle had been gouged by rough hands; there were no electronic equipment, clothing, utensils, flight recorder. The shell had withstood attempts to tear it apart; the place was dry, and there were only a few rust spots in its dents. He did not touch it. The registry number on its side showed clearly through dust and scratches. It was half-a-century old.

He threw back his hood and reached into the neck of the robe to unbutton the high collar of the suit, dragged at a chain around his neck until he was holding the silver locket. He pushed the manual release button in its center.

"König recording." His voice was quiet but clear. "Shuttle found and corresponding. Equipment removed. No GalFed ship in orbit, probably long captured by scavenger." He turned unwillingly to the skeleton of bone. It was sitting on the dusty floor up against the wall, bending forward slightly and saved from collapse by the propping of a pitchfork whose black-stained tines pierced its ribs. It had been stripped by theft and decay of everything but a few shreds of cloth and several swirling locks of faded hair hanging from patches of dry scalp on its skull. Though the body seemed longer than his own he thought by the bone shapes it might have been female. "Also in hangar skeleton of body stabbed with pitchfork staining tines and breaking ribs, presume caused death. By body size not a native of Colony Vervlen." Perhaps he should have brought the camera; but he doubted it would have made a difference. Especially to the bones. "Long narrow structure. Strands of fair hair probably faded, long and straight. Pelvis shape suggests female. Almost certain this is the . . . the body of Signe Halvorsen."

Why the quivering lip, König? If she'd lived she'd be dead by now.

Pitchfork . . .

König, lots of people in the Department think you're a bastard. I'm not sure. Others work on tiptoe, and you take a bunch of grumbling colonists and con and bully and kick them out of danger farside or offplanet. I'm not sure, because

*you've always saved them, no matter how much they've
wanted to kill you. This thing that's come up—you might say
it was made for you—and maybe you'd like to leave this one
to rot . . .*

But he was here, and he wondered if it was the colonists who
were in danger. His feelings shifted, his plans changed every
minute . . .

He switched the lights off, rolled under the door and shut it.
There was the subtlest of pale shading on the eastern horizon
and the diurnal creatures were beginning to whicker and
grunt. He rearranged the vines as well as possible, and felt his
way back to a place near his original descent. Studied the
forest, the stream, the vines. Then he rewrapped his instruments in the map, laid them on a flat stone, hesitated, added
the stunner, pulled the chronometer with its remotes from his
wrist, the recorder from round his neck. He dropped the heap
of objects into the film bag, rolled it until the air was squeezed
out, sealed it with the pressure of his fingers. He lifted the
rock aside and scratched a hole with his knife, an implement
suitable only for cutting bread and cheese; packed down the
parcel, replaced the rock. Now he had nothing to defend himself with, nothing of his that could be used against him.

Pitchforks.

He pulled off his robe, rolled it into a pillow and sat down
at the cliff's base. During the next half hour while light swelled
and birds began to caw he used the knife to scrape the an-
nealed metallic GalFed symbols from the breast of his suit.

His fingernails grew purple with cold. A drift of cloud let
down a few snowflakes and the sky cleared again. König's
teeth were clacking like a shaken skeleton's. He pulled on the
robe and a pair of knit mittens and climbed up to the forest.
An animal dancing on the lax arm of a conifer stared at him.
At first he could see only the pink bouncing eyes, for the fur
was the blue of the brightening sky. The creature was apelike,
not anthropoid but prosimian, a big lemur with a long plume
tail and sharp claws. A group converged and threw pods at
him; he went very slowly over the fallen leaves, barely glancing
up to notice that some gripped shadow-colored infants to their
breasts. None dropped to take its bite of death. The forest
cleared at last into open farmland, and he reached the mud-
track that served for a road.

• • •

Nearly three hundred years earlier an ultra-orthodox sect who lived by farming had tired of Sol III. As the world pushed up against their fences the very air smelled of spiritual as well as industrial contamination. They had decided to leave the planet in their physical bodies.

They had religious stockades to breach: they must travel by starship using the technology they repudiated; accept a world terraformed to their requirements; allow the modification of their children's genetic components to fit them for the isolated place they chose. A planet without seasons whose axis lay perpendicular to its orbit, where the equator was barely temperate.

They studied the Holy Books, argued long and loud, and in marathons of study and discussion found justification in the eye of their God.

Terraforming was a matter of land-clearing and terracing to prevent water run-off; the Vervlin knew nothing of their travels because they had been put into deepsleep before loading; their gene-pool was modified by engrafting the stock of Ainu, Inuit and other cold-land peoples who lived by hunting, herding and small-farming. Founding population was 750. By second generation census they numbered 982, a fair increase in a hard land. But some had become disenchanted; the Ninety and Nine demanded and got repatriation. Ten years later they changed heart and asked for return but were repudiated by their brethren.

Colony Vervlen lived on. At fifth generation census they had increased only to near 1200; GalFed worried at their low growth rate and slow pubertal development and prescribed dietary changes, since Vervlin would not take drugs.

Tenth generation census, in the person of Signe Halvorsen, would have been GalFed's last uninvited landfall on Vervlen, but she did not return. By last spacelight relay she was in orbit on the way to landing, and after that, nothing. There were no calls to send or receive: Vervlin would not use radio. The search team, sent a year later, had been shot out of the sky in a war between two other planets of the world's sun, and the whole system, which supported no other GalFed colonies, had been twice quarantined, for a total of fifty years . . .

• • •

Between forest and road, König paused. He did not know how to approach a people capable of murdering a Galactic emissary, even though it was half a century ago. Many colonists would have liked to kill him; none had tried. A couple had flattened his already snub nose a little further.

He squatted among bushes, half-turned to keep an eye on the blue enemies among the trees. No great antlered beasts shouldered them now: they had been hunted out or added to domestic stock. No saplings had been planted in many years. All that grew had risen from seed-droppings, in disorder. Spiralling down in darkness he had seen no roads, lights, steeples, meeting halls. Only twenty or so clumps of thatched-roof houses huddled together, perhaps a hundred buildings in all.

From the ground he could see that they were small, with parchment windows lit from within by stoked fires; wisps of smoke rose from old stone chimneys. Out of the center of each clump a taller chimney protruded like a raised finger among knuckles. East and west, Vervlen covered no more than half a kilometer.

Without birth control.

Shadows began to slip from houses and move in the grainfields—

And sharp points jabbed the base of his spine. He had left one quadrant unguarded, and rustling leaves had covered footsteps. He scrabbled round with a yelp, for he was too locked in his crouch to rise quickly. And yelped again, gawking up at the gnome.

He did not even care that pitchfork tines pierced the cloth at his breast.

"What you want?" the gnome growled in the old rough language. "Where you come, you stranger?"

König was a short stocky man with brown hair and beard, gray eyes and flat-saddled nose. The strong contour of his body was smoothed down with a light layer of fat and covered with a great deal of hair. The fatty thickening of his eyelids made them almost oriental. With darker coloring he would have looked like an Ainu, or with less hair an Inuit, for he was a descendant of Vervlin—of the Ninety and Nine.

"Where you come, say!" The pitchfork jabbed. The gnome had König's eyes, nose, hair, breadth, and was wearing the rough leather and homespun of his people. But it was as if a hand had shaped him in clay and thumped him down. Eye-slits between thick brows and knob cheekbones, lips thickened till they curled to nostril, chin vanished in beard, neckless, waistless, bandy-legged. An ancient without a gray hair.

König fell to his knees and clasped hands, begging; whined, spilled words without thinking. "Hungry, master, 'm hungry!" He had been uneasy about the dialect for fear of change and development, but there had been no change here but shrinkage and reversion. The sense of it filled him with irrational terror. He pleaded in good earnest. And doubly, because he had fasted several days. "Ha' not to eat, ha' come many day from town east—master, see!" He showed the gaping bag with its one gnarled crust. He could not keep from babbling at the terrible dull-eyed gnome. "Name of König, and a' come many days from east!"

The eyes lit briefly, the pitchfork moved down slowly. "Here's many Königs and many hungry, but a' know no man east."

"Oh, ay, master, is many men east, truly."

The tines sank to earth, the Vervlin leaned on the worn handle. His arms were thick and strong, though the fingers were knobbed like tubers from arthritis. "Will y' workn to eat?"

König dared pull himself up. "Gladly, lord."

"Lord, hah!" The slit eyes took his measure. König was nearly a head taller than the Vervlin but this did not seem to impress him. He was looking for the breadth of a hardy laborer, and where his eyes lingered was at the heavy boots. König cursed himself. His footgear was not fine, but far better than the farmer's, cut like moccasins from single pieces and laced with thongs. How was he to have foreseen that? But the shrunk man's eyes were dull. "Come with." König was careful to stay abreast of the pitchfork on the path to the nearest house.

Inside was firelit, and would not grow much brighter through parchment windows during the light of the day. König had to stoop to go through the door, and as he stepped in the gnome bellowed, "Aase!" and turned to him with what might have been a glint of humor. "Name of Rulf, König man, 'm no lord."

Aase, the female of the species, appeared round the

fireplace in homespun skirts and shawl, noted without surprise that there was one extra for breakfast, and disappeared to yell an order to someone unseen.

König himself was a result of genetic engineering, and he had seen many others, but none so grotesque, so terribly wrong. Inbreeding? Isolation? He simply let his mind go out of gear and ate the porridge with its milk and butter at the table before the fire.

The interior of the house surprised him: it was neat and clean, and seemed to mock the bodies that lived in it. The furniture was well joined and sanded, softened with knit cushions; the old chimney was freshly tuckpointed, the plank floor smooth as if it had been varnished. He heard slight noises underneath, and wondered if there were a cellar with mice. One glance into a corner showed him a trapdoor latched with a wooden bar and an iron loop; in his state of mind it would not have surprised him if a monster lived in the cellar.

But the porridge bowl emptied quickly, and the hard hand on his arm invited him to labor; he dared not look more.

And he labored. The barn was filthy and ramshackle, a big rough shelter patched together and used in common with the community of dwarfs in the house-group. Whatever explanation Rulf gave his fellows he did not hear: there were five or six of them, slightly bluer or grayer in eye, darker or lighter in hair, shorter or taller by a few centimeters—cousins or brothers. None questioned him and he did not speak. Where stupidity reigned he obeyed. Forked hay, yoked oxen, shovelled dung. At noon women brought baskets of hot cakes; he ate, standing in mud, and worked on. Once when a plough stuck in a furrow there was a yell of "König!" and he started and looked up quickly. But a stunted man dropped his spade and shambled out to help. Cousins.

The day clouded over and promised rain. The forest turned pale under the cloudlid and rustled, but no animal ventured from it. Men raked and hoed and ploughed and stacked. They did not joke or curse or discuss or quarrel, and left their work only to relieve themselves in an open pit outside the corner of the barn. When he was forced to use this, König, whose sense of privacy was acute, suffered bladder spasms. They were the day's only stimulation; he began to wonder if stupidity was contagious.

Toward sundown he pulled his mind back into operation.

Men work outside, women indoors. No children in sight. Why? Why filthy barns and spotless houses? Implements old and uncared for. No metal work done now. No poultry. Too hard to run after? There are a dead calf and two dead piglets in the stalls. No one has noticed them yet. The woman who brought the midday meal hasn't washed in a thirtyday. By rights they should be buried in their own dirt. But the clothes are well-made. The cakes were wrapped in a clean cloth. Maybe elves are doing the work for them. Why would they bother? The food is good, but no one says grace. Where are the churches?

He leaned on his rake handle and watched Rulf leading in the oxen to unyoke. The wizened man stopped at the entrance, eyes glazed, mouth open. After a few moments he blinked, closed his mouth, and moved on.

Epilepsy? No, they're all like that. Degeneration. Worse than we could have expected. I wonder how old they are. . . .

When a bell rang among the complex of houses to signal the evening meal the rest of the men came in from the fields, dumped their rakes and hoes in a corner and left without a backward look. Rulf finished unyoking the oxen. König untangled the rakes, spades, forks, hoes and hung them on rusty hooks set in the barn wall. He wanted to provoke a little reaction, but only a little. Rulf's beetling brows rose and settled. When König plucked up a handful of straw to wipe the mud off his boots he found the eyes on him and met them with an ingenuous stare. Boots you may need, Rulf, but why did your grandfathers strip the electronics from Halvorsen's shuttle? "Eh, master?"

Rulf grunted. "Y' want eatn?"

"Oh ay, thank y'."

In darkness the hearthfire burned brightly, and within the limit of movement he dared allow himself König tried to examine the place. The massive fireplace projected into the room and to either side was an inglenook. One was filled by a standing wardrobe and a wooden bedstead with an oil lamp above it, but the other was in shadow and he could not see where it ended. Since there were no stairs or any other door visible he presumed it led to a kitchen; Aase had gone there to call for and bring the food. Elves' cooking.

Supper was meat stew with barley and root vegetables, a few raw greens like cress on the side. Rulf and Aase gobbled. So did König. He was hungry.

The mice/elves under the floor were busy tonight. Almost, his imagination gave them voices. Perhaps they would come up at midnight and lick the plates clean with small pink tongues. Rulf stood and dumped the bones into the fire: König followed, and Aase took the rough-glazed bowls back into the shadow.

Rulf stared at König during the slow turn of his cogs of thought and said, "Y' work morgn?"

"Oh ay, master."

Grunt. "Here y' slep." He opened the wardrobe and a jumble of odd ragged things bulged; he heaved and tugged at an old bundled mattress of rough cloth with straws sticking out of its holes and unrolled it on the table, disregarding food scraps and gravy puddles. König moved the table slightly, away from the fire's heat, not too near the cold of the walls. He looked up to make sure he had not offended Rulf by this rearrangement, and his glance was held at the mantel-piece. There was a big clay bowl on it, half filled with ashes, and, perching on the rim, back resting against the bricks, a wooden figurine. He squinted against the glare of the flames and saw its shape was that of a forest ape, just over half life-size and roughly stained blue, lower part blackened with smoke.

Where the churches had gone.

The sight of the idol crystallized a decision he had been slowly approaching all day. At midnight, when the trolls were asleep, and no matter what the elves or mice might do, he was leaving.

There was no kindness he could do these people and no harm he would be willing to commit upon them even if their ancestors had been the bugbears of his childhood. Leave questions unanswered, let failure smudge his record. *Maybe you'd like to leave this one to rot.* No, Director. You decide.

Rulf knocked the logs down with a poker and the flames lowered. He blew out the lamp above the bed and yelled, "Aase!"

She came shambling. "Still y', still y'." She dropped on the bed and pulled up her skirts. Rulf flipped the lacing of his breeches and fell on her.

König hastily climbed his table and lay with knees drawn up and back turned, still wearing the robe, suit and boots he had sweated in all day. It was the style here. Folded his arms against the cold, tried not to hear the grunts and whimpers from the bed. Rain beat against the walls. His back was warm, there was still heat in his full belly. He was weary, his eyes closed.

He did not want sleep, but sleep was coming—not as sweet release from labor but as a dark imprisoning lid.

Drugs. He could not move.

He thought he heard steps from afar, and the scrape of wood on iron. The lid fell closer, blacker, hands grasped his ankles and pulled him straight.

Boots.

His arms were unlocked from his chest. Unconsciously his mouth opened for the last cry of the pierced man.

König, you bloody fool, murdered for a pair of boots!

Voices: he was not dead. Possibly.

Speaking in *lingua*: "He can't be one of us."

"But he's like them. Even hairier."

Fingers moving in the hair on his belly. Damned cold fingers. His robe must be off, he was unbuttoned to the navel.

"Must be thirty good year anyway."

"Thirty-five!" König snarled, simultaneously opened his eyes and sat up. "What the hell do you think you're doing?"

His sight went black and starry; he blinked darkness away with the force of anger, hands pulled back, voices stilled. On a table again. He swivelled and hooked legs over the edge.

An underground room, a vault supported by beams, opening almost endlessly into the flickering lights and shadows of wall-sconces. Around him were children, children, twenty-five to thirty of them. Real Solthree children. Dressed like the gnomes above, in clothes rough-cut but carefully sewn.

A child began to weep.

"Shut up!"

A firm-voiced girl slapped the table. "Don't be rough! You will wake *them* up and you are scaring him!"

"What are you trying to do to *me*?" He zipped thermal underwear, buttoned furiously, fingers half-numb and all thumbs.

Children . . . as he had been? The ones he should have? Curly-haired small and medium Königs with blue, grey, blue-grey eyes, sharp bright ones here under the eyelid fold. Smooth faces, sweet mouths. Girls rough-breeched like the boys, hair scarcely longer because it was so curly.

"Why do *you* have buttons?" They spoke *lingua* in the rough cadences of the Vervlin tongue. He studied the speaker. First beard-hairs showing. Not so sharp, this one. On the way to changeover. But not stupid either. He knew a foreigner when he saw one.

König felt even duller. "I come to where buttons are used." He looked for the robe, saw it crumpled on the floor and left it. The air was warmer here. Far among the beams stood a huge complex of fireplaces hung with pots and ladles, source of the big outside stack.

"Your buttons are riveted," said the girl, as if she were joining a game with infants. Fifteen, perhaps? She might be the leader, for a while.

"Technology," said König. "You don't do badly at it. Do you drug people often?"

"Sometimes to make them sleep longer when we want freedom."

"Where did you learn *lingua*?" She was as pretty as a Vervlin girl might become. Her hair was a little darker and straighter, she had pulled back the strands over her ears and tied them with twine.

"We always had it as a second language. Starwoman taught us more."

"Taught *you*?"

"The ones of us here when she was."

"Signe Halvorsen?"

"Starwoman. You with the riveted buttons and the thirty-five years, you are Starman, who lied to the Elders about far towns in the east. Why are you not surprised, Starman? The other one was."

"That you are children? I knew there had to be children somewhere. I didn't think of here. I thought there were mice in the cellar."

Giggles all around. A shiver went down his back. They were so normal, so innocent, Halvorsen stabbed with a pitchfork.

"You answer no question, Starman." Cool voice of a boy farther back. "Why no surprise that we are not as the Elders?"

His mind was too foggy to explore a dangerous question. He answered with the simplest truth. "I have already been surprised by the Elders. I knew something of what was happening, but not that it had gone so far. And my name is König."

"So is mine—and ten others here."

"I know: many Königs and many hungry. But I am tired—and drugged, thanks to your cleverness. Let me go back upstairs now."

"No," the girl said. "By morning they forget everything. You stay down here, Starman. You have much to tell."

He let it go. He could not fight even one of them now. "What is your name, Younger?" A little touch to the word.

She reddened a bit. "Ehrle."

"And mine is König. Why are you kept down here?"

"We do all the work that needs cleverness, and they are afraid we order them about. It is all the same to us. We have ways out, when we choose to use them, and we have not to work in the stinking barns."

Nor would she, as an Elder. Aase lay above, gibbering under pounding Rulf.

"And why are you here, Starman König?"

"To find out what became of Signe Halvorsen—and my people." He yawned, fought dizziness once more to retrieve his robe and roll it into a pillow.

"But you must tell us—"

"Later. I am asleep."

And he was, folded on the table, knees pulled up, robe under his head, asleep.

"Wake up, Star-König, we want to use the table."

He got up very stiffly, even though some of them had been thoughtful enough to slide folded blankets under him. His first thought was: they don't have a spare bunk; you'd think they'd prepare one if they expected company. But when he looked up he saw groups of them gathering bedrolls from the tables as well as from the tiers of shelves on the walls, and realized he had been given the spare bunk.

He had a headache but was not nauseated; there was no brightness to hurt his eyes here either, only the firelight he had seen so much of already, and small squares of dusky sky where the ceiling joined the walls. Openings screened with fiber meshes, presumably to keep out small animals, they were not quite big enough to let out small humans. They also had wooden louvers to shield from rain and snow.

He wanted to see more of these surroundings, but there were children, children, children who wanted to see him. Some, he was sure, from the groups of houses beyond this one; they wove and cut their cloth a little differently, sometimes with a stripe or a twilled weave. Did they come overland, or were there rabbit-warrens of tunnels with lookouts, codes, sentries? Why not? They knew all he had done and said above. And had children killed Halvorsen? Not these.

He looked at them. There was a hare-lip, a few cases of cross-eye and a few with buck teeth. Some scars from cuts and scratches, but no boils or impetigo that he could see. Halvorsen had been a doctor. Probably those who were badly crippled and could not be cured were kept somewhere together not to be hidden but to be cared for efficiently. From what he could tell of these children, they were efficient. "Don't smother me," he said quietly; the table was digging into his back from their pressure. "I'm like you, only bigger, is all."

"You are not like *them*," said Ehrle.

Three or four bells chimed at once, from all the houses this cellar must run under. Half the children ran away, and to the others Ehrle said sharply, "Get the pots stirring, Willi, and you, move away before you spill something hot."

The lightly bearded boy who was a bit dull went to supervise the porridge-making, others to different tasks, some, reluctantly, to sit on benches by the tables. All eyes on him. Their candle-power was nerve-wracking; compared to it the stupidity of the Elders was soothing.

Troops of servitors worked without bumping or slopping: one to send bowls of food upstairs on dumb-waiters, another to man their ropes, a third to serve the seated ones.

"Don't spit, Mooksi, you need not be a slob." Ehrle was a super-martinet.

König said, "Will you rap my knuckles if I ask for a little more milk?"

There was a ripple of laughter around the table. König locked eyes with Ehrle and wished he had not spoken. He understood what was happening.

The children were clean, cleaner than he was, and more disciplined than an armed force. They were, after all, fathers to the men, and would play later in as much filth as they chose. A clumsy Gulliver might upset an inverted social structure that was the only basis here for existence and continuity: a structure balanced on a very sharp knife-edge.

No one knew just how much time there was, for Ehrle or anyone else, but she seemed determined to extend it by the pure force of her personality. Uselessly.

He took a drop of the milk he was offered and said, "Yesterday I saw a dead calf and two shoats in the stalls."

A boy said, "I know. I got rid of them last night."

"I wasn't sure you'd noticed them."

"We know about everything here."

"Yes, of course. You knew of me."

(But not where he had left the ship and controls. He hoped to God not.)

He was reaching for equality—to be neither overbearing nor overborne. Sophisticated Gulliver. For König there was far too much intelligence and organization here. He must leave before he was overborne.

As the bowls emptied he was quick to rise and stack them. Ehrle said, "You need not serve, Star-König."

"A' mus workn for to eat, not?" He laughed. "If I break things you may put me to scrubbing floors." He joined a line of children waiting to put crockery in a tub of soapy water. Eyes on him, always. Questions to come.

The floors were worn brick, neatly grouted and well scrubbed. Probably torn from old houses. Population did not quite replace itself and as it shrank, living-space compacted for warmth and the ubiquitous efficiency. The children surely lived better than their elders. Building bigger houses to their standards would require greater strength, and more knowledge and equipment, than they had.

The eyes, pair by pair, moved away from him and turned

their attention to scrubbing, spinning, weaving. Bone needles, bits of metal to pierce leather. Sacking and woolen cloth grew on the unwieldy looms; some yarns tinted, probably from dyes scraped out of the soil. Water boiled and food simmered by the fires; dough was rising.

"You don't do tanning here, surely?"

A voice at his elbow laughed. "Would raise a mighty stink if we did. Shed's outside with the kiln and smokehouse."

"I think you're spoiling *them*."

"Ehrle doesn't let them push us too far."

A voice at his shoulder said, very quietly, "That one, there, thinks she'll never change. All them do."

"Which them, Willi?"

The boy was standing awkwardly, looking into the top bowl of his pile with its milk puddle and cereal lumps, broad thumbs hooked carefully over the edge. He raised his eyes.

"Leaders, like." He was a burnt-out lantern compared with the others, but his features had coarsened very little. "I was one. It's like I did wrong, growing. But I want to go upthere," he made it one word. "I want a woman. 'M not right, here." He spoke without lust or anger, facts.

A voice hissed, "Shut up, Willi!"

"I'll get there." Willi set his nest of bowls into the water and turned away.

And she would follow. And perhaps be his woman and bear his children . . .

König gave them a day of work, as he had done with the Elders, but for more complicated motives—aside from discouraging questions before he thought of the answers. He did not care for idleness, nor wish to set himself above them, and he did not want to become indispensable, like Halvorsen. He was trying to bond himself to them just enough so that they would think twice before taking extreme action. He felt this might be possible because he himself was a Vervlin. On the other hand, for the same reason, they might expect more from him . . .

He knew from long experience how to be helpful without getting in the way. He wiped up, swept up, changed diapers in a roomful of babies, and stayed away from those with organized serious tasks. One or another of the children was always with him, usually the boy with his own name, who was near Ehrle's age and probably the next contender for leadership. In all, they were the most solemn group of children he had ever seen. They never smiled, and rarely laughed except when he provoked them purposely. A few of the babies chuckled when he nuzzled their faces; several were wasting with dysentery, but most seemed quite healthy.

"Are these fed on cows' milk?"

"Only when they can drink from cups. It is too hard to make bottles. When we find a good milker upthere we keep two or three babies on her until weaning. She never knows the difference."

"Do you know your mother?"

"No. How can I?"

None of them had parents, except for their siblings, the busy ones who, humane as they might be, did not know how to be kind or joyful. The babies had a few stuffed toys, but there was no other sign of game or toy, no tag or rough-house. He picked up a fretful child; it fitted the curve of his arm quite properly, and fell silent pulling at the fine chain around his neck.

"What is that on your neck, Star-König?" Puzzling at the square centimeter of filigree.

"A Galactic Federation emblem. Do you grow sugar-beets?"

"A small crop. Why?"

"And put a little sugar in the cereal you give the children— or let them suck on a piece?"

"Sometimes."

"Keep it away from the ones with loose bowels."

"You have children of your own?"

"No."

Serious face close to his again. "What are you, König?"

König put the baby down; it whimpered for a moment, and slept. "A person who travels to new communities on strange worlds and tells them to move or leave because of dangerous conditions."

"What kind of conditions?"

"Disease, poisonous land or water, approaching war."

Genetic instability, he did not add.

"And you come to ask us to move?"

"No. To find out how you are getting on, because we could not come earlier on account of wars on the planets near here. To help you stay healthy and live—" he caught himself before saying, "longer,"—"more easily." He watched the babies playing with their toes. A short youth and a stern one. He added, "I was chosen because I am descended from Vervlin."

"Yes," the boy said contemptuously. "The Ninety-nine who ran away."

"They tried to come back and were not allowed by the others here."

"I didn't know that."

"Now you know, it doesn't make much difference."

"Yes it does, Starman. You are a normal adult, and we want to know why."

He was becoming tired of crowding and pressure, of attention, nudging bodies, endless murmur of voices. The focus. The wrong choice. What was the right one? An armed fleet, against despairing children? He took it head on.

"Galactic Federation made a mistake when they formed your bodies in the shape you have. There was a flaw in the seed, and because everyone had it, and had children with someone else who had it, it stayed. It took a while to show itself, so nobody was warned soon enough, and it stayed in the generations. Most flaws of that kind are weak and wash out in descendants, but this was not that kind. Many of the Ninety-nine married stranger-peoples before the flaw had time to affect them so badly, and if they thought they might be affected they had no children." Before young König had time to react he asked, "Didn't Starwoman talk of this?"

"I believe so, but no one understood. This we can understand." König shut up and let him think. "Galactic Federation must owe us something, not? Our fathers sold rich lands on Sol Three and paid to come here."

"They owe you something," König said grimly. Try to collect.

Out of mercy the bells rang for lunch.

"Today we have light lunch and early supper," Ehrle said.

"Is something special happening?" König roasted on spit.

She smiled without humor. "Tonight they have their Sabbath celebration and we get out and watch them behaving like fools.''

"They are not all such fools," said Willi.

König said quickly, "Do they know you get out?"

"Likely."

"They're not afraid you will run away?"

"No." The word cut like a knife. Of course not. The runaway would turn into the enemy.

König asked for and got the favor of a tub of hot water. While it heated he squatted in an empty niche, to be alone, unregarded for the moment. He did not want to see how the Elders would celebrate; the prospect repelled him. But for the children it was probably some kind of object lesson in superiority; actually, in futility. In spite of the regimentation, the industry, the cleverness, the almost purposive lack of differentiation between the sexes. *I want a woman.*

The niche was not bare: it was lined with shelves piled full of worn things for which uses would be found. He ran his hand down them idly. Old leather, sacking, wool. And something hard. He pulled apart two folds of blanket and found it: a heap of the fragmented pieces of Halvorsen's radio and electronics. He smoothed down the blankets and got out of there in a hurry. There were not many pieces, nowhere near enough to account for all of the instrumentation. Perhaps every housegroup had its little heap. Perhaps it was the equivalent of the carved blue god of the Elders.

He found a shadowed corner for his bath and took it in a worn wooden tub which appeared to be the community bathtub. The lye soap did not smell pleasant but it washed well, and, watching his toes curled over the tub's edge he allowed himself to relax to the point of mild relief that these colonists at least did not apologize for the primitive conditions that for him were merely a commonplace of the many outworld communities he had visited.

The moment he was aware of relaxing the trapdoor grated and opened, and Aase came downstairs. The children whispered and muttered, and began deploying themselves to keep her turned away from König. König came out of his lull into the sense of a loose situation with an open door: he sat up and reached for his clothes, ready to call out. A hand snatched the

clothes away; another grabbed a fistful of his wet hair and
pushed his head back: "Keep down, Starman. Do you think
she will fight for you?"

He clapped his mouth shut in a fury and watched her between bodies, peering into the steaming pots, poking about
like a supervisory witch. Once when she found one of the little
ones in front of her, the one Ehrle had called Mooksi, she
stopped and put her hand on his head. He turned his face up,
they looked at each other, but neither knew what to search
for, and she went on, and finally up the stairs again, and the
trapdoor slammed.

König, left to himself once more, dried himself with his
underwear, put on his suit and washed the underwear in the
used water; he wrung it out with the anger he would have liked
to use on a couple of necks, and hung it on a wooden rack by
the fire along with diapers and other clothes. The sight of this
garment, with its long sleeves and legs, gave rise to the first
spontaneous burst of laughter he had heard on Vervlen, but it
did not temper his mood. A few of the older boys, and perhaps girls, for all he knew, whispered and giggled a bit on the
possibilities of physical strength and sexual prowess in a person big enough to wear such clothing; much as the Lilliputians
had done with Gulliver. König was wondering how much
strength was necessary to knock aside all those hard young
bodies. But Gulliver had been a prisoner too.

He went into the room where the babies lay, stood with
arms folded and watched them, because he knew he could not
be angry with them.

He did not speak at supper; though his face was calm. The
whole area seemed subdued: no one was willing to break his
silence.

At the end of the meal, Ehrle whispered with some of the
others, and said, "Please, König, don't be angry with us. We
need help."

König said, "You cannot get help from a prisoner."

She was no longer imperious. "We are prisoners—of—of
ourselves and them. Give us a little time, tell us what can be
done. Then we will let you go. You have a ship and a radio,
and can bring help."

"We don't *know* he has a ship and a radio," said young
König. "Might be he was dropped here."

König said, "I have a ship and a radio, and you have a strategy." He stood and began to gather empty dishes. "You are playing hard against soft, and that is a very old game. It is no longer clever. It is against Galactic Federation's rules for me to tell you where my ship is, because there is no one to guard it, and if you try to force me to tell my conditioning will break my mind and you will be left with a real drooling idiot. I will tell you where it is not: it is not in the hangar with Halvorsen's bones and the remains of her ship. Nothing else is."

"Hangar! Bones!" Surprise and horror swept the vault.

"You didn't know! I see, I'm glad to see that." And he was, for no lie could be so well orchestrated. "And yet you have pieces of her equipment in your stores."

Ehrle's arms went out involuntarily. "You—" it began as a yell and she brought her voice down, "you think we, us down here, killed her!"

The movement had pulled the collar of her shirt apart and he saw the silver glint on her neck. The last thing. He sat down. "None of *you* killed her. She stayed quite a while—perhaps more than a thirtyday—and then what became of her?"

"One morning she was gone."

"As you had been told . . . and the ones here, did they think she had gone in her ship?"

It was someone else who muttered, "Until the broken pieces were found on a midden heap."

"The Youngers would have used the radio to call for help, but the Elders smashed it," König said. "Vervlin never did care for radio . . . and I suppose the young ones thought she had run away, and eventually died somewhere on this world." Slow nods. He was giving an out which both parties needed very badly. "But she was stabbed with a pitchfork. No one knows who killed her, and I don't want to know."

"Someone on Vervlen killed her," a hardy soul ventured, reaping black looks.

"Fifty years ago," König said. "Galactic Federation can punish no one here for that."

"But they will not want to help us," Ehrle said gloomily.

"They will want to help. I can swear that." But, the one last thing. "You are also wearing something on your neck,

Ehrle." Halvorsen's recorder. He could not do what he had
never done before: find a way to be alone with her and take it
by seduction or force. There was no time, no room, and he
had no talent for it.

She said nothing, but pulled up the chain slowly, unwillingly, until she had the silver locket in her hand. Then, "This
was in the trash, also . . . it did not seem to belong there. We
thought it was a thing a leader might wear, and the leader in
this group has worn it for many years." She looked up.
"Swear again that you will help. You lied to the Elders."

"About the men to the east? How many ears you do have!
There *are* many men to the east, Ehrle, all over the universe.
But I do swear. That is the recorder from Halvorsen's ship.
Would you like to hear what she has to say?"

"Starwoman's voice . . ." Whispers spread.

"Will she tell who killed her?" young König asked.

"I doubt she would have been recording then. If you let me
have that I will show you how it works and give it back to
you."

Slowly she drew the heavy chain over her head. "I often
thought this was some kind of instrument but I push this button often and nothing happens." She gave it to König; her
eyes held a trace of fear.

Young König, leader-in-line, said, "We should call all of
the others and let them hear Starwoman too."

"When I hear, everyone will know," said Ehrle, rap-on-the-
knuckles. "Go ahead, Star-König."

König took the fine chain from his own neck.

"You said that was a Galactic Federation emblem. Was that
a lie?"

"No. It is what I said, but also a key, something that opens
things. Each one of these is made a little differently, to fit one
recorder." He did not know where the fit was on this one, the
light was dim. He moved the side of his key around the edge of
the locket until it was retarded by slight magnetic force, and
pushed. The filigree slipped in with a click. He pushed the button. Silence. "Reversing." Click. He pushed again. Squeals
and whines. "Those are coded records of distances and directions; this piece is connected to the controls when the pilot is
aboard." Click.

Signe Halvorsen recording . . . The voice was dry and

matter-of-fact, but breaths drew in. König held his own.

And Starwoman told what they already knew: that Vervlin were degenerating in the pattern already suspected, and accelerating; that the Elders were unintelligent and almost helpless, and the children astonishingly bright, efficient and well-organized, as well as self-sacrificing—the voice wavered and lowered a bit . . . *and very brave* . . . a pause. *Halvorsen recording* a new day, voice crisp and cool, describing organization and communal practices . . . slightly longer pause, and König said, "I think it needs rewinding," pulled the key half out and pushed it in again. Nothing else then, except a faint buzz and crackle. "No . . . it's very old, and probably broken." Not really; he had wiped it. Halvorsen was dead and he was alive and he truly did not want to know more about her death.

"Very brave," Ehrle whispered. Leave it at that. "I wonder why she was killed?" Question asked for the first time.

König thought he knew. That cool fact-gatherer would not swear to bring help. König had sworn to try, because he was a Vervlin. And they were brave. He pulled the key out and gave it to Ehrle with the locket. "You can listen to the beginning again."

When the table was cleared he took his dried underwear and went behind the chimney to put it on. He had suppressed evidence and did not care. He doubted the missing parts were of much value and he had already allowed the most explosive information to surface and dissipate. Halvorsen could not describe her own death; he believed he could reconstruct it.

Would the Youngers have used the pitchfork? They had more subtle ways. Perhaps they had manipulated the Elders who must have seen Starwoman as an only too obvious foreign body, with her ship, instruments, authority—all things Vervlin in their right minds avoided and twisted ones hated: they had smashed them.

Children locked in cellars. Halvorsen had more sense than to decry them openly, but her attitudes would speak: *very brave* . . . But to the young, the leaders among them, her very unwillingness to rebuke their elders and make promises to themselves would speak even more loudly. If he judged it right she had unwittingly fed fears and prejudices until she became to each party the ally of the other: a mutual enemy. And she had not come back, and the youngest had been allowed to build a legend.

A conjecture. Director, you decide.

He came round the chimney to find a group of younger adolescents choosing straws for baby-sitting and guard duties. The bells began to ring, old church bells struck with broom handles. The hammering of their clappers in confined spaces would have loosened teeth.

"Put your robe on, Star-König. It's cold, the night," young König said.

He did not want to watch the Elders degrading themselves, and he did not think he would be given the opportunity to escape. The young knew the night terrain better than he did without his direction-finder, and he wanted to leave freely with their good will, and keep his promises. He doubted Gal-Fed would expend another search team for dead König. He tied the drawstring of his hood beneath his chin and accepted the loan of a pair of mittens. Except for the very young, all Vervlin had big hands like his; most, like him, were left-handed.

He thought Willi was a certain candidate for guard duty, but he was among the dark bundled figures shifting aside a cupboard at the back wall. There was a niche to get through on hands and knees for a few meters until the ground lowered and allowed standing; the natural cleft had not been dug, though a few heavy uprights and crossbeams warded off collapse. The passage curved down for twenty meters into a shallow puddle, and rose sharply until a cold wind flowed in from the starry opening and the lantern was blown out. The children were quiet, almost solemn, like a tribe preparing for religious rites themselves.

They squatted in the brambles of a hillside looming over a trampled area back of the sheds where the tanning and smoking were done. Beyond them the houses crouched like tame beasts; above, the two bright planets moving among the stars had made the long wars of fifty years ago.

König was relieved to find that the ceremony was no orgy. In the center of the trampled area a larger carved ape crouched on the edge of a much wider basin in which something was burning, and around it a circle of fifteen elders was moving slowly in a simple dance, shuffle-hop, shuffle-hop, each dipping a stick with its end wrapped in rags into the basin until all held lit torches. The wind carried an aromatic breath of the burning stuff, perhaps a psychotropic; after some minutes the dance quickened, though not greatly: the bodies were thick and graceless, the legs crook-shanked. The faces only firelit blobs.

The children did not giggle or whisper but remained silent, crouching, arms on knees, chins on arms. The jigging torches dropped sparks that shook themselves off clothing almost miraculously without scorching their bearers.

In the distance among branches König could see three more circles of dancing light from far houses. He was squatting among thorns, shouldered by bodies. The area was bordered by sheds, houses, hill-slope and crest, only a thin wedge of forest visible to his left. He thought for a moment that he heard the *chirr* of one of the blue apes, and the hairs prickled on his neck, but there were no trees for them here.

The dancers started to sing tunelessly, "Ay-yeh!" shuffle-hop, "Ay-yeh!" shuffle-hop. König was wondering how long it lasted, how long he would be forced to last it out, when a figure behind his shoulder sprang up with a yell of *"Ay-yeh!"*, ran down the hill in leaps and grabbed a torch from its bearer, joining the chanting circle.

The children called in low urgent voices, "Willi! Willi!"

Ehrle said hoarsely, "Shut up! Just let him go!"

König realized why Willi had been allowed to come. Ehrle, after all, knew her limits.

The dancer deprived of his torch staggered round outside the circle for a moment and sat down scratching his head in great puzzlement, but Ehrle was already slipping down into the opening of the hill and summoning others after her in silent procession.

No one reproached her aloud; a few hard looks were directed at her. In the cellar each child seemed to want to get as far away from any other as possible.

Ehrle threw off her mittens, hooked legs over a bench, sat, propped elbows on the table and covered her face with her hands.

König dropped his borrowed mittens beside hers and

loosened his drawstring to pull back the hood. "They all go that way?" he asked, very quietly, to let her ignore the question if she chose.

She pulled her hands away, down the length of her face; the displaced flesh suggested more age than she had or he had allowed her. Her eyes were a bit reddened. "Everyone chooses . . . what seems the best way." Then her eyes lit with anger and she pounded both fists on the table. "König! Star-König! Tell us about the Ninety-nine again, the normal ones!"

There was a little stillness following her change of mood, a stopping of motion by König and everyone else.

He heard the *chirr* again.

A few more children had come into the room, and one, an older girl, he thought, was wearing what seemed to be a blue fur collar. He watched, he could not turn his eyes away, as the blue fur sat up on her shoulder and began to eat some morsel it held in its claws. He stood very still.

"What are you looking at?"

"What do you call that blue animal?"

"An ape. Why?"

"We also called them apes. Is it dangerous?"

"Only if a bite or scratch becomes dirty, and they don't bite or scratch often. We bring one in sometimes to feed."

They were immune. It seemed it had come with the genes. And they had playfellows.

"Why are you afraid, König?"

"In the beginning—" Dared he give them the weapon? The story would be a lie without it. "In the beginning a bite or scratch would kill."

The girl launched the ape: it leaped from shoulder to table to shoulder toward him. He did not move. "Dead Königs don't help much, not?"

Ehrle snapped, "Helig, take that thing away!"

Someone grabbed it, it chattered wildly, and the girl retrieved it sullenly, muttering disgust to match; it disappeared into the cleft.

König folded his arms. "I don't like that. It is not a joke."

"There is not much joking here."

"That I agree with . . . The story is not long or complicated, and it has little to teach. The first settlers were used to cold weather, but not all year round, as here, and they were given

a body inheritance of even colder-weather peoples, so they
could hunt and fish and work in the woods if crops were bad.
They trained with those Solthree peoples to learn the work
before they came. They found the land quite good here, and
the farm animals grew well, but they took care of the forests
as they had been taught in case of hard times. Some grew to
enjoy that very much: they cut wood, replanted trees, gathered
what they could eat, fished and hunted. They left their land
shares to the ones who preferred farming and went on living in
the woods. That was a mistake."

"Why, Starman? It seems well-thought."

"Because the Vervlin forgot what they had learned in their
histories and holy books. Among many Solthree peoples, and
others for all I know, free-living hunters and herdsmen don't
get on well with farmers who stay in one place. Not if a hunter
chases some great roaring beast out of the woods, breaking
fences, trampling crops, galloping through the sheds sending
the pigs running squealing their heads off and scaring the milk
out of the cows—I'm glad to see you laugh, but where would
you be for all your work without the farms?"

"I want to see the roaring beasts," said Mooksi, chin
cupped in hands.

"Long gone," König said.

"Were the Ninety and Nine farmers, then?" young König
asked. "I thought they were not, but you seem to feel sorry for
them."

"They were hunters and woodsmen. But Vervlin have
always been respected for their honesty, and these ninety and
some wrote down what had happened in their journals as
honestly as they could. They had no wish to hurt the farmers.
There were no apes here then. Galactic Federation knew about
them, but they lived far across the continent and bothered
nobody. Then something happened to their forests—disease
killed the trees, or earthquakes disrupted them, or they caught
fire—or all of these things. The apes moved and settled here.
They disturbed the woodsmen, scared the big animals, and
whenever they scratched or bit, people and animals died. Their
spit was poison—then. Careless children . . . dead in a few
hours. Men, women, animals. Not so very many; enough to
frighten them out of the woods, back to the land. But the
farmers were angry and told them . . . told them it was the

wrath of God upon sinners . . . and would not let them on the
land, even to hire out for their keep . . ."

"Another mistake," said Ehrle quietly.

"And when the Colonial census people came the woodsmen
asked to return, and made still another. They had become very
angry. They didn't tell about the poison deaths. A few of them
hoped the apes would attack the farmers. I know this because
I've read what was written . . . and they were very ashamed of
it later . . ."

"If they had told? What difference would that have made to
us?"

"Very little. GalFed would have moved the colony or
destroyed the apes, the woodsmen would have stayed and kept
fighting the farmers."

"Why did they want to come back later?"

"I think they enjoyed the free way they had lived here
before the trouble. They got over their anger, and thought
they might fight the apes, or the farmers, to a standstill, or
find other land here. But the colonial Vervlin thought they
wanted the original land, and threatened to abandon the
whole colony and go before the law and demand repara-
tions—"

"And that was a mistake," said Helig bitterly. "They
should have abandoned. Because you were saved and we not."

"There was really only one mistake," said König. "The
first one made by Galactic Federation when they believed they
could join parts of seed to make people who could live com-
fortably on this world." He was beginning to droop from lack
of a good night's sleep.

"And how can they repay *us*? Your fathers were normal
when they left here."

"No. The ones who mated with normal people right away
had mostly normal children, but some were not, and those
were discouraged from having children." Forbidden. "And a
few had abnormal grandchildren. They would have liked to
stay together as a group, but could not last without bringing in
new blood. The ones who tried to intermarry, about a third of
them, had to give up. They were given land and money and
whatever else they needed." Like sterilization. "Very few were
lucky." When his raw energy was spent he wearied quickly
and completely, and he was very tired now.

"But some were, like you," Ehrle insisted. "What can be done for us?"

He took a deep breath. Halvorsen would not have touched this one with a pitchfork. "You would have to stop mating among yourselves and take the seed of normal people, or give it to normal ones. That would not help you at all. It might help a few of your children. Changes in diet with some hormones—the chemicals the body makes to control growth and function—might help you a little, might help your children more." But not untie that unholy knot in the chromosome. "Your children's children's children might be pulled up little by little." The silence tightened like parchment and he let his arms drop. "You are young. It's hard for you to look ahead to the hope that you might have a few normal great-grandchildren . . . when I can only ask Galactic Federation for help." He was nearly asleep on his feet.

"How long do *your* Vervlin live, König?"

"To our fifties. It is a short life for Solthrees."

"We die before forty," said Ehrle.

"You are the adults here."

"Yes. We have four or five years of that."

"What shall I tell you?" There was nothing. He was desperate. "GalFed will come here with medicines that will make you three times taller and handsomer than I and you will live to be three times my age!"

"Perhaps it would have been better if you had, Starman," Helig said.

"A child's story? Broken promises and battered hopes make people sick and cruel and ugly." And how far they had been driven along the road, the brave children. "Youngers, am I on trial, or may I sleep? I got very little sleep last night."

The lamps were guttering, and upstairs the floors were creaking as the Elders stumbled into their beds. König smelt once again a cold drift of aromatic herb washing in through the screened conduits. Thunder whispered far away, rain pattered softly. The youngest children were being put to bed, the oven fires banked down with ashes.

But Ehrle and the other eldest ones surrounded him, heads tilted, eyes far away. Duty had burdened them; as soon as they could walk or grasp they had been made to heed. If they were by some miracle created whole down generations, how many more generations would they need to recognize an instant of happiness? Even he had had to learn his meager share through outsiders. He said in a low voice, "If I don't go back no one will come here again. No one will help."

The children turned away and began to blow out lamps; a few murmured together. One pulled down the shelf that had been Willi's bed and piled blankets on it, motioning to König.

König lay down on his side, facing inward, and through half-closed eyes watched the shadowed figures moving. It was cooler by the wall, he warmed his hands between his knees and let sleep gather in him. Sentence in suspense. He wondered how long Halvorsen had really endured this place, and how to break the flesh-and-blood prison wall . . .

"König!" Intense whisper. Ehrle. Hand on his shoulder.

"Let me sleep," he begged.

"König, you!" The hand became a fist that shook and pounded. He cared little for touching, and surely not like that.

"Oh God, what now?"

"Quietly."

"Mustn't wake them upthere," he muttered and tried to turn away. The grip held.

"Down here you must wake now!"

He pulled himself up on one elbow, his head was sagging. "What then?"

"König, I am eighteen years old, and I have had my bleedings for over a year. Helig is half a year younger than I, and there are two other girls in this house who bleed. You can give us your seed and we can begin the new cycle of children, even if we never know what becomes of them. It's no use to keep you here longer, but you can do that much for us before you go."

König felt his soul shrivelling and the flesh withering on his bones. "Good God, Ehrle! I'm not some kind of—some kind of animal you can use to improve the stock! That's a danger-ous idea."

"We don't care about that! No one who comes here will know of it."

He sat up. "I cannot . . . I cannot service a bunch of you like—"

"We will wait as long as need be," said Ehrle, every word a bell tolling.

"I'm so tired . . . I can't think straight. Please let me sleep and we'll discuss it tomorrow."

"We will discuss it when you have agreed, König. A grown man like you must still have—"

"It's impossible. I can't—"

The hand had never left his shoulder. "Why are you shivering?"

"I told you," said young König. He was dipping a stick into the fire to light a lantern. "A man grown for nearly twenty years and he has no children, when his people are dying out." He came holding the lantern before him, face lit yellow from below. "He knows how to care for children and seems to care about them but he has none. He is telling the truth at least this time. He cannot."

"Maybe he is one who goes with men," Ehrle said.

"He would still have the seed," said Helig.

"This one has none," said young König.

"Goddamn it, if I did such a thing I'd lose my—"

"I think you have already lost," the boy said.

"You cannot have children. Not at all," Ehrle said, and took her hand away at last.

He yelled, "I told you there were those who were not allowed—"

No one woke. He wondered if they had been drugged, if there had been a plan. The faces of Ehrle, König, Helig, others surrounded him. Hard composed faces.

Ehrle said flatly, "Those who were not allowed, you said, were defective ones or had made defective ones. Do you have brothers or sisters, König?"

"No."

"But you are a normal grown man of thirty-five."

His face was beaded with sweat, he wanted sleep as if it had been a drug in his own system. "I made promises, I will keep promises. But I will not make children."

"Why can you not make children?"

No promises were enough for them, for that accumulation of anger and frustration. These would kill, if others had not. The smooth fresh faces. He had no ghost to give up. He had never been quite alive. Hands gripped his shoulders, each finger pitting through the cloth layers.

"Goddamn you, I'd run through the lot of you and the

cows too if it would do any good—and don't think I'm joking,
you don't have to put on the laugh this time! I am not normal,
damn you! I am not a man. I am a clone, a being in the shape
of a man, made from a store of cells kept alive for two hundred years. That was the kind of reparation we got! Without
internal sexual organs, that means no seed at all, only hormones to make us look like men and women, perform like
them, only it doesn't work quite that well and oh God this is
the first bloody time I'm glad I never took a clone woman and
raised a clone child and my family weren't part of those—''

"There were none! There were none! And you made promises to us!"

"There were a few of them! There were! I told you the
truth!"

Helig sneered. "And the truth is, if men come here from
your damned filthy Galactic Federation they will not let us
have children at all! And we will *all* live as idiots in filth until
we die with Vervlen! And then they will sell it all over again!"

The hands pulled, tore, dragged him from bed. He beat
about him with his fists. "I told you—" He did not know if
more had gathered or it seemed so; the hard bodies walled
him, drove him the length of the vault, into another opening,
this uphill, tripping on hard granitic edges; his head knocked
against the ceiling, he was dizzy.

And out into the forest trampling moist dead leaves. The
rain had stopped, but wind still rustled the trees and the blue
apes woke and chittered.

They pushed his back to the trunk of a great conifer,
plucked the cord from his hood, dragged his hands around the
tree and tied them, ripped down his clothes to bare shoulders
and chest, the cold struck him. One of them, he could not see
which in the dark or in his terror, shinnied up the tree to grab
boughs and shake them, mimicking obscenely the noise of the
apes, jumping down and pulling back. All of them in a circle
about König and the trunk; and the apes dropped squalling,
scratching, biting at his head and shoulders, tangling their
claws in his hair, in as great a panic as he; left him clawed and
bitten, scampered to find other trees.

There was no mercy to beg for. He had stormed, cajoled,
commanded in his life, never begged. Never died. The lantern
disappeared and the children were absorbed in darkness. His

mind twisted like a worm in contemplation of dying, he sagged against the trunk. He was not a man for contemplation and had never studied the holy books of Vervlen. Had not the farmers driven woodsmen back into the forest to die?

He let himself slip downward until he was sitting, in order to shrug his body into his clothing against the cold. He was still bare about the head and chest and the wind plastered dead leaves on his sweating skin. His nose was running, his breath rattled. He waited for cramps and retching and hoped they would bring death with them quickly. His stomach knotted sooner than he had expected and he twisted grotesquely in order to vomit on the planet rather than himself. So much for revenge. *Murdered for a pair of boots*. That was simpler. And he had turned his eyes away from Halvorsen and the pitchfork. That had been quicker. Cramping and vomiting drew up his legs and wrenched his arms again and again until his mouth ran with bile. The wind stung the sores on his bared skin, the trees whispered in darkness. He thought he heard laughter, but it was only the barking of blue apes and the hooting of strange birds he had not had time to notice. He had never feared the entity Death but was often afraid of dying. Now it was only a matter of waiting out the pain. He was terribly angry, but not afraid at all. The anger dulled at last and the world turned black.

"Oh ay, Master König, what y' doin' here?"

He knew the voice: Willi.

"Willi," he whispered. His eyelids were cemented shut. He forced them open, blinking away crust and film. His mouth was dry. Alive again? Maybe.

"What y' doin' here?" Willi repeated. He was bending over König, head against black trees and gray sky, one hand holding a string of fish.

König did not say, *What the hell you think?* but only repeated, "Willi," as if he were as stupid.

But he was unjust. Willi dropped the fish and knelt beside him. The sun was about to rise, the forest blew and flittered and spoke the sounds of its creatures. The boy reached into his tackle bag and pulled out a knife to cut the cord. He dragged the limp hands about until they rested, two hairy purple things, on König's knees, and rubbed them between his own

warm ones; then paused a minute in thought as visible as if his
skull were transparent, pulled his mittens from his pocket and
forced them over König's hands.

"Thank you, Willi." He was alive. He was immune. He was
a true citizen of Vervlen, the blind gut of humanity.

Willi flushed with pleasure at thanks from a man half dead
and wholly stupefied. "Y'r hurt. Come with me to home and
get help."

König shuddered. "No thanks. Just help me up, please."

His legs shook. He clung to the trunk and giggled helplessly
because if he had been a fearful man he would have killed
himself with the poison of his expectations. He pulled the
clothes about his neck and the hood over his head. His
shoulders ached, his hands were turning hot and stinging.
"Where was the stream you were fishing in?"

"There," Willi pointed. "It's the only one about."

"Good. Here's your mittens."

"Oh no! Y' keep those." Willi picked up his fish, odd
shapes with fins like wings. He drew close to König and said in
a loud whisper, "But watch out. They're a bad lot, them,
sometime. I know. I was a leader."

"Yes . . . good-bye, Willi."

He staggered from tree to tree, working life into his fingers,
easing it into his shoulders. He did not touch the crusted cuts
on his flesh. On the way there was a little valley, like the dip of
the forest floor where he had landed, but not the one. The sun
was up.

He sat on an outcropping in the valley's shadow to rest, and
though he still felt like giggling he began to weep. He had
often cursed himself for whining at his own fate. It was at least
permitted to weep for them, the Elders turned useless and the
Youngers already warped in every part of their lives, in intelligence, determination, bravery. And cursed both them and
those who had created him. The apes threw pods at him and
the wind sang an old song his people had found somewhere: —

> *Yellow leaves are flying, falling*
> *where the King sits, lonely one*
> *flocking birds are crying, calling:*
> *withered, wasted, dying, done . . .*

• • •

He pulled himself up the hill and across the wooded land to the cliffside, slithered down vines and saw the pool Willi had fished in where the half-winged creatures leaped and flopped gracelessly splashing; followed the stream upward until he reached the hangar wall. He did not go near the hangar. He regretted not having taken the pitchfork from Halvorsen so that he might arrange her bones with dignity; likely they would merely have scattered.

He found the flat stone and examined it: one among many, it did not seem to have been moved. He worked his fingers inside the mittens. The stinging and the heat were going with the stiffness. He heard footsteps in the leaves above, looked up and saw Helig, ape on her shoulder. He clenched and stretched his fingers, and stood still. So did she, a few meters away from the cliff's edge. The ape leaped from her shoulder to the fir above, ran cackling to its topmost branch.

König did not take his eyes off her. Squatted and dropped the mittens. She took a step forward. He flung the stone back, grunting. From the corner of his eye he caught a glance of another figure on the cliff, upstream. Young König. No sign of Ehrle. He whipped his head about and back: no one across the stream.

Eyes on Helig he groped for the bag, found it, ripped it open, plunged his left hand in, the stunner seemed to leap into it. Helig took another step forward. Young König took two steps toward her.

The stunner was a little thing, standard issue for colony-shifters. König had practised much and seldom needed it.

Helig stepped nearer. "Can you kill us all, König, before we find your ship?"

König aimed dead on and thumbed the stud.

The tiny nerve-poison capsule burst in the corner of the blue ape's eye. The animal squawked horribly, seemed to try to keep balance for a moment, fell sliding down the eaves of the conifer and landed with a thud at the girl's feet.

She gave a little shocked cry, grabbed up the bruised and paralyzed creature and ran sobbing. König was more shocked than she. "Dear Lord, you can cry for *that!*"

He shifted aim to young König, gloving his gun hand with

the other: a gesture; his stance was as hard as a rock. "Which eye do *you* want it in?"

Let him believe it kills. Let him believe.

Young König stood a moment, empty hands at his sides, and backed away. He would not run.

"—alone!" a voice rode on the wind. "Leave us alone, König!" Deeper in the forest he saw Ehrle, hands resting on the tines of a forked tree. Her cheeks were reddened with wind, a wisp of hair blew across her forehead. She had not come forward, not to lead here.

"Alone," the wind cried.

"You will be left alone." Against his will he saw her in a year, a little more, waiting in line awkwardly with head down, splayed thumbs hooked over the tops of the dishes.

His mouth tasted of bile, of failure. The shadows moved and she was gone.

He put the stunner on the rock, pulled the recorder from the bag and looped the chain over his head, slid the chronometer with the remotes over his wrist, pressed a colored button for the thin beep of the direction-finder; shoved stunner and bag into his pocket, scrambled up the vines, panting and clumsy. He followed the cliff-edge, gun in one hand and infrared scanner in the other. Its light-strip flickered with the movements of small animals.

When the hypnoformer was reversing he waited listening and scanning for the moment it took the field to dissipate. The shuttle broke like sun through cloud, white dappled with shade, gold numbers burning.

He saw no more Vervlin, and when he had climbed in and locked down looked no more on the world. The ship lifted its feral beak to part the sky, pulling after it a whirlwind of yellow leaves that reached the tops of the trees before they drifted in slow circles downward to the forest floor.

– Phantom Foot –

Phelps was in the dayroom watching Beal and Twelvetrees playing *blitz,* a roughhouse performed in a six-foot chalk circle, crouching in the sumo position, but with pronged fingers aimed and darting. It was stuffy; suddenly the grunts and jibes, the glistening shoulders, and the clang and shuffle of heavy boots on steel plates oppressed Phelps; he turned away and reached for a stereo reel. There was a gasp and thud, and when he looked back Twelvetrees was doubled on the floor, choking, most of his body well outside the circle. Beal was pulling in shuddering breaths, rubbing sweaty hands on his chest.

"Pay up, buster, I got you square."

"Hell with you." Twelvetrees bent over his clenched arms, retching.

"Sell your butterfly collection!" Beal sniggered. "Borrow from Towser!" He roared, and his laughter redoubled on the metal walls. Phelps rubbed his leg and wished he were elsewhere, wished there were a big enough elsewhere on the cramped ship to give him privacy and silence for his ravaged body and his nerves. His fear.

Beal turned. His sneer glanced off Phelps and settled on Dionisi, who had fitted his shoulders to the corner of the cabin, and was drawing the last sustenance from a mangled cigarette butt.

"Come on, Kos! Play the winner."

Dionisi took the butt out of his mouth and said, "No thanks, I don' like your style." He dropped the butt down the airsuck; Phelps parted his lips to invoke Regulation 86/493a, recollected what and where he was, and shut up.

Beal's eyes narrowed. "You weren't so particular when you knifed Halloran in the sweepstake on the *Nicholas of Cusa*."

Dionisi fished out another cigarette. "You are mistaken. He pulled a knife on me. I killed him with my hands. And got suspended for it."

"He ain't around to talk about it," Beal said. "And you got plenty of money out of that deal." A switchblade flicked out of his closed hand. "I think you ought to play *blitz* with me, Kos."

Phelps found his voice. "Stop it, Beal. Put it away before it gets bent. We're going into orbit in an hour and we need Dionisi."

Kosta Dionisi grinned. "Yes, Beal, I am a very valuable member of the crew."

"Yeah," Beal stowed his knife away, "an' you'll make as good-lookin' a deader as the rest of us." He tossed Twelve-trees a shirt and buttoned on his own; then he found his target in Phelps. "You're pale, Joe, you're shakin' like a leaf. What in hell's name made you volunteer?"

"I didn't," said Phelps. "I'm a conscript." He limped out of the room, and when he was in the passageway with the door closed behind him he leaned weakly against the wall.

The *Cayley & Sylvester* went into orbit; it wheeled like a yo-yo going round-the-world, centering on the planet Qumedon, and waiting.

Towers faced Phelps across the *go*-board in his cabin. The board was a magnetic slab with black and white metal stones. Towers was a fifth degree player, but he did not expect to dedicate four or five days to this game. He doubted he would be alive that long. He faced Phelps wishing he had something more than empathic feeling for this thin-lipped white-lashed shadow. He had been against taking him on but there was no other arrangement possible. He could think of half a dozen thick-headed louts who might have proven more useful; but the choice had been made for him.

Shiptime it was 1934 hours, fifty-ninth day out. They had been in orbit for two hours.

Towers said, "That means we have anywhere up to twelve hours."

"Anywhere at all," said Phelps, retracting his last move. Towers ground his teeth, but there was nothing to do but wait, and nothing mattered. To cover his annoyance he picked a turnip-shaped chronometer off his desk and studied it.

"Five-ten P.M. EST Solthree. . . . My four kids are sitting around the Tri-V watching *Jett Winslow of the Solar Patrol* and wishing they were out fighting ten-legged Vegans."

"I haven't even that," said Phelps.

Towers sighed and fished his mind in vain to find something worthwhile in himself, his work, his mission—and Phelps. The veined hands, pale blue eyes, pale red hair cut close to the scalp, seemed extensions of raw nerve. Phelps might have been at home stalking errors in a roomful of IBMs; as a conscript on the *Cayley & Sylvester*, sunk in apathy and self-pity—and yet the only survivor of contact with the Qumedni—Towers would have preferred the company of Beal and Twelvetrees, whom he considered worthless anywhere else.

Air pulsed through the arteries of the ship with a faint but pervasive noise; the magnetic board pulled at the descending stones with an unpleasant snick; Phelps rubbed his leg and a roughness in his fingers rasped on the cloth; a flaw in the air-conditioning which Towers had cursed many times pulled in rowdy voices from the mess-room in one of the innumerable variations of the "Battle Hymn of the Republic":

"*She went into the water and she got her thighs all wet
   But she didn't get her* (clap, clap) *wet, yet!*"

Still, he would not have shut them up.

The intercom buzzed. Towers glanced at Phelps. Dionisi was up ahead with the instruments, alone. He pressed a button.

"Dionisi?"

"They—it's here, sir."

Towers thought the voice was trembling. "Just what is it, Dionisi?" He spoke softly. He was called Towser because of his bite.

"The Qumedni ship is pacing us, sir—just like Phelps said." He gave the coordinates in a calmer voice.

"Stay on autopilot and come down here in ten minutes," said Towers. "Bring the others."

He said to Phelps, "You're sure, now, we have a little time, half an hour at least?"

Phelps twisted in his chair. "Two hours, more likely." The voices in the mess-room stopped, leaving a gaping hole of silence beyond the other noises.

Towers tried to make human sounds. "Leg bother you?"

"No more than usual. Nerves. I get, you know, the feel of the foot. . . . I had a sore gall under one ankle. . . ." He forced open a clenched fist to rub his jaw.

"Why don't you take it off? You might as well be comfortable. . . ." He put away the *go*-set while Phelps loosened his laces.

"I don't know if I—"

"Don't worry, just go ahead." Towers gave him a brief, rare grin—then his eyes caught sight of the chronometer. At home it was 5:29, and on Tri-V red, green, and yellow Chucklies were popping musically in the cereal bowl. He pulled his eyes away, and yanked levers that folded up the bunk, washstand and table. Phelps pulled off his shoe and the aluminum foot inside it and rubbed his stump in the white sock marked with the constrictions of the laces.

"Now come the sentences," said Towers.

There were four tense faces in front of him. The crew knew almost as much as Towers; there was not much more to know. The spread of information had not been encouraged, though there had been rumors of sealed orders. Towers himself had not wanted to ask Phelps any questions.

He said, "You know we were sent here to contact the Qumedni and that three ships were lost trying."

They shifted about.

"Nobody ever said what happened to them ships," said Beal. "Sir?"

"They blew up," said Towers.

Beal squeezed his eyes and pawed his bristled cheek. "But if we gotta fight—we ain't armed. Sir? How do you expect—"

"The Qumedni don't attack with guns," said Phelps.

Three pairs of eyes turned to him. "Go ahead," said Towers. "There's your sealed orders. Anything you want to know, ask Phelps. He's the only one alive who's had anything to do with Qumedni."

They had grown too familiar with him to become respectful now. Dionisi said, "If they are so hard to reach, how did you do it?"

"I was the captain of the third ship," said Phelps.

"A thousand years ago a Qumedni ship crashed on Bellisarius VI. The crew died or somehow disappeared, but the log and some other records had been stored in a black box and were found almost intact. They'd never gotten in touch with the Bellisarii before, and it was believed they meant to stop for repairs and try to get away unnoticed. We first heard about this twenty-five years ago, but we haven't been the first to try to visit the Qumedni."

"What have they got that we want?" Twelvetrees asked.

"Technology. Of course, you can't get much technology from a simple record like a logbook, but the account of places visited and distances covered is unbelievable. . . . They've gotten out of the supergalaxy—perhaps even into other dimensions. Peoples of far greater technical development than ours have tried to establish relations with them, but they've all been pushed off. . . . The Qumedni seem to want to keep to themselves."

Privately Towers agreed with them. In twenty years with the Service he had seen enough of Earth's meddling with planetary peoples to stuff his craw.

Dionisi said suddenly, "I think we have nothing they want."

"It's a point," said Phelps. "I don't know what we're going to trade with, and I can't imagine setting up the kind of formal contracts we've used on other planets—but contact comes first, and we've got to play it by ear."

"What do they look like?" Beal asked.

Phelps shrugged. "Nobody's ever seen one. We suspect

they're energy-forms of some kind. We know they can communicate when they want to, they're telepathic—and they have other psi powers." He paused, and his face became drawn. "They have also a cruel humor."

"Killing people is not humor," said Dionisi.

"It is certainly not." Phelps stared him full in the face, and Dionisi flushed.

Towers said, "You'd think if they were telepathic they couldn't be really cruel."

"When I was being put through Psych—afterwards—I was told that degree of empathy could kill off a race in two generations." Phelps looked at the blank faces of Beal and Twelve-trees. "Their coarseness is a kind of tranquilizer that lets them register pain without being disturbed by it. That's why we want their technology, not their art or philosophy." He rubbed his stumped leg and tucked it under the whole one.

"Now I'll tell you what happens. They pace a ship, as they're doing now, and send out telepathic feelers. They play a few table-rapping tricks to get us off guard, then they probe, and find out what makes us tick. . . . Nobody's ever lasted past that."

"But if you say they don't attack," said Beal, "how did the ships—"

Phelps read the faces carefully. "The men blew up the ships themselves."

Dionisi poured a round of coffee from the pot on the desk.

"That's why we have no weapons," said Towers. "So—so we won't use them against ourselves." *What form of madness would make men blow up their own ships?*

"They get at the nerves," said Phelps; his eyes became vague. "They pick at the weakness. . . ."

The men shifted in their chairs, rustled their dry palms together in the silence to reinforce reality. Phelps pulled himself together.

"When we were going through all that, something . . . went wrong with the reactor. The others were—weren't in any condition to attend to it, so I suited up to have a go at it myself, but as soon as I was ready the ship blew up. I was blown clear but a piece of the hull sheared my foot off. . . . The suit sealed it and I radioed and they found me two days later. That's it."

His flat dry voice broke off like a biscuit; he leaned back, licking his lips.

"Time for one more question," Towers said. "Anybody?"

"I have one for you, sir," Dionisi said. "Of all the volunteers, why did you choose us?"

Towers hesitated. Dionisi was the best pilot he had ever known, and had a strong and simple view of a world which had never treated him kindly: life was hell, but it was not necessary to behave like a devil; Towers felt that was as strong a protection as anybody could want for this task. He had chosen Beal and Twelvetrees because they were a pair of roisterers with thick wits and superb reflexes. But he was spared the trouble of deciding what to say aloud, because the lights went out.

"Just sit still," Phelps said tensely. The lights went on again.

They looked at each other. They waited like a man in a dentist's chair watching the dentist's hand hovering over a row of drills. The papers on Towers's desk began to rise and stir, eddied once like leaves, and settled in their accustomed places. The Qumedon force ransacked the place lightly, touching and turning articles as if it were looking for a map or key.

And all at once there was nothing.

The night before takeoff.

Dionisi took a woman up a hill under a red August moon low over the ripe fields. At the foot of the hill the mist was so thick it moistened their lips in invisible droplets. They scrambled up hand in hand and at the top it was clear. Below the fields were broken by thickets of fir that turned ghost in the shifting mist. He spread his coat and they sat on it. When he had kissed her she laid the flat of her hand on his chest, and he could feel his heart plunging against it. Her hand moved to his face.

"Don't go now, Kos. Not when things are like this."

"But I will come back; I always come."

But she shook her head, shivering and clasping her arms. "I'm frightened."

"You're cold," he said, and covered her with his body.

•　　•　　•

On the night before takeoff Beal was lying on the bed in a cheap hotel room. Under the bed there was a pile of whisky bottles that spilled out around his shoes and the clothes he had dumped on the floor; there was only the sick light of a parchment-shaded lamp in a porcelain wall bracket. He was conscious but paralyzed with drink and every once in a while his consciousness took a dive into the interior darkness, pulling his senses reeling with it. The blinded window flickered as if flames were licking it, and he heard sirens in the street. Terror welled in his throat and he couldn't lift a finger. He rolled his eyes desperately and saw something growing in the corner of the ceiling where the light was too feeble to reach—a smoke, a shadow under the buckled wallpaper. It grew, red and purple, writhing at times, running down in streaks like ink. He wanted to scream but he could hardly croak.

"Me with the D.T.'s," he whispered. "Christ!"

The stain widened and spread; the light dimmed; as the room darkened the thing grew phosphorescent, the ancient glue of the wallpaper parted and cracked under the pressure. He knew the light would go out, he knew that as it failed the paper would burst and the thing with its horrid glow would reach slimy tentacles and engulf him.

And still he could not move.

Twelvetrees helped his mother serve supper to his four younger brothers and his three younger sisters, and gave a hand with the dishes when it was done. He was touching the thick cracked mugs and blue-rimmed plates for perhaps the last time, but that was how it went. After the younger ones had been put to bed his mother put on her good black dress and pinned on a hat with raveled veiling. "I'm going to church, Roger," she said. "If you go out don't forget your key."

"No, Ma."

He watched Tri-V and leafed through a magazine for a while; then he got up and put on a leather jacket. His brother Herbert looked up reproachfully from the welter of glue-tubes and the half-completed model of the *Nicholas of Cusa*. "What's the matter? You so sick of our faces you can't stay around a while on your last night?"

Twelvetrees stopped at the door. "If you were leaving Earth knowing you'd probably never come back, I'd think you might want to see a bit of it before you went."

He closed the door on his brother's shocked face. He'd never said anything like that before, but it was true, so what the hell? Herbert wouldn't tell their mother. She always half expected it with every trip anyway, or thought she did. She was sure it was a deadly sin for Man to leave the Earth and poke his nose in the heavens, and if the Lord had wanted Man to, etc. But as a widow with eight children she was glad to accept a good share of his pay.

Tonight there was enough left to do what he wanted. He walked rapidly down toward the waterfront. Earlier there had been foghorns and a close red sullen moon, but as evening wore on it had paled and receded till it stood white as salt against the basalt of the heavens. He had ridden in those heavens; he had crossed the deserts of that moon. It was a place like any other, good or bad they were the same to him. Yet it made a pretty light on the water. He stood on a bridge and watched, first the moon and then the colored lights of the dance-hall down along the curve of the shore. Those lights glittered on the water richer than the colored stars he had passed in ships. He would find a girl there, they would drink and make love, and he would waken with the taste of the scotch tightly coated on the back of his palate; it was what he had to have once more. Still, he waited for a while, watching the multiple fold and flow of the moonlit water. He was very much alone.

Towers stayed up late with his wife and four children, sitting in the living room watching green flames in the fireplace that were chemical but warm as any that had lit the arthritic passions of men in caves. He wanted to go to bed with his wife, and yet he wanted to see the children as long as possible, so he stayed, watching the children as they drowsed by the flickering light.

Then it seemed, perhaps by a trick of the light, that he could see his children's thoughts rising above their heads in the warm air, like heat-waves above asphalt on a hot day. They were simple, rather meretricious thoughts in primary colors.

From the baby's rose-and-gold head came the dream of a curly-haired doll; one child was forming a devious plan to forestall a bully who had designs on his coptercycle; another was hoping to negotiate a loan from his father for the down payment on a secondhand chronometer he needed very badly in order to tell at any given moment the exact time at any spot on Mars or Venus.

Smiling, Towers turned to tell his wife about his amazing vision; and he saw that she too had thoughts moving in a cloud over her head. She was thinking that tomorrow night she would see her lover.

And Phelps—

Dionisi laughed. "Oh no. No, you cannot catch me that way," he told the invisible Qumedni, and the rest of the men looked up, dazed and blinking. For a moment they swam together in the bowl of their accumulated mind, and all knew the thoughts of the others. They laughed with him, a little stiffly, trying to orient the truth of what had happened to the twisted visions the Qumedni had tried to unbalance them with.

It seemed funny enough to Dionisi. The night before take-off he had picked up a whore at the corner bar; later she had emptied his pockets while he slept. He was neither surprised nor disappointed to find his wallet gone: it was what happened to Kosta Dionisi. He laughed. Poor bitch with a handful of silver; he had hidden his folding-money and spaceman's papers under a loose tile in the shower-stall.

Beal was puzzled and insulted. He had actually celebrated his departure by rolling two drunks on Main Street as a valedictory gesture to his old hometown. He had given Officer Martinez the slip, hired a Fli-Rite from the local U-Driv-It, killed a mickey on the way to the rocket port, made a perfect landing, and slept sweetly in the best hotel room available. He didn't know what had prompted that horror—unless . . . There was an LSD experiment he had tried when he was fifteen that—ugh! He clasped his head in his hands.

Twelvetrees opened and closed his eyes dreamily. Neither imaginative nor guilt-ridden, he had relived his evening truly.

Towers, for a moment, fought sickening doubt. His children's thoughts had been genuine, perhaps, but his wife's? He had been married seventeen years; he loved his wife. For the first of those years he had tortured himself with jealousy, but the love and intimacy they had built with whatever time they had—if all the years of mutual trust were nothing . . . He smiled at a sudden memory. He had watched her face, thoughtful in the firelight, and said, "What are you thinking of?"

She grinned. "My secret lover."

"Is that all?"

"Oh—your farewell dinner . . . that sirloin tip—do you want an oven roast with garlic or a pot roast with bay leaf and cloves?"

He laughed. "Make it any way you damn well please! Just come up to bed with me right now!"

And Phelps—they turned to him. He had not been in the pool of their thoughts, he had been outside alone somewhere. He gripped the edge of his chair, contorted with bared teeth, contracted brows over eyes squeezed shut. Was he in space among the shards of his exploded ship, with the pain of his sheared leg?

Towers barked, "Phelps! Come out of it!"

Phelps came out slowly, grudgingly, almost cracking with strain, like metal cooling from white-hot. As his features loosened the flesh seemed to ebb from the bones till he had the pinched nose and upper jaw that rises from the mummy's skull. His mouth worked, he blinked, passed his hand over his head; the scalp was shining wet. He reached down, half in dream, to find the contraption that housed his stump.

"I—" he began. But as his fingers touched the edge of the corset the foot rose up and sailed across the room, rebounding from the walls with a ringing that echoed deafeningly in the stillness, then to the ceiling and the floor and the walls again—*clang!*—corset edges flapping and the light tattoo of lace points.

"For God's sake!" Phelps jerked up galvanized. The men stood and reached for it, but even in the small space it eluded them, slipped from their arms and flew, an ungainly albatross lurching and crashing.

Towers remembered Phelps's earlier advice. "Stop! Don't go after it! Don't—" But Phelps, broken by whatever terrors had attacked him, was beyond advice. Standing awkwardly on one foot, fists clenched, he cried out, "Stop it! Come back, damn you!"

The boot crashed and lurched. Phelps screamed in a high thin voice, "Give me back my foot!"

"Sit down," Towers ordered the others. "For Christ's sake, Phelps—"

"Shut up! Shut up!" Phelps whispered. But he sat down. Towers took a deep breath. But Phelps was groping with shaking fingers for his handkerchief. He grabbed one of the polythene cups from the desk, wadded the handkerchief into it and then crammed in his stump. "Bastards," he whispered, wincing. He got up and flung himself across the room, lurching more drunkenly, more crazily, than the foot he was trying to capture, shaking with pain, shrieking in his cracking voice, "Gimme back my foot, you buggers! Gimme back my foot!" There was a giggle of hysteria, a hand moved out to stop him.

Towers snarled, "Stay still!"

Each time the cup struck the floor they shivered. But Phelps went on yelling, "Give it back to me! Give it—"

They gave him back his foot.

He stopped, choking on a sob of frightful impetus.

He stood perfectly still. He looked down.

On the floor beside him lay the stump sock, the cup, the handkerchief. At the end of his leg there was a foot, made of flesh and bone, pink and new as a baby's. Under the outside ankle there was a small red raised lump, the gall he had complained of. He moved the toes.

All of them saw it at once, within a second. But before the second had passed they knew something else. Each man raised his own left leg and found himself without a foot. Sheared an inch above the ankle it terminated in a stump, tightly bound in ridged livid scar over the shivered bone-end.

Then they knew what Phelps knew, and swung alone past the stars in forty-eight hours of pain and terror; each cut nerve end telegraphed to the empty air beyond it that here had been a foot with its experiences in the spring and pressure of a thousand steps, and whatever weariness and joy there had been in them.

Singly, each of them might have borne it; together their minds balked and sank.

They opened their mouths to scream; their risen gorges choked them. Their mindless, soundless repulsion beat against the walls of the confining ship like the wings of a great moth in a cyanide jar.

Drowning in panic, Towers battled to the surface of his consciousness. He forced himself up through a blind torrent that made him want to break out of the ship and find a suffocating freedom in raw space. Eyes up, away from the horror, he saw Phelps standing solidly on two feet as if he were frozen to the floor.

Phelps's eyes were pools of icy calm. They said: revenge. Every insult Phelps had suffered, or thought he suffered, was caught there: broken ship, lost foot, days wheeling in space, the probing indignity of Psych, the desk job for a ship's captain, months watching the rolling muscles, the hard whole nerveless bodies of men playing *blitz*, every coarse word from an ignorant tongue.

Towers whispered, "Phelps," but he did not know if sound, or any reality at all, existed around him.

Phelp's eyes slid back and forth over the semicircle of gaping statues. He took two steps on his new foot and looked down at it. He licked his lips and turned, searching for something.

"Thought you'd play with me," he muttered. "Thought because I was crippled you could . . ." His head swung back and forth. He found what he wanted: a long-necked metal decanter clasped to the wall above the desk; Towers kept it for the rare moments when self-doubt engulfed him, and now Phelps jerked it from its prongs and hefted it. He struck it against his cupped palm and it rang softly.

Towers worked his throat desperately and croaked. "Please! For God's sake, Phelps!" *For the love of God, Montresor,* bells jingled; he wanted to giggle. Phelps smiled once. Then he sat down on the floor and raising the decanter above his head brought it crashing down on his bare foot.

There was a black fall, as if the laws of the Universe were repealed, and inseparably welded atoms dissolved. The decanter, coming down, had burned an arc of light across

Towers's retina, and when he was able to see again, he found
Phelps sitting on the floor, calmly smoothing on his stump
sock. There was no foot.

Towers crossed glances with the others, afraid to look
down.

"Gotta do it sometime," said Beal, and looked. He found
his booted foot where it belonged. Then the others dared look,
and found themselves whole.

"Jesus Christ," Twelvetrees said softly. Then a new
thought struck them together. This might be illusion, too.
Dionisi raised his foot and stamped twice, like a newly shod
stallion breaking sparks in a dark smithy.

They relaxed; if this was an illusion it was the one they knew
how to live with.

Towers picked up the decanter; it was undented; yet when
he closed his eyes he could still see the arc of light. "How
much of that was real?" he wondered.

With savage jerks Phelps tightened the laces of his artificial
foot. "Yes, how much?"

The tone of his voice made Towers turn. Phelps pointed
down. On the floor, on the dull green metal, there were the
prints of a bare left foot.

"What now, Captain?" Phelps asked. He had been shamed
and degraded, and his voice was bitter.

Towers sighed. "Out of here while we've still got our skins,
I guess, if they aren't illusory."

"I don't mind keeping on," Phelps said.

"No, Phelps," said Towers gently, "there's nothing more
you have to prove. Dionisi, are you all right? We're going
back."

:So soon?:

He whirled. "Who said that?"

But the words had been spoken in their minds.

:The Cayley and Sylvester? The Cayley and Sylvester?: The
metallic *whang* of hallucination under anesthesia.

"What do you want?" Towers called aloud, ridiculously
loud.

*:This is the Amhibfa of Kwemedn. Will you talk with us? If
it is more comfortable to use the radio our call signal is . . . :*

•   •   •

"The way it looks," said Towers, "you may get that foot after all, Joe."

They faced each other across the go-board. Although it was 0335 hours shiptime they were both too wrought-up to sleep. But contact had been made, negotiations arranged, and over-drive and autopilot were set for Earth.

Phelps shook his head. "It doesn't matter. I mean, not in one way. . . . I could have a whole new body every year and I'd still be amputated inside." He added hesitantly, "My family has a long record in the Service. I was expected to go in, and I let them push me without thinking, though I barely scraped through the Physicals. When I finally started having doubts, I thought, well I'll go out once more and call it quits for a while." He lit a cigarette and watched the smoke work its way toward the airsuck. "That one more time the Qumedni called it quits for me. And I let the guilt nearly kill me for three years. . . . I felt my authority was weak, it was my fault the ship blew up. If I'd had a tighter grip—"

"But that wasn't so."

"No, I don't believe it now. But I did for three years, and I didn't like it."

"And you won't go back?"

Phelps looked away. "No. You said yourself, I don't have to prove anything anymore. And I don't want any presents from the Qumedni."

"I'd like to know what the brass back home think we're go-ing to be able to trade for what we want."

"Beads, maybe." He grunted. " 'If you will find it more comfortable to use the radio—' Huh! Specious bastards. They know they're calling the tune. We surprised them a little, caught their respect somehow, and they want to know why. Now we've really got to be careful. Soon as they think they know—" he drew a finger across his throat.

"Yes," said Towers. "I'm tired of being a foreign devil, but this one's going to be interesting." He looked at his chronometer and found it was 2:26 AM at home. The chil-dren, in crib and cot, would be dreaming of patrolling the stars with Jett Winslow. His wife, he trusted, would be asleep in the middle of the double bed with her hair in curlers and two pillows piled under her head—as he had found her once on an unexpected return.

Rubbing his head with one hand, *Phelps* retracted his previous move with the other. Towers sighed. *You'll be back, all right*—he watched the thin nervous hand hovering over the board—*but not on my ship, by God!*

Beal was strangely glum. He undressed and poured water over his head, and toweled his face, snorting. But he said nothing.

"What's the matter, Beal?" Dionisi taunted. "Every trip we come back, you say, 'Now we got them buggers where we want 'em!' Why not now?"

"If I had 'em—" Beal mashed his hands together so tightly they popped with vacuum when he pulled them apart. "Jeez, if I had 'em—" He flung himself into the top bunk and slept.

Twelvetrees thought of the dance pavilion on the glittering water, and sang softly to himself:

> *"I been to the stars*
> *   that shine in the skies,*
> *I never seen any*
> *   that shine like your eyes,*
> *Oh, dum-diddly-dum. . . ."*

No ripple stirred the calm littoral of his mind, and he fell asleep at peace even with the Qumedni.

Dionisi, in the middle bunk, lay awake. Thinking about the face of that woman in his dreams. He remembered every feature as if she had been real, and he wanted her. Surely, once seen so clearly, she existed somewhere. He had only to use his eyes and he would find her. Somewhere . . . he slid toward sleep.

Suddenly he jerked awake with a force that cracked his head against Beal's bunk, drawing a cry of anguish from himself and a curse from Beal. In his half sleep he had remembered the face of the woman he had picked up, and something about that face, some line of it under the thick and tawdry makeup—suppose her face had been scrubbed clean, perhaps . . .

He swore, because now the two faces were inextricably mingled. Damn the Qumedni! They had played with him, given him a vision and taken it away. Suppose he went back and found her again? She would be what she was, and no more. She was too far gone. It was a long time ago, and for someone else, that she had been the girl on the hill. Yet he wanted something, and he had a quickened feeling for her, for once a painful sense of the derelict flesh he had used and forgotten. He fell into a troubled sleep.

And the *Cayley & Sylvester* spun the first fine warp thread between Earth and Qumedon.

— A Grain of Manhood —

She was lying formless; the contour of her body was lost except for the white ring of pain that worked its way downward every so often like a wedding ring over a swollen knuckle. All her other miseries were encompassed by this masterpiece of nature, a force at one with lightning and thunder, the hurricane, the great reach of the four-thousand-year-old sequoia.

In the intervals she was a person again, and she turned her eyes to James, who was standing at the window watching white peaks rising out of the shadow of night. She asked for the first time, "James, what will you do when this is over?"

"I don't know." He spoke through the window to the sky. In spite of the unexpected hurry to the hospital he was wearing his dark suit, pressed and fresh, and a tie knotted with painful neatness.

"Why do you always call me James?" he asked suddenly. "Why not Jim or some other kind of short thing?"

She would have said, Why not, it's your name, but she was too miserable for even the feeblest humor. "I don't know. You always looked like a James to me. Hair parted neatly, folded handkerchief in pocket, buckled briefcase." And on Earth perhaps a bowler hat and tight-furled umbrella. "It seemed suitable."

"You mean stodgy and prissy."

"No, James, just suitable. It's right for you, and I've always liked you as you are."

But he kept his lips compressed and his eyes on the white peaks.

The hospital lay in the crater's plain circled by the mountains of Axmith's Territory II. Not a person in the whole of the Community who did not know them, and all he had ever wanted was to dissolve among them like a grain of salt without much more color or savor. She liked him as he was—and what she had done to him!

"You never did explain—" he began.

"Oh, James, let it go!" She tensed on the bed and then tried to make herself limp and slide under the coil of pain. "You wouldn't let me, all those awful months. Now I don't want to."

Light reflected back on his face from the mountains of Axtu, and for a moment it showed open and vulnerable. She set her hands warily over the frenetic writhing in her belly and said with bitterness, "A virgin birth would have seemed more reasonable to you."

He said in the precise way she claimed she had never hated, "There are at least three people on Axtu beside us who know I am sterile."

Shut up! Shut up! You married me because there was a good job for a married man out here! Shut up! "And of course no one could want me but you, James, you're pretty sure of that." Perhaps not. She stared at the pale green ceiling, green walls, palely enameled night-table, water-pitcher, callow-colored with the uncertain light reflected from the western wall of the pumice crater. All things sullen, solid, a hard shine to them. In her mind colors flickered, shifting pure prism-hues, only paled and whitened by pain, till she opened her eyes to the nothingness of reality.

She said, "What's there to explain? The old story . . ."

He opened his mouth and closed it. Then he said, "When *that* is born—"

"I'll go away, if you like. You'll never have to see me or it again."

"Don't be foolish. It can't be hidden now. Damn it, why couldn't you have gotten rid of it, like any other woman?"

"Why couldn't you have had children, like any other man?" she said softly. It drew the blood to his face. Could she

ever have pretended to love this man, who used so much nasti-
ness to cover his vulnerability? With an effort she kept her
voice gentle. "When we found we couldn't have children, I
couldn't help being restless . . . all the money we'd saved with
my working, and I hadn't seen my people for three years . . ."
The time-old tale of alien grain. No use saving money for the
child, and she used it to visit Earth.

But she had forgotten that life on Earth was what she had
married to get away from. There was nothing for her, and all
she had was the return fare to Axtu, and she started back.

But the shipwreck changed it.

She shared the life raft with the mutilated body of an old
woman who had taught her the Italian hemstitch a few hours
before; it took three days till the boat homed on a safe planet
and landed battered and useless on the rocky shores of a lake.
The equipment seemed crushed. The radio had told her that
the air and water were usable, but now it was silent, and she
had no idea whether it was still sending the automatic SOS,
nor how to repair it or use it.

She crawled outside at last, poising on jagged rocks that
bruised her feet, and looked out over the grey expanse of the
lake, flat and sunless.

Nothing worse than the hell I've always lived in. She
grinned in despair and went back into the boat to salvage
food.

The lake was in a craterlike depression, a stony saucer of
water, and she was unable to see beyond the rim. When the
boat landed she had been asleep and had not seen the planet's
face—a grim tumbling sleep with the consciousness of the
blanket-wrapped body beside her, the vacuum of loneliness in
an old woman who had died without her descendants around
her. There was only one other blanket. She stuffed it into a
canvas bag with some concentrates and a canteen and slung it
over her shoulder. There was not much to eat. Even if there
were her survival would be only a matter of inertia.

She stared around once more. There was no sign of movement, not a wind carrying gull-cries, scuttling run of lizard, or
oozing of any alien life she might have imagined. The air and
water might be all right, but the planet gave no sign of being
any more generous than that.

There was a tinge of chill to the grey air; she wiped sweating palms on her skirt and began to climb the rim. Once her foot dislodged a stone; it rolled downward for a few feet, and that was the first sound she heard beyond the beating of her own heart.

She climbed, and before she reached the top she began to hear something more: the trill of a pipe so faint and uncertain it might have been the singing of blood in her brain. But it grew and paced her as she stumbled on; it traced the whorl of her ear.

Light grew overhead, palely, and then burst into a burning sun; the sky became blue, as if she had risen out of a cloud. The points of the rocks dulled, the ground softened. She was walking on clipped green turf.

She stopped, took off her shoes, and stood with her toes pressed in the grass, dropping the canvas bag from her shoulder. The piper was walking beside her, fingering the stops. His scales were blue, green, amber, and silver; colors writhed on him like the lights on a peacock's neck.

The unfluid walls of plaster and fiberboard faced her, and the falsely soothing colors of metal-frame tables. "That was Kolanddro," she said. "I didn't have to explain anything to him. He knew already."

"The way I never did," said James, and added half under his breath, "—and never will."

She remembered the months of nights she had lived alone with the half-formed creature in her, screaming in nightmare that it was clawing and ripping its way out through the frail membranes of protection that were all she had been able to give it—or maintain against it. . . .

The former face of the planet had crumbled like a clay mask. Here there were heavy-leaved trees; grass grew damp and cool beneath them. But in the sunshine the strange people who lived here had raised gaudy paper pavilions of pure color. They came at the sound of the pipe and gathered around her. She would have said that they were dressed, but they were wearing only the fur, scales, or bat-wings their curious nature had given them, and there were no two alike.

They were humanoid, but flat-nosed and narrow-jawed; it

was hard to find the form beneath the skin. Some of the feathered and crested ones looked like the eighteenth-century Romantic's idea of the Noble Savage, but she was able to find neither nobility nor evil in their faces.

The scaled man beside her said, "This is Nev; I'm Koland-dro, and you see these are my people. You came from the wrecked boat."

"I did. How could you have learned my language?"

"I translate alien tongues. I'm the Interpreter." That explained it to him, perhaps.

He lowered his shining lids with the effect of a smile. "You'll understand it later."

"I see. You people are telepathic."

"No. *I'm* telepathic. That's why I'm the Interpreter."

"And I don't have to tell you that my name's Lela Gordon, and I'm from Earth, etc."

"Nor ask to see anyone more important than me, because no one will understand you."

She smiled, then sighed. "It doesn't seem very easy to leave here. Can you help me?"

But he had turned to speak to someone, and she looked around at the Nevids who had approached her. They returned her interest with a kind of inoffensive curiosity, and when they had seen enough left to go about their business. Kolanddro brought her a bowl of fruit and fresh bread.

"We don't make this kind of thing with our grain, but we baked it when it became evident that you would be with us."

"Are you clairvoyant too?"

He made a glittering gesture. "I have great range. There's little I can't do here." He blinked. "No, I can't repair your boat. We haven't many hard metals—and we don't need them." He pointed out a winged man who resembled the Spirit of Communication which for centuries had graced the telephone book. "We have Messengers." He tapped his head. "We have Interpreters." Recognizing the panic rising in her he said anxiously, "Please eat. You won't come to harm here."

She said, "I believe you . . . but the strangeness . . . is overpowering." But she calmed herself enough to eat her meal under the tossing shade. The bread was rather heavy, but good enough for having had the recipe drawn from a fleeting picture in a sleeping mind.

Kolanddro blinked and asked, "What is lemon soufflé?"

"Something I'm glad I didn't dream of while I was sleeping," said Lela. She added very gently, "I really don't like having my mind read."

"While you are staying here you will have to get used to it."

But I don't want to stay here. She was uneasy with the strangeness, the sense of having already become completely integrated into the life of the planet in an hour's time. She thought of the old woman dead in the boat who might have been happy to spend the last years of her age under this sun, and brushed crumbs from her skirt.

"I think I'd better stay near the boat in case the signal's working."

He stared at her with his black-and-green eyes. "You'll never reach the boat without my help," he touched the pipe, "and if you go you won't come back, or even remember all this. There'll be no more food or shelter for you."

She said slowly, "Open Sesame?"

"The connotation's unclear. . . . I see, an old story (perhaps you'll tell it to me sometime?)—yes, something like that."

"Kolanddro . . ." she spoke to his still shadow on the grass, ". . . are you an illusion?"

"You will have to decide that for yourself."

The chill that crimped her skin was not an illusion, at least not more so than the whole cosmos of matter. Where in relation to this place were the grey lake and the overcast sky?

"There's nothing to be afraid of. Believe me." He ran a pearl nail around the rind of a yellow fruit and halved it. "But if you stay here you must live as one of us. We like privacy and we don't let anyone leave us who'll endanger it."

"It's beautiful here," she said reluctantly.

"It is. And we know what kind of things aliens will bring us. We've had experiences with them." He stood up. "I'm busy now, but most people like to rest in the heat of the afternoon. I think you will be glad of a rest; you may have my house." He pointed out a particularly vivid pavilion of crimson and purple. He swallowed the rest of the fruit, spat out four green pips into the palm of his hand, and cast them to the winds.

"Four more zimb trees," he said.

"You had already forgotten me by then," said James.

"James, I thought you would have been glad to forget me.
. . . They wouldn't have taken your job away from you here
just because your wife was lost in space."

"That wasn't why I married you."

"If there was another reason it was because feeling so trod-
den on yourself you had to have someone to hurt in return."

"Don't, Lela. I never meant to hurt you."

But she was thinking of the last few months of sullen meals,
crushing silence, and loneliness. *What in hell are we going to
do with a little bastard who looks as if he'd escaped from a
prism, no matter how appealing he may be aesthetically? How
can we keep him here? Where can we hide him?*

The color flows on you like the broken light of a prism.

"All you people," she said to Kolanddro, "have the same
form basically—I think—but no two of you are alike on the
surface. That seems impossible."

"Not when our germ plasm is almost infinitely tractable."

"What do you mean?"

"We can take in any form of intelligent alien life. The children become pure Nevids within three generations."

"How?"

"All psychokinetic faculties on Nev don't rest in the Interpreters—although I will say," he added complacently, "that
most of the intelligence does. All Nevid parents have a choice
in deciding before the child is born what form it will take—
externally, not in the vital organs."

"And the child has no choice in the matter?"

"No. His happiness depends on how well he lives with the
shape we give him."

"And if he doesn't?"

"He'll have an unhappy but interesting life."

She shivered. "I don't think I'd like that for my children."

He waved his arm at the Colony and the multicolored flow
of the strange people and the wind-rippled walls of their
houses. "A quarter of these people are descended from aliens.
We've found for every alien an Interpreter who could bring

him into the life of the planet. I don't think any of them have been unhappy."

"I can't believe I could ever be a part of your life."

"I'm no more part of the life here than you are. The Interpreter is born, not made by the longings of his parents, and he comes no more often than"—he searched her mind for the parallel—"the true genius on your planet. Man or woman, he gives up private life."

"Your laws are cruel."

"Only as cruel or weak as the people who live by them. Do I seem that way to you?"

She never really knew the shapes of their souls or the range of their emotions, and only had rare glimpses of the mines and orchards, weavers and gold-beaters, that produced what she used and ate. Sometimes she thought she had glimpses of city spires beyond the forests, and though she knew that the Colonies often shifted with the seasons, there was no change as long as she was with them, and she never found out what they traded for with coins or feathers, or if they sacrificed the living on stone altars, or the names of their strange gods.

She woke late one morning after a restless night; she was queasy and aching, and was struck with the sudden fear that she was going to have a child. She made breakfast, and when Kolanddro came in and stood silently looking at her, her teeth began to chatter. He only smiled, and loosening a strand of her hair laid it across his green-white palm, where it lay very black, as if he were matching samples of material.

"I can't go through with this," she whispered.

"You've accepted the conditions . . ." He became hesitant and faltering for the first time since she had known him. ". . . I have had to accept them." But she turned away. What had he had to give up?

Late afternoon when the sun was falling toward the west, a woman dropped down from the sky. She did not come directly into the encampment where the cooking-fires were going, but folded her wings and waited at the edge of the clearing, searching in the shifting colored frieze her people made of their most commonplace actions.

Kolanddro noticed her and moved forward; Lela turned from her task to watch them as they spoke, soundless shadows in a green shade. Something in their attitudes made her very still, though her halting command of the language would not have allowed her to understand them even if she had heard their voices.

The Nevid woman pointed toward the west; her downy hands flickered and her head lifted urgently to his calm face.

Then she turned away and came into the clearing where there was a late gold patch of sunlight lingering; she stopped and stood with her head bent down, almost as if to thrust it under her wing. Soundless and motionless she waited for the desire for flight to thicken her wings with blood. When the great delicate membranes opened she rose against the sun in a blaze of heraldic red, diminished, and was gone.

But Lela soared with her in imagination over thickets and rolling hills, perhaps past stone towers and shimmering rivers, half-blinded by the deep light that warmed the clear air, and without pleasure in the flight.

A voice murmured in her ear that the meat was scorching, and she felt both foolish and sick; she recognized Kolanddro's sacrifice to the laws of Nev. When she looked again, she saw that he was gone. He came out of the pavilion a few minutes later; he was wearing an obsidian dagger.

It was not until after supper that she saw the stranger emerge along the forest trail from the same direction the woman had come. He was a crested and feathered man as splendid of his type as Kolanddro; Kolanddro washed his face and hands in a basin and went out to meet him.

They faced each other in a pantomime of tense hieratic gesture; Kolanddro spoke, unfastening his belt with the dagger and laying it on the ground. He moved his hands in a wide gesture, as if to erase whatever angers were between them, and they turned and separated.

Lela sat waiting for him in the pavilion. The sun had almost set and the evening air had thickened to sweet dusk heavy with the smells of flowers and fruit. Indoors was the heart of a rose. The simple dress the Nevids had made for her slid over her body in rich folds; the sky was mauve and pearl flowing with the last of the sun.

Kolanddro came in, his mind so full of his own affairs it was quite blind to hers. He murmured, "That was a long journey for nothing."

"I think he'll make it again," she said. "I'm going back."

He stared at her. She went on falteringly, "I know it will be a lot of trouble to put things right—but they will be right. . . . I thought I could be a moral person simply by accepting the inevitable. Now I no longer believe it's inevitable."

"If you leave we can't take you back—you understand?"

"I understand—the kind of law that lets you risk death fighting a rival even when you're the most important member of the Community."

He said, "A superman on your world would have to live by the same laws as the rest."

"I agree. I don't think your laws are unjust, or even inflexible—but they aren't sensitive." The word conjured James, with his capacities for loneliness and self-laceration and suddenly time, even a lifetime, seemed very short. "They've gotten stunted along the way, and on Earth they're always reaching, like a tree, for the ultimate justice—not only in lawcourts, but in relations between persons. . . . This justice, it's a clumsy, top-heavy thing, full of stupid mistakes and dead ends —but it grows."

"If people on Earth are much like you they must make themselves terribly miserable for nothing."

"They do. Will you let me go?"

"No one may ever find you out there."

"I have enough food for a while, and there's water."

"My son?"

"I think you'll have other sons. Please."

"What can you and your husband make of him on Earth?"

She winced. "Perhaps someone who can love both Earth and Nev."

"No. He won't know anything of Nev." He watched her gravely a moment, and she waited. He said, "When everything is quiet I'll take you back to the boat. I'll break the law, for you."

When the night was dark and quiet I took off the dress the Nevids had made for me and put on the one I came in. Render unto Caesar. *We went down along the smooth grass and the colors shimmered on him even in the dark. All I could think of, feeling so foolish and sick, was that he was going to kill that splendidly feathered man, or be killed, and there was nothing to say, because I'd told him what I thought of his laws.*

"But we don't fight to the death."

"Thank you."

"Our law would never allow anyone to leave as cold and un-protected as you are doing. I must bring you food and clothing."

"No . . . they'd make me feel worse." But there was one thing I wanted from him. I knew he guessed it, but I said it anyway.

"Kolanddro. Don't make me forget Nev."

I found my canvas bag. It was weatherproof, but the shoes were rotted from nights of dew and days of hot sun.

He put his pipe to his mouth, and I had one glance of his fingers glittering on the stops and then the stones

cut her feet. She stood on the sharp edges like the trans-formed mermaid who walked on knives of pain as long as she had legs. She thought she could hear a last thin echo of the pipe, but it faded into the hollow lapping of the waters on the shore under the night wind.

There was no clear memory of how long she waited on the shore, days and nights. She ate concentrates when hunger became painful, and drank water when her tongue rattled in her throat, and nightmares chattered around her. She wondered that the baby lived, but it clung fiercely to the fetal stalk and thrived, walled away from her terrors.

She could hardly move when a loud bleep sounded in the boat at last, and she crawled into the terrible place on hands and knees to pick away at the wreckage and find the source, and push the switch that told them she was there. When the rescue ship lifted, she was in a bunk tossing with fever; she never saw the face of the planet.

"Lela."

She was fastened in one clench of force. "Please call the nurse now, James," she whispered. He pressed the buzzer.

"You came back, even when you could have died out there—"

"James, I could fall downstairs on my head anytime, or pull

a hangnail and get septicemia; it's a chance. But I don't care now. I just want to die."

"Don't talk like that! I want you to live and be happy. With me, whatever happens! I love you, Lela. . . ."

But the mist was rising before her eyes, red as the blood in the wings of the Nev woman against the sun.

She opened her eyes once out of the chaos of pain and sound; a rubber-gloved hand was holding a shining thing by the heels, a baby gleaming with the detritus of amniotic fluid. She sank back.

He was a complete and perfect replica of James, down to the last neat lock of dark hair on his forehead. A stranger in the world, he lay beside her; his arms and legs trembled, his face crumpled, his pink hands moved aimlessly with unconscious grace.

"I can't understand it," James said, ". . . but he is beautiful. Lela, I have to tell you this now; I thought I could get away with it, but I can't. I knew I was sterile before we were married."

"I guessed it," she said. "That was really why I went away. I was going to leave you. But it doesn't matter now."

"But you did come back."

"Yes. I didn't expect much." The months gone, the long slow growth of a child in her, the woman's right she had wanted so deeply—eclipsed in bitterness and recrimination. She smiled without joy. "The tie that binds."

But he said quietly, without arrogance, "No. This depends on us."

She bent to smell the newness of the child's flesh, and to feel the hands on her face. "All right, James."

The white sun of Axtu was very clear and warm in the room. She moved her clean drained body under the sheets, grateful enough to have her breasts ripening with milk, the baby in her arm, and James beside her with the faint pulsing of hope between them.

– ms & mr frankenstein –

Scarpino and I had this thing
going upstairs in a downtown house
he dismantled the skylight first I
mean a thing with an old wroughtiron fence he got
from a contractor for the armature
comission he said
that's what he said
built up past the TV antenna   landlord
picking up Pittsburgh yelling *Get that thing down!*
NEXT WEEK says Scarpino don't ask how welding
letting fly
rust jets and paint curlicues
into a black stick man NOW
says Scarpino EPOXY MASKING TAPE and ARTIFACTS
MAN OF THE CENTURY!!! MADE ON THE
PREMISES!!! gluing
cuphandles dented percolator baskets
potlids nonreturnable bottles
twisted tinties coffeemill-wheels
cracked dollsheads rundown alarmclocks
paperclips shoelaces nailpolish-brushes
typewriter keys
that made ½ a leg
and the night I spent hacking him out of the epoxy

gave the thing most of a pair of overalls & a jockstrap
    we still had
        lampshades windowblinds
cornpoppers shishkebab-skewers knifesharpeners
    bent forks axehandles beercans shavingcream containers

Scarpino wild with welding gluing winding
    till we got what looked like ⅔ of
       Ozymandias King of Kings
and I begged, Scarpino, don't you think enough—and he
  BELOVED gave me an abstract kiss could have
    got more juice out of a Rodin marble DARLING
    WE MUST SCROUNGE AND SCAVENGE
      he always talked like that
   IT IS ART DEAREST HEART!!
if it had been January he could have gone to hell
        but what with night youth and the May moon
I mined the dumps for paintscrapers andirons winecorks
  tin funnels paperweights runningshoes raingauges
    dull hacksaws sprung springs bicyclespokes tenpenny
           nails
gum erasers toothpaste-tubes broken staplers spent matches
  plugged nickels
       he welded wild and mad
     arm & thigh of his mighty man
  & I was getting a little off on the thing myself maybe
      the glue
        some weird trip good God
      how we'd get it out of there
     or where
          it grew
  smashed headlights ashtrays burnt bulbs
    popcan-rings empty ballpoints cereal-boxes
crochet-hooks pacifiers cigarette-holders
last year's calendars candle-stubs speedometers
    tongue-depressors dipsticks
  lipsticks ticket-stubs ladles without handles
    strawberry-hullers china dogs
                I'm out of breath
& flat on the floor by the time Scarpino says
       DONE!!!

•   •   •

there stands Man Matterhorn
by Easter Island out of Las Vegas
   & a soupçon of King Kong

   COLOSSAL breathed Scarpino and fell to his knees
   well its head was up there in the stars
   25 foot high and every inch a junkman

so being a bit woozy with this bottle of Old Bubble
   not having magic names or electric jolts
          and it didn't have much of a noble brow or prow
       still I felt it needed a little ceremony you understand
up there on the scaffold Scarpino dancing around singing
   THERE'LL BE A HOT TIME IN THE OLD TOWN
          TONIGHT
   climbed up dizzy don't ask   ·
   & bashed Godzilla's eyeless head with Old Bubble
               and he gave some kind of shiver ·
               and his mouth opened

          honest I wasn't all that scared
          just thought he'd say something friendly like
          hello there honey   but he jerked
          and squeaked
                    that was the wroughtiron innards
          and blinked
          and ticked and whirred and whirled and went
          ma-ma ma-ma
          and sparked buzzed clanked cracked flashed
                    foamed
          twanged squirted spilled snapped tapped
          stapled snipped crackled crocheted
          sharpened sawed slurped threaded popped
          hulled honked scraped crunched zinged

             scaffold shaking like oyoy old Scarp
               down there
               doing Yoga exercises singing
          GOT IT ALL TOGETHER YEAH,
          YEAH

that mindless mouth *wa wa wa*

I wanted out

slid down the shook frame
chachachattering and whooee
a kind of cloudy glory
gathered from the sky
and Thing just raised his arms twitching forty ways
and cleared his throat and cried out

COSMOS I COME!

zapped out the roof on a pillar of fire
blowing a hole clear down the cellar
knocking the landlord out taking along
Scarp's wig & false teeth my fillings
& the bandaid from my thumb where I'd
cut it on the damn thing

neighbours yelling

Lightning, by Gawd!
we ducked out before the landlord came to
also slipped the cops the Fire Dept & the Board of
Health
sleeping in weedy lots under newspapers
about *RCMP Probes Bomb Plot   New Comet Sighted*
Scarpino
half off his nut for days raving

HE IS OUR EMISSARY TO THE UNIVERSE!!!!

he she it shit I wonder
just what kind of garbage they're gonna be sending us

anyway old Scarp got over it looking pretty thin
without the rug & choppers and my teeth hurt
so we split he went up to Inuvik to learn
bone carving from the Inuit
and I moved in with a plumber and that's the story

– was/man –

whenever the moon went into eclipse he became a man
lost quite a lot of hair, his fangs pulled in about half an inch
and he put on heavy muscle in shoulder, buttock and thigh
he wasn't bothered losing the tail and claws so much, it was
growing that crazy complex inefficient
nose vexed him. sometimes the transformation
caught him in the middle of a howl & he sneezed
his eyes stayed harsh and feral. the moon darkened
he picked up on it quickly enough, bathed in the windblown
rainpool, shaved, kicked the year's collection of
bones out of the closet looking for the roll-on
shook the moths from the woollens, shoved his feet
clumsily in the shoes, dragged on an old
trenchcoat & a fedora and caught the fast freight

town wasn't much, a few bright lights in the plaza
and the all-nitery. people in that place
were rather morose and surly, but it
suited him down to the ground.

                                              he enjoyed
a few cigarillos, and whiskey in moderation
girls who didn't mind the hairy type liked him. he never
bit them, just grizzled a little.

                                      at first he found all that

grown flesh of his luxurious, new senses nipping him
every minute, but when the moon's scythe edged out
he wanted to gnaw on himself, drag off the excrescence
caught himself thinking of barred places, jail, cage, zoo
got scared he'd be trapped in his strange meat, man till he
     died.
found he wanted to pick fights with dark grumbling
figures in the eye-stinging smoke. he lit out for home
under the quarter-moon

not snapping back in 2 flicks like some movie monster
he knew he'd be at it again, folded & packed the trappings
     neatly
but his wild thighs tightened, went to the sweet ground
the claws sprung,
he dug his beloved snout into the scents
of wood-rot and wet leaves, sharpened the fangs
lengthening from the roof and floor of his jaws, he had
an hour or two of the moonlit night to run in
though his eyes were redrimmed from the smoke
of the bar and poolroom
               and he
dashed water in his thickening fur to douse the rank
civil insidious urge of the secret man

— Son of the Morning —

By the time Khreng and Prandra came out of deepsleep the ship was in Sol III orbit. Lights warmed around them, the deep yellow of their sun; they slipped the clasps of their webbing, leaped out snarling and yawning hugely, stretched to the limit the hinges of their fanged jaws.

Khreng was a seasoned traveler; he had been twice to the system called the Center of Worlds, where Galactic Federation was based, and once to Sol III. Prandra had never before lifted off Ungruwarkh, but her mind broadcast no complaints, and he asked for none.

The ship was wakening, systems quickened from maintenance level. Khreng's blood rose with the heat, and he wrapped his tail around Prandra's waist; she tapped his nose lightly with the pads of her hand. "Food first."

He growled without malice and dug in the food locker. "Dog food!" That's what it was. Meat for cats was as scarce in the Center as it was on Ungruwarkh, but colonists demanded and got amenities for their dogs.

"Wuff, wuff!" said Prandra. "I can eat dogs too. Little things you say they are? Why do I leave Ungruwarkh?"

"On Sol Three you get meat."

Nice fat people, she thought slyly.

"Then you get killed. They have death bullets there," he pointed through the viewer to the blue-brown globe stippled with white, "not stunners like the GalFeds'."

She spat.

They ate and got full but not satisfied; then they coupled, combed each other, and bathed. "Now the ESP."

He picked up a small blunt rod and pushed a button. Ungrukh fingers were too broad and padded, and their prehensile tails too thick, to handle the controls designed for humans and many other life-forms, but they had a multitude of small implements, some they had made, others had been made for them; no task they were determined to perform was impossible for them.

At the press of the button the ESP's case opened slowly to the warmed air, and the ESP began to waken.

His name was Espinoza, but he refused to be called ESPinoza, said it was too robotic. He was a brain in a midnight-blue glasstex globe, three hundred years old, and he had spent seventy-seven of them as a man. His self-image was this: a man thirty-eight years old, of medium height, brown-skinned and wiry, black hair and mustache, deep brown eyes, white even teeth. Scarce as ESPs were, even good second-graders, over two hundred years was a long time to spend as a brain in an upside-down fishbowl; he often said he was tired. "How can you feel tired?" his superiors asked with unconscious cruelty. :*Believe me, I know when I'm tired.*: Brain cells number in the billions, but they die eventually without regrowing, and he knew he was raveling around the edges.

His thoughts gathered:

A string of onions hanging on the wall, my mother's house . . . like everyone else's his oldest memories were the strongest.

Diego! Diego, it's morning and he had grown up in a slum in São Paulo, what was there to wake up for?

Dvora, will you

"Espinoza," Khreng said. "We're in orbit."

:*Present and accounted for,*: said Espinoza. :*Home already?*: A thought shaped like a sigh.

"What next?" Prandra asked. She too was an ESP and she would also become a brain in a globe; it was part of the price for the ship, the instruments, the meat. Her eyes were wide apart, bad for close work, and she peered with difficulty through the blue glass, wanting to see what she would become.

The brain, freed of its skull plates and suspended in the nutrient bath, had become smooth and spherical, anchored by the pink cables of the vertebral and carotid arteries leading down into the pump that fed them with blood. It was not a dramatic brain, it did not throb, bubble or blurp, but the pump hummed steadily, or it would have died.

"What's next, Espinoza?"

:Pick up the radio messages, eisenkop!:

Khreng grinned. He was not hungry enough to eat a three-hundred-year-old brain. He turned a knob.

The computer rattled, squawked and said:

GALFED RELAY STATION OF FIJI TO SHIPS IN SOL THREE ORBIT: THE FOLLOWING SHIPS ARE IN SOL THREE ORBIT, DATE 7572/58/186/1132:

ANDROMEDA STAR, ORE CARRIER FROM SOL NINE. MESSAGE TO JOE WISNICKI OR WARSAW, SOL THREE, IT'S A BOY, CON-GRATULATIONS, MOTHER AND CHILD WELL—

"How long does this go on?"

:Be patient.:

YSKELADAR RUXCIMI, QUARANTINED HOSPITAL SHIP CARRY-ING 172 CASES FUNGUS PLAGUE, STAYING THREE MONTHS:

Khreng yawned.

ZARANDU OF THANAMAR SIX, BENGTVADI SECTOR 221-278, SUPERFAST CRUISER, RELAYS MESSAGE TO *GALFED SURVEYOR 668X327* FROM GALFED CENTRAL—

"That's us!"

—ORIGINATING FELDFAR 553, ANAX TWO, LOCALLY UNGRU-WARKH, TO KHRENG AND PRANDRA FROM GALFED OBSERVER STATION. MESSAGE: ALL IS WELL, THE (WORD UNCLEAR—KITS, KATS OR KIDS) THE KITS, KATS OR KIDS IN GOOD HEALTH, TUGRIK HAS HIS SECOND TEETH—

All those light-years for this? Prandra wondered.

"Be quiet, that is my son," Khreng said.

—AND EMERALD LOOKS LIKE A FIRST GRADE ESP.

"Ha." Prandra grinned. "And that is *our* daughter."

"It's time for a male to have the ESP." He raised his hand over the switch.

:Wait—:

WARNING TO ALL SHIPS IN SOL THREE ORBIT. QUMEDNI SHIP TENTATIVE IDENTIFICATION: *AMHIBFA'S DAUGHTER OF KWE-MEDN*, IS STILL ORBITING BEYOND GALFED LANES, EXACT

WHEREABOUTS UNKNOWN. DO NOT ON ANY ACCOUNT REPEAT
DO NOT ON ANY ACCOUNT TRY TO CONTACT THIS SHIP: THE *RUX-
CIMI* TRIED CONTACT AND BURNT OUT A CLASS-ONE ESP.
REPEAT—

:*Switch off.*:

"What is that about?"

:*With luck we won't have to find out. If you have messages
home, send them now. We go down in two hours twelve
minutes:*

"First I want to see what is in this place once more,"
Prandra said. "There is not enough time before lift-off."

:*Don't be long.*: They left him, but his mind whispered
behind them: *Burnt out the ESP? lucky devil* . . . the shape of
a sigh hung like a raindrop from a branch. . . .

GalFed Surveyor 668X327 was a good used ship with a
class-two ESP, a new hypnoformer, and a late-model computer; and it belonged to Khreng and Prandra for as long as
they wished to use it.

Khreng and Prandra were a pair of big crimson cats
weighing about a hundred kilos each, Khreng slightly heavier,
Prandra's fur a little darker. Digits rather more elongated
than those of Earth cats gave them almost plantigrade feet
and, with the help of the prehensile tail, fairly manipulative
hands. They could walk on their hind legs with some discomfort, preferred to go on all fours and squat on their haunches
to free their hands. It was hard to estimate their intelligence
since no Ungrukh had ever agreed to be tested and there was
no arguing with their fangs, claws and muscle.

The first GalFed surveyor team to touch down on Ungruwarkh stepped out on the barren plains, sniffed the air and
coughed, and declared it a poverty planet. Their ESP had
reported traces of primitive civilization, but they did not
expect to find much.

While they were unloading, a big red cat appeared half a
kilometer distant and loped quietly toward them.

:*He likes your smell, he's hungry,*: the ESP said, and they
stiffened. :*But relax, he's much more curious. . . . his name is
Khreng.*:

He stood among them very still, and a cat-fancier from

Solthree slowly put a hand on the massive head. A comparative anatomist from Sirius V considered bone structure, and had a stray thought of a lab and dissecting-table; Khreng grinned, and within fifteen seconds seventy-five cats, claws out and fangs bared, appeared from behind boulders and out of fissures and cracks, and ten minutes later truce terms were arranged. The ESP had been working so hard on the receiving end that he had not given thought to the possibility of telepathy in Earth-like jungle cats.

The planet, out on the tip of a Galactic arm, was a bit smaller than Sol III and a bit denser; it had a distant yellow sun, rarefied air, and was half-covered in water. Life spread thinly over a great chain of archipelagos spiraling from pole to pole; the climate ranged from semitropic at the equator to cold plains of red lava in the temperate zones; the cat-civilization, numbering about a million, lived in tribal units wherever food and water were available; competition for them was intense. They had never been threatened by larger predators—the meat animals, now near extinction, ran to pig and rodent types— and they had made few local adaptations except for the red fur with which they blended into the red of the sparse soil and the lava on the plains, and the big black chevron running from the crown of the head down either flank, much like deeply shadowed fissures in lava, centered with a thin white stripe resembling the salt and snow crystals that sifted into the cracks. They did not need weapons for the few animals they hunted, but they had developed sophisticated builders' tools for their shelters against the treeless cold of the plains, and the flotillas of rafts they used for fishing. They hated the fish, which harbored parasites that gave them enteritis, but they were starving.

Fortunately, GalFed was happy with the Ungrukh. (a) About a third of them were telepathic, most often the females, and many of these at least second-grade; ESPs are rare, particularly where language is advanced, and for Galactic liaison and socio-biological sciences they are invaluable; (b) they were an evolutionary puzzle, very nearly Solthree cats with big brains, language, and a civilization only a few thousand years old and no relatives to evolve from or with on the planet.

So GalFed got their proto-ESPs and Khreng and Prandra

their ship with its ESP and equipment, and they were coming to be educated, like cat-Candides, in the ways of the world, the enriching and sowing of their meager soil with grain for fodder, the raising of cattle from stocks of frozen embryos.

:Time to go,: said Espinoza.

They wheeled him into the shuttle on a dolly and bolted him in. Khreng checked the ship once again. Everything was neat and tight. He stepped into the shuttle and pulled the switch for the lock doors. Then he strapped himself down alongside Prandra.

:This boat's very light and it might yaw,: Espinoza said. *:Don't be nervous.:*

"Why are we nervous? There's nothing fearful here."

:I wish you people would learn to use something beside the present tense.:

"Why must we?" Prandra asked. "It always is the present."

The radio beeped and said:

GALFED SURVEYOR, YOUR CHANNEL REQUIRED FOR EMER-GENCY LANDING. WILL YOU ACCEPT COURSE CHANGE OR WAIT ONE ORBIT?

ACCEPT COURSE CHANGE, Khreng answered. The last landing had given him a terrific case of motion sickness, and he wanted to get it over with.

Then for half an hour they spiraled downward. There was no yaw, no nausea. "This is much bet—" Khreng began, and Prandra screamed.

Something was going round and ringing. Them? Over and over and over. Warped, they elongated. Transparent, they contracted. Star-spirals every-which-way. Nothing to them, not a sound or thought, and the planet below them and above a cloudy rope. Then they went everywhere. And all black.

Still.

Khreng snarled, "That is something new GalFed does not trouble to inform us ignorant Ungrukh."

They were landed, evening sky in the viewer.

"No," Prandra said. "The ESP is unconscious. Something is wrong."

"Dead?"

"No. The blood supply is cut off and comes back."

"That is much quicker than the other landings and much more unpleasant."

"I tell you something is wrong! Espinoza!"

:What? what?:

"What is happening?"

:You're asking me?:

"Who else do we ask? You are the ESP. Are you hurt?"

:What have I got to hurt? If I had a head I'd have a headache.:

"Espinoza! What is happening?"

:Something picked us up and put us down. You tell me.:

"I look and you esp," said Prandra.

:Trees, land, sky . . . that's good to know. We seem to be in a blackberry patch. Give me latitude and longitude.:

"51' 30"N, 20' 17"E. Where is that?"

Espinoza considered. *:About halfway between Lublin and Warsaw. . . . :*

"But what does that mean, Espinoza?"

:We're in Poland, not far from Warsaw, where Joe Wisnicki comes from, and mother and child are doing well, with congratulations. Only half a world off course.:

"You are making some kind of game."

:No, I'm not. It's nothing serious, we're down safely, we just went off course.:

Khreng said, "The course record is the same as on the indicator." He played the taped directions from Fiji Station. "I make no mistakes."

:Raise them on Fiji then, nudnik!:

After a moment, Khreng said, "There is nothing anywhere on the band. Static only. No disrepair indicated."

:Try the ship computer.:

"There is no answer, Espinoza."

It was growing dark. The evening star rose in the viewer.

We are on Earth . . . the thought was a whisper, a mutter . . . finally he said, *:Hypnoform the shuttle compatible with surroundings—if it's working.:*

The hypnoformer was not exactly a cloak of invisibility; it generated a hypnotic field around a person or object that convinced the viewer that he was seeing something else entirely, and was useful for contact with fearful or suspicious aliens. Khreng set dials, knobs, switches. The machine was built into the bulkhead; a growl began in its base, rose gradually to a whine and then a sound beyond hearing; in the distance, dogs were barking. . . . "It's working," Khreng said. The barking stopped; the sound had reached its peak of silence.

:With our luck it could just be pretending to work.:

With real luck the shuttle had blended into its surroundings and was invisible to all external eyes. "You expect enemies?"

:No . . . not yet.:

"Then let's go out and greet the friendly natives." Khreng didn't mean that literally but as a gesture of solidarity with an ally, a custom of his tribe, to show that he had no fear, and he made it because he sensed fear in Espinoza. A brain in a bowl is not supposed to be able to feel or fear, but a glandular body might impose certain ineradicable habits on its brain over seventy-seven years of existence.

"You say the Solthrees have death bullets," Prandra said.

:Children, it's more complicated than that. . . .:

"What then?"

:We'll scan and find out.:

No person lives in this thicket, hermit or woodcutter; there is not enough for him, nothing to attract even Khreng and Prandra, hungry as they are for meat. But there are many small animals: birds above, then squirrels, chipmunks, a few pheasants and rabbits, a bat swooping, flittering moths; and below, moles, grubs, worms. And insects, smaller and smaller sparks of life, each emits its own whisper. Life proliferates helplessly wherever it touches, and even on Ungruwarkh, where it has to make an effort, there are many forms beyond the microscope. But on Sol III, officially designated a Mother-of-Worlds by GalFed, the noise of life currents is almost deafening to a telepath.

"I don't know that I like it here," Prandra said.

:And I can't promise you will, either.:

Beyond the woods a stream with a few unremarkable fish; beyond that a village . . .

:No power, they aren't using power. . . .:

"If there is no radio working—"

:There can't be a power blackout over the whole—no planes in the sky, no—check radiation.:

"Nothing beyond normal."

:Then it's not a war. . . .:

Prandra's fur stood on end, and Khreng said, "Stop that. You are making me feel ill."

"I am not as brave as you, big man," Prandra said, and pulled her mind away.

"What you are thinking . . ." Khreng said to Espinoza, and his voice lowered till he sounded like a tiger with bronchitis, ". . . at GalFed Central they tell me there is no such thing as time travel. . . ."

Three hundred and twenty-four people live in the village. Two will soon die and three more hope to be born; the rest are making a tremendous earthly din. To the Ungrukh, who don't talk much and have fine-tuned ears, it is fearsome, even strained through Espinoza's mind. Women are banging pots, yelling at quarreling children; merchants bargain with farmers, all weary now, they want to go home to supper; boys fight in the dusty streets, are pulled apart and slapped; in the House of Prayer forty-odd men and boys are making extravagant promises to God and demanding Heaven and Earth in return; at the village's northern rim, farthest away, the blacksmith is shoeing the last mare of the day—there's a piece of meat for you!—and the distant *tink* of his hammer is almost peaceful. . . .

"What language are they speaking?"

:Yiddish, mostly.:

"I am told nothing of that one. Is it spoken by many?"

:Nobody. It died almost a hundred years before I was born. . . . I took my Hebrew lessons from the grandson of the last Yiddish scholar. . . .:

"But just for this reason you cannot be sure—"

:Let me tell you . . .: Espinoza pulled his mind back into the silent boundary of the little ship. *:At GalFed you heard that we don't use time travel, not that we don't have it. There was a device built right on Sol Three: a fifty-two-year-old man was sent back fifty years. They brought him forward again well*

*enough, in good shape—except that he had a bad case of
diaper rash, a compulsion to suck his thumb, and no memory
of anything that happened.:*

"Then it is useless," Khreng said.

:It is to us.:

"But there is somebody else that uses it," Prandra said.
"You are thinking of the Qumedni . . . and of the Qumedon
ship in orbit, the one that burns out the ESP."

"That's right.:

"You cannot be sure of that."

*:Not until we find out much more. Just the same, I think
they may have set up a time-vortex here.:*

The Qumedni make their home in the Galaxy, but they
don't belong to GalFed. They don't need to; they have so
many talents, powers and dominions that they hardly know
what to do with them, and sometimes they make mischief.
Most of the time they coexist peacefully with GalFed and occasionally even make contact, trade bits of information and
warnings of local conditions for small souvenir items they consider quaint. No one has ever seen a Qumedon or wants to;
perhaps they are pure energy forms: they surely have a
repellent field about them, and their powers are so supremely
discomfiting that the more one knows about them the less one
wants to know.

They travel back and forth in time as they please, shape the
worlds of their dominions to their fancy, set up their time-
vortices where they choose. One concession GalFed managed
to wring from them was an agreement to set up a warning
signal around every vortex.

"There is no warning," said Prandra. "We come straight
down without even stirring the leaves."

"And in one-tenth the time," Khreng added. "That at least
is good."

*: . . . And a Qumedni ship burning out an ESP, behaving
like an enemy—though they've never exactly been friends.
Perhaps some kind of renegade . . . :*

"Tell us what to do, then Espinoza, and what time we are
in."

:Listen . . . listen to the people. . . . :

• • •

ten zlotys is nine zlotys too many for such, what did you expect, gold with bells around it? didn't I tell you (slap) not to
(slap) climb trees? what can I help it if, leave off already, how
can I study when, where did you put, I told him and told him
and he went, tell me what do you want from my grey hairs,
hah? tell me? *oy Zevi, oy Zevi, what did you do that you
should die?*

"This is a hard place, it's hard," Prandra whispered.
"Everyone here is hurt and bent, even the children . . . except
for that blacksmith, maybe."
    :*And he's a bit of a simpleton.*:
"Like the people of Ungruwarkh, Espinoza?" Khreng
asked with a fanged grin. He was neither hurt nor bent.
    :*I'll tell you, if the Ungrukh break off relations with GalFed
and stay on Ungruwarkh and starve, they might possibly
escape getting bent.*:
They waited, crouching like hearth cats in their small space.

Among the people of the village no one clear voice rises to
describe itself in terms of time and the world. But it is night,
they close their mouths, bite their tongues if they have to, fold
away their grievances. *Tomorrow is erev Shabbas, tomorrow,
tomorrow* . . . A few students read by candlelight, the black
letters shimmer on the white paper like the flames of their
candles, the rest lie down on beds, cots, feather tickings, most
of them trembling with weariness, and sleep. Rats and mice
scuttle among the weathered timbers of the houses; a stray pig
grunts in the street (and Prandra's ears twitch, her eyes spar-
kle . . .)
A voice, in a small tuneless song, quavers on the light wind:

  *"Chava, shtel' dem samovar, ai lyu lyu, ai lyu lyu;
   Chava, shtel' dem samovar, ai lyu, lyu!"*

The rabbi is sweeping the synagogue. He is thinking of hot
tea with lemon, his wife's hands around the samovar, her
family's treasure. . . .
Espinoza fishes deftly, not to disturb, comes up with a

name: Eliohu ben Shmuel Greenblatt, big name for a thin little man, about forty, looks much older, thick grey in the hair and beard—so call me Reb' Elya, everybody else does, I'm not proud! He sings:

> *"Come children, drink the Rabbi's grace*
> *and eat his Sabbath bread;*
> *the wisdom shining in his face*
> *will multiply in light and place*
> *its crown on every head!"*

That's not me! I'm not wise, and my beard is full of sweat.

All right, but why is the rabbi sweeping up?

Espinoza gave Reb' Elya's neural connections a nudge. Even a humble village like—what's it called? Kostopol?—even Kostopol should be able to afford a shammis to take care of the shul.

Reb' Elya turned silent, rested chin on hands clasped around the broom handle and watched the lamplight flickering on the walls. An uneasiness which the merchants, scholars, workaday people had managed to push down below the level of consciousness rose in him like a bloated thing surfacing out of the depths of a pond.

The shammis is dead, that's why! Dead for no reason. Zevi-Hirsch Dorfman, a little sour apple of a man who never opened his mouth except to curse his life and the lives of his wife and children, had flown into a fury at Janchik, the big peasant boy who helped the blacksmith. For what? Janchik, a sleepy good-humored farmer's son who had drunk tea often enough at Reb' Elya's table, and who hardly ever got drunk— liquor made him even sleepier—had started shouting in the middle of the street, things about poisoned wells and Christian blood used in Jewish rituals, things no one would have suspected seeping into his mind let alone coming from his mouth. And Zevi, with Passover coming in midweek, had opened up a mouth back at him; and Janchik had clenched his huge fist and killed him with a blow. Last night, at the end of the evening. . . .

The street had cleared like dust beneath a broom, and when

they had all crept back an hour later in the silence, the darkness, the body was lying there in the mud, flat as it had fallen, a pig rooting in its belly. . . .

Even for Kostopol it was not a pogrom, but—
Reb' Elya shook his head, swept and sang:

> *"For all of time you long to fly,*
> *you build a pair of wings;*
> *and in one teardrop of his eye*
> *the Rabbi sails across the sky*
> *to meet the King of Kings . . ."*

Reb' Elya giggled. "Wings, wings! Sweep, wings!" he told the flying broom. Dust obeyed him.

The shul is a small humble place, dusty, the windows are dim, and there is no obligation to make it a shining Temple when you can never own the land it rests on, but Passover begins Tuesday night, there is no time to elect another shammis with the usual politicking, and Zevi had a habit of hoarding cheese rinds and bread crusts in the cupboards and on the shelves behind the volumes of the Talmud; Passover uses no bread. Besides, Rabbi Yaakov Yitzhak of Lublin, the great Seer, will be staying over this Sabbath on his way home from visiting disciples all around the country. . . .

Espinoza said, :*Early nineteenth-century Poland, things were fairly quiet, maybe early Alexander the First . . .*:
"Explain, Espinoza, what is this?"
:*A village of Jewish merchants and traders surrounded by Polish farms. Look, I was a Solthree historian, but I don't know everything that happened on Earth, and I was a Jew, am a Jew, so you know something of what that is—but these are Eastern European Jews and my ancestors were from Spain; I don't know everything that's going on here because the speech and customs are not all the same as I learned.*:
Prandra said, "They are disagreeable people. I think they are screaming prayers even in their dreams."
:*They think they have a direct line to God and they want to keep it open.*:
Prandra sniffed. The Ungrukh living on the temperate

plains were very possessive about their volcanoes, where the
Firemaster they worshiped had his dwelling places.

Now the shul was clean, for the demons and dybbuks who
slept there after midnight. Reb' Elya flung his broom in the
corner and listened, half-fearful, for the whisper of Lilith on
the wind, for ghosts scuttling in the beams, chirping and
scampering in the rafters. The dogs had set up a furious barking a short time before, and he wondered what wandering soul
had aroused them. Oy, Zevi-Hirsch . . . he sighed and sang
again:

> "Whatever price the Czars may claim
> he praises One alone;
> the Rabbi sings the Holy Name
> and laughing, climbs the steps of flame
> to sit beside God's throne . . ."

Ai, ai! He sang:

> "You, Reb' Elya, know no Names
> you, Reb' Elya, are an ignoramus
> you have your Rebbetsin,
> and your Rebbelach,
> and your samovar, bim, bam!"

He blew out the lamp, closed and locked the door behind him,
and went home to the Rebbetsin, rosy-cheeked Chava, and to
the Rebbelach, four little boys who slept tumbled together on
the bed in the corner, side-curls tossed out over the featherbed
or lying along their cheeks and trembling with their breaths.

And to the samovar, *bim, bam!*

A weary thought: sleep/home/twilight from Espinoza. He
gathered, directed himself to the matter at hand:

*:I think we've been sent backward about seven hundred and
fifty years. I take the number from local conditions, and from
Reb' Elya's thought of the Lubliner Rabbi who was well
known around here in the early nineteenth century. . . .:*

"Could all this be something like the 'plains-companion'?"
Prandra asked; she was thinking of the hallucinations that

sometimes plagued lonely hunters on Ungruwarkh.

:Not with three hundred and twenty-four complete and distinct people, as well as all the animal life . . . and a natural time-warp only turns up in deep space under conditions that are extreme and peculiar. No, I think the Qumedon has set up a time-vortex, and it's pulled us in. He may be some kind of renegade or criminal among his own people; the hostility and the lack of warning seem to go together. Sometimes a Qumedni ship won't answer a message, but it almost never attacks the sender.:

"You think the Qumedon is down here?"

:We got dumped here. If there's a Qumedon, I don't know where else he'd be.:

"Do you really believe in that Qumedon, Espinoza?" Khreng asked quietly. "I think you are only trying to give us hope where there is none."

:What can I say? Assume there's a Qumedon and a vortex. If we came down in it, we have to go up in it. I don't think his shuttle would have enough power; it's probably generated by the mother ship—and he could go off with his vortex and leave us. Or he's gone. So much for hope.:

"There is no sign of aliens here."

:Except us . . . still, the shammis and the blacksmith's boy behaved out of character, and that's typical of Qumedni mischief.:

"It is also typical of many peoples in every time and place," Khreng said dryly.

:Yes, but it's really odd that Zevi-Hirsch went into such a rage.:

"What is strange about a man fighting back?"

:When your method of survival among hostile and suspicious people is to keep the peace at all costs—it's lethal—but so are Qumedni.:

"All right, Espinoza," Prandra said. "You convince us we must look for a Qumedon. Or more than one."

:You realize that if he's here he's hostile, and he can esp you but you can't esp him. He may have taken on the shape of a Solthree.:

"I go scouting and find that out."

"No, you do not," said Khreng. "I am the one to go out,

and you can read me back here.''

"You know that's not close enough for good cross-readings.''

"I am going! Otherwise you are giving me hell and blazes for bringing you across the Galaxy for nothing.''

"Oh, you always think you must be the big man just because you are first out to meet the GalFed surveyor team.''

"That's right,'' said Khreng. "And it goes very well, too.''

"Because the rest of the tribe is together waiting to jump out!''

"You are only thinking of that pig running around the streets!''

"Of course. I come here with the promise of meat and a great deal of knowledge from wise teachers, and I am stuck in an iron box with death and dog food!'' She lashed her tail, endangering everything in the vicinity. "I must get out!''

"See? There are the hell and blazes already.''

:Oh for God's sake be quiet, you pair of actors! You're sending my blood pressure up.:

"The pump is working perfectly,'' said Khreng.

Prandra said, "Look, Khreng, on Ungruwarkh I am your choice because I am a good ESP and know where to hunt. You are mine because you are clever and strong and a fine tracker. Here it is a case of being an ESP and knowing where to hunt when there is no track.''

"You cannot esp a Qumedon.''

"When the valley people come to raid us with that spy who cannot be esped, do I find him or not?''

Khreng grunted.

:You cross-checked. . . . :

"Only go round them, I can shield a little, and make a network, because each is known to so many others, and finally there is one the others know whom I cannot esp. I must be out near them; I cannot do that from this place.''

:A Qumedon can take almost any shape.:

"If it is not a Solthree, we find that out and try something else.''

"I wait for you outside the ship,'' Khreng said, determined to salvage something. "If you are in trouble, I am not wasting time fiddling with lock doors to come after you.''

"I am always grateful for help," Prandra said complacently.

:*And luck,:* said Espinoza.

The planet teemed with strange odors. Khreng's and Prandra's were not among them; they had decontaminated and deodorized so that the local animals wouldn't jump in the air at one sniff of them. They had nose filters to lower the oxygen to its level on their own planet, but there was more life here, more to smell: earth, air, water, animals, men. . . .

Espinoza had said: :*You should hypnoform into a Solthree, or at least a blackberry bush, make yourself inconspicuous. . . .:*

"Espinoza, as a Solthree I must go on two legs and I get nowhere; in my own shape, if someone sees me—well, the people here believe in demons, and whatever they are, I am not far from what they look like—so they say, 'Oh, God help me, there goes a demon!' and shiver and say their prayers. If they see a blackberry bush running by in the street, they think they are going crazy and start screaming. Forget it!"

She left Khreng hidden in the shadows; opened her mind, her senses; padded easily among the thickets, tail curled around her rump to avoid breaking branches, could feel her shoulder blades, her haunch bones working freely under her skin in the cool air.

She crossed the stream and the dirt road and went up the village street. Houses clustered at either side, and it widened at midpoint into the marketplace; the synagogue was here, and it sheltered bats and mice; if there were demons, she missed them. The pig was here, too, grunting among the burdock, thinking of sleep. In a while it would get more than it wanted; she passed it without a glance. She was not wearing her harness with its civilized implements, only a belt with a pouch and a knife.

Back on Ungruwarkh the thought of coming across the Galaxy had not dismayed her, but she had been disturbed at the prospect of going among so many beings, not of her species, who had so much flesh on them. Down among them she found it was not their flesh that disturbed her but their noisy heads. Being with Espinoza had prepared her for complex

multilayered minds; now she was surrounded by hundreds of
them, dreaming and weeping; their bodies were only unregarded appendages. She thought it might be more pleasant to
make the acquaintance of some of Solthree's big cats, even if
they were a bit backward.

She went round the houses, silent, twitching her tail, not
understanding all she picked up, leaving Espinoza to sort and
collate; plucked out one thread of identity and another and
another, tying knots of relationship in them.

A thin current of odor from dough for the Sabbath bread,
rising on warm stoves, flowed about her; one more strange
smell among thousands for an Ungrukh who knew nothing of
cooking except sometimes to roast those detestable fish.

Fish and edible birds were being stored here too, in cool
places . . . there was a lot of food in the little house of Zevi-
Hirsch's widow Tsippe, whose neighbors had provided for
her: she was asleep, salt crust on her cheeks;

(What is that?) *(tears: weeping/grief)* (for
that mean little man? does he leave her then without provi-
sion?) *(she helps support the family taking in sewing—make-
and-mend-clothing—because the sexton gets more honor than
pay)* she sniffed (what an honor)

The one whose helper started it all,
Shloimeh the blacksmith, sometimes called King Solomon,
Shloimeh-ha-Melech, because he was a bit of a fool: snoring
happily beside his wife (bleeding? blood?) *(she's
menstruating, too bad, so he's—hoo, what a sinner!—dreaming of dancing a kazatzka with)* the servant girl who worked
for

Reb Zalman Dorfman *(the Rich Man, cousin to Zevi-Hirsch
Dorfman the poor man)* who was taking in the Lubliner Rebbeh for the Sabbath; wondering how to impress him, for a rich
man in Kostopol was not much better than a poor man in
Lublin . . . turning his mind away from the death, the funeral,
the weeping widow (fear, discomfort—don't be scared, big
man, she's not planning to beg). Prandra passed him by with a
last wisp of thought: idiot rabbi . . . still, the cantor (prayer-
singer? oh, like the rabbi in the synagogue—not much better
than an Ungrukh) . . . the cantor

Nachman Klein, had a fine voice, doubled as (slitting throat of an animal? blood again?) *(ritual slaughterer)* (don't bother explaining), was dreaming of singing in a fine synagogue in Warsaw (wearing no clothes?) *(typical Solthree dream)* (if you say so) . . . his demon daughter Sheyndl, a tough little girl, wakeful, sucked her braid and planned to drive a goat into shul one Sabbath in the middle of the most tearful and dramatic part of *Ribono shel olom* . . . (poor man) . . . and

Reb' Elya, the innocent, dream rising from him in a perfect sphere of light, wearing a white silk caftan and embroidered yarmulkeh, broke the Sabbath bread at the table of the wise and the holy . . .

(nothing here . . . tomorrow three boys come home for Sabbath from the? yeshiva, and some others . . .)

:All right,: said Espinoza. *:Come back.:*

:About that pig . . . .: She had a sting of conscience. *:Does it belong to someone here?:*

:Jews don't eat it. It does belong to someone, but I guess it could drop dead anytime from disease or old age. Give it a merciful end and hurry back. Don't eat any till it's irradiated.:

She found the pig drinking from the stream, stunned it with a blow of her tail before it could squeal, dragged it through the water into the thicket, dug a pit with her claws, used the knife to slash its throat; the blood sprang into the pit—

:You'd also make a good kosher butcher,: said Espinoza.

—and the entrails followed; she covered them over, stamped down the earth, took a film sack from her pouch and packed the meat in, sealed it . . .

And felt a most peculiar sensation at the back of her neck. The fur rose.

Espinoza asked, *:What's that?:*

:I don't know.: She put down the package and stood still. Nothing but the night and its small noises. Her pulse was steady . . . and a little tingling went along her nerves, a physical sensation raising her hairs of their own will.

:Some kind of radiation? . . . a force-field?:

:I go look.:

:Take care,: said Khreng.

:No!: Espinoza called. *:Come back!:*

She disregarded them, crossed the stream, and stood at the edge of the road. This way Lublin? That way Warsaw? She didn't know which. She chose a direction and walked, meter by meter; early spring night, branches studded with leaf buds against a dull sky; and the moon, finding a space between clouds, silvered the air for a moment, but there was nothing to see in its light.

The small tingling intensified, spread over her body; the air trembled as in a heat wave, then rippled and warped; the skin was writhing over her muscles.

:Don't—: Espinoza was whispering (something); but she was not afraid, did not feel under personal attack or in the presence of an enemy, only intensely interested, able to turn back at any time, and went deliberately toward that strengthening source, out of all contact with Khreng and Espinoza, padding down the silent road at midnight in a deafening silence.

She stopped, not knowing or wondering why, very still in the center of her being, though every hair of her body was on end, the knife burned against her side, her skin writhed and swirled over her body like an oil film on water.

A small whiteness spread behind her eyes, grew till it blinded her, went down every nerve, into every tooth, set her brain on fire. She sprang up on her hind legs, savaged the air with her claws briefly, and fell into blackness.

Khreng was pawing, pushing, growling at her.

"Where is this?" she whispered.

"One kilometer from the village, where do you think?" he grumbled. "You are a great traveler."

She lay panting. Whatever she had run into was gone, but she ached from the crown of her head right down her spine to the tip of her tail.

:Are you all right?: The image of Espinoza, quick swarthy man, touched her on the head, lightly. *:Are you all right?:*

"I am stupid."

"There you are not mistaken." Khreng pulled at her this way and that, heaved her on his back, her head lolled as if her neck were broken, her legs hung. "You are damn heavy." She was as limp as a trophy skin.

He headed back toward the shuttle at a slow trot, the piston-bones of his shoulders moved beneath her jaw. In a great effort she stretched her neck, touched the tip of her tongue to the hairs in his ear. "Don't forget the meat," she whispered, and fainted.

She came to again in her couch in the shuttle. Khreng was rubbing down her sides and back with his pads, lightly oiled. "Now who is playing at great heroics, ha? I come looking and find you with your hair all on end as if you are struck by lightning."

"I am struck by lightning," she said sleepily.

:You sure you feel better?:

"I don't ache so much now. Do I find the Qumedon?" Khreng brought her a cup of warm herb tea, one of the few vegetable products Ungrukh enjoyed, and she lapped at it.

:Not exactly. You ran into his shuttle's energy-field. He was starting up the engines.:

"Why don't I turn back?"

:There was nothing you could do against it. It paralyzes the nervous system, like a GalFed stunner, only this can be deadly.:

"Is he gone then?"

:I don't think so. From what I could see through Khreng, there was no blast-off, and there wasn't a cutoff as if he'd been sucked into his time-warp. It increased gradually and died down the same way. I suppose he was testing.:

"Does he esp me?"

:I don't know. He's not too far away.:

Prandra sniffed. "He's no Kostopolier."

:He may become one yet—and you certainly will. Tomorrow you'll both practice two-legged walking; if you want any chance of leaving this place, you'll have to hypnoform, get out there and find him.:

And suppose they found him, what then? Espinoza was grateful that Khreng and Prandra didn't ask silly questions like that.

Prandra didn't dream often, but perhaps she was stimulated by all the minds she had been esping. She found herself running shoulder to shoulder with Khreng across the red plains, as they had done often enough on Ungruwarkh. Tugrik and

Emerald on their backs, each one a small warm weight with little claws prickling into the skin. And Espinoza, a young brown-skinned man with black hair and white teeth, quick-tempered and sharp-witted, was running lightly between them —how, when they were touching?—seemed to be blended half into each, with a hand resting on each of their necks, laughing. Was it her dream alone, or one she was sharing with Khreng? Or Espinoza?

Friday morning they were up early; Espinoza had not slept. *:Everybody tells me I don't need sleep. Liars.:* His consciousness had been lowered by drugs for the Jump, but at his age they were too dangerous to use regularly. *:Anyway, this is my last trip.:*

"What do you do afterward, then?" Khreng was stalking stiffly about on two legs, preparing to hypnoform into a Solthree. He and Prandra were going to be a pair of travelers stopping over in Kostopol for the Sabbath. For some vague reason, possibly tribal conditioning in conformity, he felt all this business was unnatural and immoral.

:Not more so than coming across the Galaxy in the first place.:

"In the first place, I am better to stay home and die fighting."

"What do you say you do after you go back, Espinoza?" Prandra asked.

:Get put into some library think-tank as part of historical reference. Students come around, ask, "How long did the Thirty Years' War last?" That kind of thing. I'm too old to travel anymore . . . you've got to get that tail curled up or you'll look like a pretty damn funny Solthree.:

"It's a meter and a half long, Espinoza. Do I chop it off?"

:No, but you, Prandra, will have to chop off your whiskers. No use swearing. Solthree women just don't have long red bristles sprouting out of their faces.:

Friday morning everybody gets up early. Chava and Braina and Freyda and Reisel and nearly a hundred other women jump out of bed while their husbands are still groaning and snorting with the misery of waking; wash hands, pull on old dresses, tie aprons, kerchiefs, flick the cloth off the risen dough, punch it down and turn it over to rise again. It smells like life, like a baby's flesh. . . .

Reb' Elya gnaws a crust, gulps tea, grabs shawl and phylacteries, and runs to shul. There is a film of dream around him yet, like a bubble ready to burst.

It never quite bursts, only rises and floats above him like a balloon on a string. Reb' Elya does not live in a bubble; he runs so that the damp from the early rain will not soak his old shoes, mud splashes his tattered caftan; supported by an impoverished congregation, he is a "poor man in seven edges," as they say in the shtetl, and he clasps to his breast the tallith and tefillin in their velvet drawstring bags so they will not be spattered.

:*Stop and eat now,*: Espinoza said. :*But don't gorge or you'll be sleepy.*: He enjoyed watching Reb' Elya, resting along his consciousness.

Espinoza was interested in psychodynamics, not physical or emotional privacies; he was not a voyeur, only an enforced observer of sentient life. He had a great fondness for Khreng and Prandra: they were fierce, quick, direct, integrated; their conjoined mind was a crystal globe without bubble or ripple; Reb' Elya's was faceted, asymmetrical, flawed and striated with pressures. Many parts of it were painful, some silly, some fine qualities blocked and thwarted by circumstance, and all of it fascinating. Sometimes Espinoza wished he had been a class-one ESP, could have had a ready insight into the psychological structures he had to build with so much time and effort. Sometimes, but not often. First-grade ESPs dealt with medical and psychiatric problems in many kinds of life-forms; an ESP who could think like a psychotic decapod from Arcturus IV was as uncomfortable to be around as a Qumedon.

Reb' Elya pulled the string with the synagogue key from round his neck and unlocked the door. He knocked to warn demons, and opened it. A bat flew out. Reb' Elya smiled and called out half-seriously, "Good day, Ashmedai!" But the demon-king did not hear, or did not choose to answer. Elya slipped inside, whispering as always, "Lord, I love Your house, the place where Your glory lives. . . ."

• • •

Khreng and Prandra ate cubed meat out of bowls, licking their jaws and grunting with pleasure.

Espinoza said, :*We have tapes for English, French, Russian, Chinese, Japanese, and Spanish. Unfortunately the languages you need are Polish, Yiddish, and Hebrew. What I don't know I'll pick up and feed you.*:

"Eat now, think later," said Khreng.

:*Think now, because you don't know what the Qumedon will do, or when. Remember: the rabbi doesn't like to speak Polish, the women don't know Hebrew, the scholars don't read or write Yiddish.*:

"You remember," Khreng growled. "I become a deaf-and-dumb Solthree."

Reb' Elya shook out the folds of his tallith and wrapped it round him. Having blessed this act, he sat down to wait for his quorum. Some of his congregation would be saying prayers at Tsippe's for the last day of Shiva and enjoying a bagel and a little schnapps too; a couple of schnorrers, who went where the food was, Shloimeh ha-Melech likewise, Reb Nachman and Reb Zalman who were important . . . He could count on the company of Mordcha Pipick, whose huge belly was caused by a tumor, not by appetite. . . . He had an inspiration: he would use his small authority to appoint Mordcha temporary shammis. . . . "How can we do without a shammis over Pesach and with the Lubliner coming? Who'd complain? Who'd worry he'd hang on too long? Except for that pipick of his the man's thin as a pipe-stem, and, God be merciful, I think he'll soon be—oh."

Oh. The soul drained out of his body leaving Reb' Elya white as his tallith. Words said themselves:

HE'LL SOON BE DEAD HE'LL SOON BE DEAD HE'LL SOON BE DEAD DEAD DEAD DEAD DEAD DEAD DEAD

:*Oh . . . oh . . .*:

Khreng belched and scratched his belly with the tip of his tail, but Prandra cried, "Espinoza! What is it?"

There was a whimpering in Espinoza's mind. :*Dead. Dead. Oh, I don't know. Oh God. Tell me if there's something happening in the village. Quick!*:

Prandra scanned. "Twenty-three people are vomiting; eleven babies have begun to scream; seven men, thirteen women, and eighteen prepubic children have burst into tears; two old men and one woman have pain in the chest and trouble breathing; fifteen assorted people have headaches."

:*And Reb' Elya?*:

"The rabbi . . . faints."

Reb' Elya opened his eyes, pulled himself up to his knees, and began to weep. He gathered the fringes at the four corners of his shawl and kissed them, with trembling hands picked up the phylacteries, which he had pulled down in his fall, and kissed them as well.

"Blessed Lord our God King of the Universe, what have I done? Why have You struck me down? Lord of the Universe, did I sin when I said that Reb Mordcha would die? Perhaps the Evil Urge made me call him to the attention of the Angel of Death? Spare the life of Your servant Mordcha, O Lord our God and forgive me, forgive me!"

Still weeping, still trembling in every limb, he pulled himself to his feet and began to wind tefillin, straining with all of his will not to drop or tangle them, crying out the prayers through chattering teeth:

"On the arm in memory of His outstretched arm, opposite the heart to subject our hearts to His service, opposite the brain to subject all faculties to His service, blessed be He . . . bring me long life and holy thoughts, and free me from the Evil Urge. . . ."

"Solthrees live half again as long as Ungrukh, and they are still afraid of death," said Prandra.

:*I am not afraid of death,*: said Espinoza with asperity. :*I have already died once. Something has constricted the cerebral vessels of everyone around here. Didn't you feel anything?*:

"A bit dull and sleepy. . . ."

:*You have a high metabolic rate, and you've just eaten heavily; that may be why you missed it. Turn up my oxygen a bit.*:

"Can you do anything for them?"

:*Plant a suggestion that they'd feel better with some fresh air. It's passing off already. The men will be praying, and that will get the air in their lungs. That was a very unpleasant feeling.*:

"What causes it?" Khreng asked.

:*Who would you suggest? Who do you know in the district with power to do that?*:

"*We* don't do that," said Khreng, with what for him was a great deal of forbearance. "There is no need to be sarcastic."

:*Sorry. I guess it's the effect.*:

The people of Kostopol did not quite know what had happened to them, or realize it had happened to all of them. It was variously a sudden unease, nausea, depression, fear, headache, shortness of breath . . . a something. And it went away. Not quite. A thing, perhaps as small as a sand grain, perhaps as large as a flake of stone, remained. Lodged beneath the skin, or behind the eye, or back of the throat, or under the breastbone . . .

The quorum who had been saying kaddish for Zevi-Hirsch came out of Tsippe's house in a peculiar frame of mind. They had eaten bagels and hard-boiled eggs, and had drunk schnapps, and the food knotted in their bellies and the liquor burned. . . . They did not speak much, and for them this was as if the world had turned upside down and day become night. They came raggedly across the marketplace, blinking, though there was no sun, scratching their necks, though there were no flies; bearing toward the smithy where Shloimeh would leave them.

On the farther side, Janchik had just turned off the road and was shambling toward his day's work; sleepy-eyed, grinning foolishly, big shoulders swinging and coarse red hands hanging loosely.

They watched him.

That fist of his had gone crack! so, and the little man had fallen, scraggy beard jutting at the sky. . . .

"Big loshek, what he did . . ."

"I don't know what got into him—"

"But you keep him around!"

"Give him meals, yet . . ."

"When he ought to be—"

"Yes, he ought to be . . ."

"—no justice—"

"Why don't we?"

"He's big, but—"

"—ten of us—"

"And—"

"Do something about it for once, instead of—"

"Why not?"

It was strange that they did not look at each other and ask if God would wither their tongues.

:I think they've gone mad,: said Espinoza. *:They're planning to kill him.:*

From the other road approaching the village, a horse-drawn cart and driver were bringing Count Rosnicki, the landowner, to collect the black mare he had left at the smithy to be shod the day before. Riding behind him were a group of cousins from Warsaw who were staying with him over Easter, and he was going to show them his stables and his lands and his budding orchards and everything else that made for good country living. He was in a relaxed good humor, a state he could sometimes maintain for more than ten minutes.

The two parties were converging on that hapless Janchik, and Espinoza's mind hummed like a bee swarm with useless alternatives. *:God help them. . . .:*

"Let us out, Espinoza."

:Half an hour apiece to hypnoform and ten minutes for the lock doors.:

"We go without hypnoforming."

:And make a big red target . . . Lord, I wish I'd never been born.:

Khreng and Prandra looked at the blue globe, and at each other.

Reb' Elya came out of shul, like the minyan, in a very uncomfortable frame of mind. He did not know why it should have seemed so sinful, just at that moment, to think of

Mordcha as a dying man, since he and everyone else knew he
was. . . . Elya pulled at the strings of his fringed undergar-
ment, the minor tallith, as if the knots would undo themselves
and solve his perplexity. He went across the market without
seeing the minyan moving forward with death in its heart, or
the count rounding the corner in a magisterial cloud of dust,
driver beating the whip-stock against his thigh.

Elya looked up and saw only Janchik, and his brow cleared.
Surely the best way to be forgiven was to forgive. Blind to
everything else, he hurried over to the shambling boy and
plucked at his sleeve. "Janchik!" he cried. "Come have a
glass of tea with me!"

Janchik blinked down at him, smiling. "I'd like that,
Rebbeh, but I have to go to work now."

"Take a few minutes. . . ."

The minyan stopped short; Elya noticed them from the corner of his eye and turned his head. He saw two merchants, a
blacksmith, a schoolmaster, a cantor/slaughterer, a cobbler, a
carpenter, and three schnorrers. "Nachman," he called, "I
have an idea, I want to talk to you . . . What's the matter?"

The ten looked at each other and saw much in each others'
eyes. Their faces burned. "Nothing . . . nothing is wrong,"
the cantor said, choking. . . .

The galloping cart pulled up to them in a shower of dust.

:*Very close, very close,*: said Espinoza.

"Gut Shabbas, Rebbeh," the count said. It was a little early
in the day for this greeting, but it was the only Yiddish he
knew.

"Good day, Count," Reb' Elya said civilly. The count was
no aristocrat in bearing, but a stocky, ruddy countryman,
strong and glossy as his horses. His shrewd slit eyes glittered
with ironic and capricious humor; he was not a wicked man,
only nerve-rackingly unpredictable. The previous summer he
had sent a couple of men to knock the cobbler around over the
quality of the leather used in repairing his boots; a few days
later he had sent the same men beating the bushes to find
Elya's Moisheleh, who had gotten lost picking berries.

Elya did not even dislike the count, but he was so far from
Elya's model of what a man ought to be; i.e., pale, with side

curls and beard, black hat and caftan—that he found him
totally alien.

The count said, "Feliks tells me his favorite sow didn't
come home last night, the beautiful Sasha." He laughed. "I
told him you wouldn't know where she is, but she likes to be
around you so much I thought I'd ask."

Sasha? The stupid animal that rooted in Kostopol's vegetable plots? Tsk. Elya kept the glint out of his eye and said
quietly, "No, Count, I haven't seen her." He added, "The
children tease the pigs but they never harm them."

The count laughed again and jumped down to collect his
horse. Reb' Elya looked round for Nachman, but the minyan
had scattered. He sighed and turned homeward. Maybe it
hadn't been such a good idea? He stopped in midstride and
clapped his hands: of course! that's why I was so upset. I was
turning Mordcha's illness to my own advantage, choosing a
dying man so no one would complain. . . . Yes, I see it quite
clearly—but God forgive me! we still need a shammis. . . .

:Now you know what you ate,: said Espinoza. *:The beautiful Sasha.:*

Khreng licked his jaws with his long rasp tongue. "I agree
about her beauty."

"It's a pity Rosnicki is not the Qumedon," Prandra said,
"nor his people."

*:He's not far away now. . . . I've heard of a quorum of ten
exorcising a dybbuk but never of any that was possessed by
one.:*

The fish are cut and simmering, spiced, in their pots; the
women have dismembered and soaked and salted the chickens
and put them on to boil; they punch down the dough, slap it
on floured boards, divide and divide it, roll it in strips, braid
and set it to rise for the last time.

The boys come home from yeshiva for the Sabbath and the
Passover week, bringing friends whose homes are far away;
they carry packs filled with threadbare clothes and books with
raveled leaves; they march, unregimented, side-curls bouncing, singing songs to ancient Biblical verses; they are seized
upon, their cheeks are pinched, to cries of "What are they

feeding you, you got so thin?'' None of their translucent spirits harbors a Qumedon.

Khreng and Prandra buckled on their harnesses, tucked away dozens of implements, clipped remote switches for the hypnoformer on their forearms, put on tinted contact lenses to counteract the harsher rays of Sol.

:*Your names are Jacob (my Hebrew name) and Sara, let's see, Katz—why not?—on your way from . . . Krasniewic—I just made it up—to Warsaw, because, oh, because your mother's dying, your brother's been kidnaped into the army, and you have to buy him off, and—and your father's in jail for not paying taxes.*:

"What a life," said Khreng. "How do I earn my keep?"

:*Buy a little, sell a little, mend a little. The usual.*:

"You must admit I have a very strange accent."

:*That's the way they talk in Krasniewic,*: said Espinoza. :*The first person you see, you'll ask where you can stay over the Sabbath. Somebody will find you a place.*:

The Sabbath loaves, risen at last into the shapes of cumulus clouds, are glazed with egg and put into the ovens. . . .

Hypnoforming an object is one thing. Hypnoforming a person into the shape of an alien being is something else: if he doesn't feel like an alien, he will never convince anyone else that he is. It's a good device for explorers as long as the two life-forms involved are roughly the same size and shape: a four-meter Arcturan serpent will never persuade anyone that he's a ten-centimeter Crystalloid from Vega, particularly since the two forms have never been able to communicate and you need to be assisted by an ESP of the race you're turning into in order to know what it feels like to be one.

For Ungrukh the process was relatively simple, but it was intimidating enough for Khreng to attach the electrodes to his skull and to Espinoza's connections.

He pulled the switch, closed his eyes . . . and over an endless half hour Espinoza gave him a life. Even if he never hypnoformed again, his mind would always be threaded with wisps of alien memory. . . .

Strange shape, strange land, cruel time, a boy three years old dragged screaming into manhood and whipped in school over the shape of every black-flame letter, trailing at dusk in a shivering crocodile of children scared of demons, that thin child who crouched beside you snottering all day dead of typhoid, *mazel tov*, Bar Mitzvah, thirteen years and you're old enough to pray in a quorum with your cracking voice, your old man's wizened face, *mazel tov*, meet your bride, *l'chaim!* you're a father—sorry, it only lived an hour, anyway the Cossacks are coming. . . .

:Not bad,: said Espinoza. *:No beautiful Jew, you're more a blacksmith than a scholar, but you'll do.:*

Khreng opened his eyes, upright, looked down and saw the long black caftan, through Prandra's eyes saw his face. Red hair and beard, fair enough; he looked in fact a lot like Shloi-meh. Espinoza had picked the blacksmith as a good model for body type, big chest and shoulder muscles to mask the power-ful torso and forefeet, heavy thighs to accommodate the tail. *:Keep your movements slow and close; any gross distortion and the field will crumble and break:*

"I am choking, I think," said Khreng, pulling at his illusory neckband.

:It gets better later on. Now you, Prandra. You'll be a big girl, no beauty, either, but we don't need the men chasing you.:

"Hah!" said Khreng. Prandra hissed, her equivalent of a giggle.

Who should be first to meet the strangers but Reb' Elya? He was everywhere, comforting the sick, pestering the healthy, blessing the newborn, collecting from the poor for the poorest. "Come home, stay with me," he said. "I have only the one room, but there's a little shed in back, where I keep the pickles—they only smell in summer—and I'll put in a stove, with blankets and a featherbed . . ." He paused, looked at them, felt (they could tell) a little shiver, and added, to cover, "Come, come, you'll have a glass tea? Then I have to meet the Lubliner, a big man, guests are coming, a busy time . . ."

:He knows something,: Prandra told Espinoza. *:I can't tell what.:*

:Intuition . . . he's not an ESP; some kind of sensitive . . .:

Chava, the Rebbetsin, was resigned to unexpected guests; they meant light eating on the following night. But lemon tea was a cheap drink and not a bad one. The Katzes refused cookies (more dog food).

"Where did you say you're from?" Reb' Elya asked.

"Krasniewic," said Khreng/Katz. He was relieved to be sitting down. Walking upright was hell; he thought his spine would crack and his tendons rip. Prandra was even worse off because she felt some of his pain as well as her own. How would they find the Qumedon if they were half-crippled?

:No other way,: said Espinoza.

"Krasniewic?" Elya clasped his glass in both hands and blinked at them over the rim. "I never heard of it."

"Oh, you know," said Chava. "That place where they all talk like Litvaks."

The loaves come out of the oven, burnished, hollow when they're knocked on the bottom. The smell is superb.

"The Lubliner Rebbeh," said Elya, "same first name as you, Yaakov Yitzhak, he's called the Seer. . . . They say he can look at a man's forehead and see into his soul. . . ." His own look seemed to wonder what that seer might find within them. He was still conscious of that something, that grain of sand or seed of doubt which had been planted in him during the agonizing moment in the synagogue.

The youngest of the little boys, not much more than a baby, crawled about them on the floor. Prandra gave him a piece of cookie and stroked his head. It might be possible to love such a creature.

Elya picked up the child quickly and put him on the bed in the corner. Then he blushed. He was a hospitable man; he did not know why he felt uneasy.

Prandra, cramped spine and all, smiled to herself because she had not thought of the child as a morsel.

Reb' Elya got up and Khreng followed; the women were not expected to meet the Lubliner. "I can make up the bed in the storeroom," Prandra said. Elya tapped the table with his fingertips, hesitating, and to calm his uneasiness she took her feelings about Tugrik and Emerald (separated by such distance and danger) and placed them as well as she could among the complicated folds of his emotions. "That's right," he whispered, nodding. "That's good."

The children played and quarreled loudly. Chava grabbed and scrubbed them for the Sabbath, rattled pots, tasted, jabbed the chicken with a fork, all the while yelling personal questions at the top of her voice and giving her life away in return:

"—terrible time with the little one, they thought I'd never—"

Prandra swept the hard earth floor, shifted the pickle crock, laid down mattresses and featherbeds, her mind with Khreng crossing the marketplace toward the road from Lublin.

"—certainly are strong, I've never been able to lift that thing, Gitte-Frima next door got a hernia—"

Scholars and schoolboys in Sabbath clothes, the rich, the poor, the important, the insignificant, all paraded to meet the rabbi of Lublin. Everyone with a question, an ache, an Evil Urge, a little money to help loosen the holy tongue. A few were women, two barren ones who wanted to conceive, and one pregnant with the twelfth who wanted to stop; the rest of them stayed home putting their houses in order and shaking their heads over the foolishness of men.

"—married to a rabbi God bless him you're better off not every schlemiel in the street he thinks can give him a holy word I tell him if he got one word just one word from every schlepper he ran after he'd be wiser than Solomon if I didn't bring him the samovar when he got married he likes his tea so much I wouldn't see him Monday to Friday—"

:Just like my aunt Lena . . .: said Espinoza.

Even the count was there, with his cousins, to see what was so fine about the Seer of Lublin.

Prandra was scanning them all, using the quick network of relationship she had drawn up the night before. For Kostopol they were a crowd, actually only a few dozen; every one of them, count and all, held that odd hard thing only Reb' Elya was conscious of; for the others it was masked by anticipation of the Sabbath, the holidays, the honored guest—or perhaps it had simply settled down among the usual griefs and terrors of their lives. . . .

"He's coming! There he is, the Rebbeh! There!"

Down the road, in a dust cloud, the rabbi came. Riding a horse, dapple-grey, a sleek trim animal, its hooves touched the earth as lightly as if it were dancing. It was like a piece of the sunless sky; behind it, six disciples marched, brisk of step and singing a song of the Joyous Festival:

> *"He has divided the sea*
> *for His children,* bim bam!
> *but their enemies drown*
> *in its waters . . ."*

As it came closer the procession slowed—

And Khreng's skin prickled, not from what he saw but from what Prandra was seeing through his eyes.

The pale horse picked its way through the dust cloud; the oiled reins rippled lightly on its neck, almost like snakes, wound themselves around a thin white hand. . . .

Reb' Elya yearned, his eyes filled. He had no wisdom, no learned tongue to speak with the holy and the pious. He would have been content with one deep look into the eyes of the Lubliner. But his own eyes were blurred with tears; he could see the billowing silk caftan, the shining black Cossack boots, the fur hat, the white hair and beard, could hear the pattering steps of the followers singing their songs of holiday and Sabbath—but the eyes were withheld from him: tears came between.

Prandra and Espinoza saw very clearly from their distance; they fixed their minds on the cloudy rider and the cluster of figures on foot behind him; they saw that there was no heart in that body, no human heart, no brains or bowels, none penetrable to an ESP. It was dense as stone, cold as ice, cruel as death.

:*There he is,*: said Espinoza. :*Now what do we do with him?*:

:*He knows we are here?*: Prandra asked.

:I'm sure he does. Why should it bother him? He realizes we're helpless.:

Prandra gave more attention to the horse: it was not a real animal, but a simulacrum created of dust and wind.

:And those who march and sing . . . they're not persons, only things made of dry leaves, branches and mud.:

:Yes. Golems,: said Espinoza.

The people of Kostopol raised their voices and sang with the shadows: *He has divided the sea for His children. . . .*

On a quick malevolent impulse, Elya's first son, Yehoshua, a boy gentle as his father, picked up a stone and threw it at the horseman. No one saw: it vanished before it struck and rebounded in three fragments. One struck Rosnicki in the neck; he clasped his hand to the spot and swore. Prandra, on the alert, picked up a message from Espinoza before he had time to implement it and covered the count's reaction swiftly: a Jew picked up/a stone/kicked up by the horse. The count only blinked and shook his head. Another fragment fell at the feet of Reb' Elya, who was standing with bowed head; in a dream he stooped to pick it up: it burned and he dropped it and stared at the small red spots on his fingers. The third struck Khreng in the forehead; he bit his tongue to repress a snarl. The Qumedon had acknowledged the presence of unbelievers.

:When do we talk to this person, Espinoza?:

:Not while he's throwing stones. I don't know if he'll ever give us a chance.:

:Is this the only one?:

:I think so . . . his operation is modest, so far. I hope so.:

Reb' Elya managed to confer the title of shammis on Mordcha Pipick, and at dusk he proudly summoned men to the bathhouse; it was never too late to become significant, and he was probably the most cheerful man in Kostopol; perhaps the others were overwhelmed by the presence of the Lubliner; the morning minyan who had prayed at Tsippe's had sweepings of guilt in the corners of their spirits; they could never know whether they would actually have killed Janchik.

Khreng sat in shul with the men of Kostopol and the Qumedon/Rabbi, cursing his aching back; he prayed to the

God of Solthrees with his voice and to Firemaster with his heart: *Unburden me of this Shape and this World, make me a man among men on Ungruwarkh and I never lift a foot off the planet again!* Perhaps the Qumedon had put flint in his heart as well.

Come in peace, crown of God, come with joy. . . .

Elya turned the pages of his siddur with trembling fingers while Reb Nachman chanted, and tried and tried to see the face of the Lubliner; always at that point on his visual field a flickering came before his eyes like the disturbances of certain headaches. *We hope, Lord our God, soon to see Thy majestic glory, when the abominations shall be removed from the earth. . . .* What have I done, that I am blinded? Whom have I sinned against, O Lord? And what is the use of searching my soul? I have not done enough in the world, good or bad, to make it worth while for God to notice me.

He turned his eyes back to the letters of his prayers; these at least he could see clearly. *Angels of peace, may your coming be in peace; bless me with peace, and bless my table. . . .*

Prandra had withdrawn quietly into a corner while Chava changed clothes and blessed her Sabbath candles. She was satisfied that the Qumedon had been found and what was postulated had been proven, shaken because a Qumedon was an unsettling creature. What did it want with these people?

:To inflame them into bloodshed.: Espinoza had been quiet for a while, and she was glad to have word from him; it was becoming very lonely in Kostopol.

:That's silly. There's so much conflict in the universe he has only to sit and wait.:

:He wants to cause it, not sit and wait for it.:

Khreng, who had been receiving in silence, asked, *:Is that why Qumedni set up the time-vortices?:*

:I think most often they use them to observe alien peoples the way GalFed Central does in controlled experiments. I don't believe they generally make mischief. I said before, this one is criminal or insane.:

:It is very hard to ask a mad Qumedon to help us get back to our ship,: Prandra said. *:One thing strikes me as very odd. Is*

he responsible for the death of Zevi-Hirsch?.:

   :Likely. You wonder why he waited thirty-six hours after that to make another move? I can't tell you. Our Qumedon is a riddle.:

   :Does he have any weaknesses?.:

   :None that I know. . . .:

   "Good Shabbas!" cried Chava, and Reb' Elya came into the house with his sons and Khreng.

Reb' Elya did not eat with Reb Zalman and the Lubliner. He would have been welcomed, only a bit grudgingly, but he was frightened to be in the presence of those strange disciples and this saint whom he could not see clearly and whose words did not seem to have any meaning. No one else appeared to be bothered by the man; he wondered if he were suffering the onset of some terrible disease of the brain—madness, degeneration . . . even his guests made him fearful, and he did not know why. His mind unfolded a panoply of horrifying images: soul struggling in the meshes of slow decay while his wife and children watched in helpless anguish, were left to charity when he died. . . .

   :Stop this, Espinoza! I can't bear it.:

   :The Qumedon's doing it. It won't stop till we get out of here with him.:

Reb' Elya smiled with all his strength and broke the Sabbath bread.

Khreng closed the door of the storeroom as firmly as it would fasten. It was dark and they had no lamp because of the Sabbath; he had a tiny penlight tucked somewhere in his harness but it was too risky to use it. "Do we wait till they're asleep?"

   "No use. I doubt the Rabbi can sleep."

Both fumbled at their wrists for the remotes and pressed them, dropping to all fours with a shudder of relief. Khreng snorted and muttered, "Trying to eat with a spoon is as bad as walking on two legs." It was chancy, dropping the hypnoform field, but they could resume it at any time using the remote switches until the machine in the shuttle had been cleared and reset, and Espinoza would warn them of danger. As uncomfortable Solthrees, they would get no sleep and be drained of their febrile energy.

They removed the contact lenses, which dimmed their night vision, and stared at each other. "I like you much better as Khreng," Prandra said.

"As a Solthree you find me tasty, I suppose."

She flicked his nose with the tip of her tongue. "Not bad."

:Take a scan with me,: said Espinoza. *:If nothing's doing, you can sleep.:*

Exhausted as she was, Prandra forced herself to scan the village and as far beyond as she could reach. The old dozed, the sick turned restlessly, the young made love in celebration of the Sabbath, babies snorted and snuffed like little animals, a child or two cried out in nightmare. . . .

:Stay with me,: she said, *:I don't understand all this about Rosnicki.:*

In the big country house the count and his cousins were finishing their meal with brandy in the company of Father Chryzostom, who was there to discuss the matter of repairs to the church roof.

Rosnicki was shaking his head. "Money doesn't grow on trees."

One of the cousins grinned. "It grows on Jews."

Rosnicki, who knew that Reb Zalman the Rich Man was no more affluent than any rag merchant in the Warsaw Ghetto, nodded. He didn't want to be shown up as a country cousin. "We don't do badly here."

"The way they go around in rags . . . you'd never know what they have buried underground in old pots and kettles."

"Those scrolls of theirs with silver crowns . . ."

". . . always money to lend . . ."

". . . give them a good shake . . ."

Among those laughing men with their heavily blued jaws and glittering eyes, Rosnicki began to feel that the conversation was running out of control. "They're my Jews—"

"No reason why you shouldn't get the most out of them, Oscar."

"I've done very well," he said with dangerous mildness. "I don't believe there's much left in them."

"Nonsense! If you were to get them together, for instance, when they are in synagogue tomorrow, and—"

Rosnicki got very red in the face with rage and brandy. "I don't—" *care to deal with my people that way,* he had been going to say, and hang city sophistication—and a small spot on his neck stung and burned where it had been struck by a stone a few hours before. "I don't think that's a bad idea at all," he said.

:Espinoza, do we warn them?:
:How? Tell Reb' Elya you had a dream? He'll think you're crazy, or else he is, and he's near enough that now. Wait till tomorrow.:
Tomorrow.
And in one teardrop of his eye
the Rabbi sails across the sky. . . .
Rabbi Qumedon, we must find how to sail you off this planet.

At the inn, a ghostly horse was tethered, and mock-men of clay and twigs lay upon benches. In Reb Zalman's best bedroom the Qumedon, a pulsing vortex of energy, spun like a star. Prandra pulled away from that quickly, and with the recoil fell asleep.

Reb' Elya did not sleep. How could he? He stared at the Sabbath candles until they guttered out in a fume of hot wax, and then at the lamp, which still had oil to use up and would be left until it went out by itself. The light meant nothing to him; his spirit was in darkness. The wife and children he loved were breathing softly around him, vulnerable and ephemeral. The people of the village, whom he had known all his life, had something wrong with them, that showed in a dulling of their eyes. . . .

No, it is I who have something wrong, my eyes . . .

Was it that which had turned the Lubliner away from his sight? Had the holy man seen something in his eyes that repelled him, and so avoided them? Even the count, with whom he had gotten along tolerably well for so many years, seemed to suggest some vicious threat with every look and gesture, as he thought back on them.

It is I! He screamed inside, O Lord our God, King of the Universe, how can I pray to You?

He pulled himself out of bed in a sudden movement of terror and despair, afraid to look at Chava and the children in case he might see something ugly and filthy in them. He grabbed his head, pulled at his hair, in a twist of anguish found himself facing the door to the storeroom.

That ordinary, coarse-looking pair, from that Krasniewic he had never heard of—who were they, and what, that they should have made him so uncomfortable the first time he had set eyes on them? In their eyes he had seen clearly enough a still, watching strangeness. No mistake, they had not blinded him. And yet their outlines, their very shapes, had never quite set or solidified. They had a shimmer to them that was—

Full of horror, unable to stop, he found himself picking up the lamp, which was never moved on the Sabbath, and walking toward the door.

Espinoza, who also needed some rest, had been drifting on the whispering memory of an old melody. Centuries of practiced instinct alerted him.

:Oh my God! Khreng, Prandra, wake up! WAKE UP!:

Prandra, chin resting on Khreng's shoulder, sniffed and went on dreaming. Padding down a vast hall till she came to the niche where Espinoza waited in his blue globe. "Hullo, Espinoza, you don't look a day older."

:Wake up, you damn fool, change back!:

"Ha, Espinoza, you always are a joker!"

In desperation Espinoza plunged into Elya's mind, but there was nothing for him to grasp at in its foaming turmoil.

Elya did not even have the choice of screaming or weeping now. His hand was rigid around the base of the lamp, his body propelled him against his will. The thought that the couple might be making love jetted into his mind, and a shameful desire to see them made him burn cold with sweat. He did not know how skillful the Qumedni were at turning a person's feelings against himself.

• • •

Espinoza knew very well, but he had no mouth to shout with, no eyes to close in despair. Khreng and Prandra were impervious.

Elya opened the door, his body vibrating like a tuning fork with internal tremors, lifted his lamp and saw the demons. Their deep-red bodies, heavy muzzles, slit eyes, and fearful claws. His trembling intensified, but he could neither move nor wake, and there was nothing for him to wake to.

One, which had been resting against the other, stirred and lifted its head. Elya's teeth unclenched at last. "Shaddai!" he cried in a strangled whisper.

"Mazzikim!"

Prandra opened her flame-colored eyes and stared at him.

:Oh God, Prandra, why in hell didn't you wake when I called!:

Prandra yawned and Elya's body jerked in terror. Khreng growled softly, his nose twitched.

Elya, in the light of the trembling flame, hair awry and nightgown bunched in his other hand, was whispering, *"For He shall give His angels charge over thee, to keep thee in all thy ways, they shall bear thee up in their hands, lest thou dash thy foot against a stone, thou shalt tread upon the lion and the adder, the young lion and the adder shalt thou trample under foot . . ."*

:He really does believe we are demons,: Prandra said in some wonder.

:Don't try to change his mind or you'll drive him right over the edge.:

Reb' Elya, in spite of everything, managed to conquer himself enough to close the door and touch the talisman on the doorpost.

"Spare Chava and the children," he whispered. "Please . . ." Under his fear there was a terrible gulf of sadness that his hospitality had been betrayed and all of his love of God had come to nothing. "You are the ones who were called Jacob and Sarah, aren't you?"

"Yes, but—"

"Then take me if I have sinned, God help me, but don't—"

"Rabbi, Reb' Elya, we do not come for you. Not for you!"

"I think you have already taken the Lubliner and left some strange empty thing in his place. . . ."

Prandra sighed. "No, Rabbi, it's not so simple. . . ." She got up on her hind legs, so that her head was level with his. "How are we to talk to you?"

Elya shrank back against the door. Her solidity, the sleekness of her belly, and the faint rank smell about her suggested that she had borne and suckled demon whelps. "You are playing with me," he said sadly. "Demons are liars. . . . I knew there was no such place as Krasniewic."

Prandra watched him a moment while he stood immobile, eyes far away, drifting toward some depthless precipice.

:Prandra,: said Espinoza, *:if you don't catch him—:*

Prandra shrugged away Espinoza's mind, dropped to her forelegs, tilted her head so that the lantern could reflect its light in her eyes but avoid the eyeshine that would terrify him further. "Look at me, Rabbi. You are blind, I make you see."

He did not want to, he tried to keep his eyes turned away, but there was nothing else to see in that room. And her eyes were not hidden from him, nor were they anything but eyes. Light reflected from the inner surfaces of the corneas onto the irises so that they were glowing translucent rims centered with black vortices; still they were calm sensitive animals'—no, person's—eyes within any accepted range of creation.

"I don't mean to harm you or even touch you, only tell you what is happening, why you are so sick and unhappy. Your arm is stiff and aching, Rabbi, put down the lamp and let the oil burn out. . . ." She took a small penlight from her harness—he noticed for the first time what a complicated piece of equipment she was wearing—turned it on and hung it from a nail; the other red shape behind her watched and blinked: ". . . You're free to speak and move. . . . If you are too frightened, if you feel sick, you can go to bed and forget everything . . . do you want to do that?"

"No!" Elya cried, astonished at himself. "I want to know!"

Prandra showed her teeth, not too many, and gave Reb' Elya the short course.

She was quick. Almost instantaneously she drew from Espinoza everything she could understand of all he had learned of the psyche for three hundred years, collated it with her own experience, and turned the walls of Reb' Elya's mind to clear glass.

It was a violent act. Elya bent over, clutched his stomach and retched, but Prandra didn't hesitate. When he straightened, gasping, before he could think or speak, she gave him pictures: . . . two demon shapes burning red in the evening light, going to and fro over the earth, lost on a journey from the unimaginable to the inconceivable/sucked into the trap laid by a sickly pale batwing creature, Ashmedai, King of Demons, who crouches over Kostopol and its people, and with a touch here, a twist there, turns them sick and drives them to rage/Janchik kills Zevi-Hirsch—Elya feels devoured by sin and faints in the synagogue—stammers his agony, his trembling hands wind tefillin/and the minyan plans to kill—

"Oh, no!" Reb' Elya cried. "Never! They'd never dream of doing such a thing! You're ly—"

(. . . picks up the Sabbath lamp and opens the door to the storeroom to see if the man and woman are making—)

"Stop!" Elya's face was flaming.

Prandra grinned with all her teeth. "That is the way you usually behave?"

"No, no, but—"

"It is the demon Ashmedai that does this," she said, "That's what I'm trying to tell you. . . ."

. . . as the minyan direct their rage at Janchik, Rosnicki is approaching . . .

"It is you who saves Janchik from being killed . . . and your friends . . ."

Janchik, come have a glass of tea with me!

"I didn't know—"

"Perhaps not, but you do what is necessary."

. . . when the minds of all Kostopol hold suspicion and unease like fragments of flint waiting to be sparked/the rabbi comes on his horse of dust and wind, with his disciples of twigs and clay . . .

"I knew when I couldn't see his eyes . . ." Tears streamed from his own. "Will he hurt Reb Zalman?"

"Not now."

"Is there no true Lubliner?"

"He exists, but I don't know what is become of him."

. . . last flicker of imagery, a fragment of stone burns Elya's fingers/stings the neck of Rosnicki, who agrees to a plan . . .

"It always comes to such a plan," Elya whispered.

"Now we ask: we want to warn your people but we don't know how."

"Do you really know what will happen tomorrow?"

"No, but this devil wants to drive men to fight and kill."

"Then what can I tell you?" Elya shrugged. He was leaning against the door, calm enough but feeling slightly nauseated, his heart bumping. "Men like Rosnicki make these plans . . . Sometimes they wake up in the morning with headaches from drinking too much brandy and give them up. . . . If they decide to carry them out, we go and talk to them and sometimes manage to scrape up enough money to satisfy them. Sometimes even then they kill us."

"And you don't fight," Prandra muttered. Before he could answer, she went on, "We do what we can and make no plans. Still . . ." she kept looking at him and he turned deeply shy. "You are a good sensible man, not cowardly. Remember you are doing nothing wrong and are not thinking evil thoughts of your own will. You have nothing to be guilty about. Shall I make you forget what I tell you?"

"No, I want to remember." He had plenty to worry about, for himself and his people, but he was free of the sick fears of madness. These demons, and their adversary Ashmedai, were very far from the local ones of his belief, which had no Satanic majesty, no smoky splendor, but were shadowy stunted things that lurked and whispered, like fear and rage, in dark places. He wondered if he had fallen into some sin by listening and believing, but—dear God, Little Father, I am free to pray. . . .

He said hesitantly, "You don't seem much like demons to me."

Prandra opened her mouth and closed it again. Khreng rose and stood beside her. "It is not necessary for demons to be what men expect," he said.

"I believe you," said Elya. "Good night."

●   ●   ●

"I almost tell him everything," Prandra said. "I want to."

:Just as well you didn't. That's a nice piece of hypnodrama you put on. I didn't know you could handle that kind of therapy.:

"Is that what it's called?" she asked indifferently. She was sulky with overexertion, crouched down and rubbed her chin on her forefeet. "It's risky, only for emergencies. . . . I do that for my sister when she thinks it is her fault her baby dies."

:Be careful or you'll end up a class-one ESP.:

"Can we arrange to give the count a headache?" Khreng asked.

:That won't stop the Qumedon.:

What stops the Qumedon? Prandra pulled a shield around her mind, not to hide from Khreng or Espinoza, but to give herself a few quiet minutes to think.

. . . Not everything he does is successful. . . . What weaknesses do powerful creatures have? On Ungruwarkh no one is stronger than Khreng and I, though there are many equal . . . the great power over us is starvation, and a Qumedon . . . needs energy most likely . . . and . . . Reb' Elya stops the Qumedon once—by being foolhardy and generous!

She snorted.

. . . But there are things we learn here that are useful, I'm sure . . . only Espinoza is too old and tired and Khreng and I are too inexperienced to use them. . . .

Khreng said suddenly, "The Rabbi does fight, you know. Otherwise the Qumedon does not give him so much attention."

She laughed. "Are you sure you're not an ESP?"

"If I am no one puts me in any bottle."

It was not quite morning on Earth, in Kostopol. Khreng stood by the open door of the shed, watching the fading stars; no one he knew lived around them in this quarter of the sky.

:I wish I could be out there with you,: said Espinoza (a young man in his strength . . .).

"The sky is clear, it means bright sun," Khreng said. "I hate these scratchy lenses on my eyes."

"So do I. . . . The sky is strange here with these clouds that move and change."

:*Move and change yourselves, friends, or Chava and the children will take fits.*:

Prandra laughed. "Maybe the children like the big pussy cats."

:*I'm glad you can be so cheerful when we have no plans and don't know what to do.*:

Khreng said, "On Ungruwarkh we act quickly and don't make secret plans because everybody knows what they are as soon as you think of them." Prandra laughed again and he grunted. "This makes the men faithful—and the women silent. I think I die here soon if we can't get back."

Prandra asked, "Khreng, when you are a child, what do you do when you meet a bully or a bigger challenger?"

"I give him a good thump on the snout before either of us has time to think, and even if he beats me up, he thinks twice before he bothers me again."

"Ha, today nobody gets a chance to think twice."

Though it had slept beneath a clear sky, Kostopol woke a little tense and irritable as if there had been wind and thunder during the night. Babies disdained the breast and cried, children woke red-eyed and whined to sleep longer, banked fires ebbed, letting the Sabbath hotpots cool, and Janchik and a couple of other Polish boys dashed about, summoned by frantic wives, to shake and relight them.

Chava wrung her hands, but Elya for once did not complain about the coldness of the tea. He barely saw around him, hardly noticed the guests at his table, and Chava, noting the strange expression on his face, did not question him.

He prepared for shul: put on a fur-rimmed shtreimel over his yarmulkeh, shook out his tallith from its bag and swept it over his shoulders. As he left the house with the three older boys, Chava following with the baby, he spread his arms as if to draw the children under his shawl, and as suddenly dropped them.

"Moisheleh, you look as if you have a cold, maybe you should stay home."

"No, Tateh, I'm all right."

The dread he did not feel for himself had driven its claws through them to pierce him. He had no desire to run, he had no world beyond Kostopol, and he did not know how to tell

others to run, or where. The curious effect of meeting the
demons, or whatever creatures of the night they were, had
been to lessen his belief in them, and though he now only half
believed, he thought, hoped, prayed that God, creator of
angels and demons, would give him a sign.

The great Rabbi of Lublin came to shul with his disciples,
their faces pale as porcelain-clay, their shadows crisp and
dancing on the rutted ground.

Reb' Elya pulled the shawl over his head and plunged his
spirit into prayer. A few shafts of light pierced the dim
synagogue windows and dust motes whirled in them briefly
and drifted into shadow. *Master of all worlds! What are we?
What is our life? What is our goodness? What our righteous-
ness? What our helpfulness? What our strength?* The white-
covered heads, striped blue or black, nodded and whispered
on the drifts of the words, raised voice and sang, the sound
was swallowed in a dead air. In his house among the orchards,
the count and his cousins were perhaps holding their heads
and groaning, swearing to leave off brandy and vodka, turning in their sweated linen sheets to sleep again. Perhaps not.
*My offering, consumed by fire, a sweet savor to Me, you shall
be careful to offer to Me at its proper time.* Jews shut into a
synagogue set afire, burning and screaming, a sweet savor . . .
the demon rabbi Ashmedai, standing on the beemah only a
few feet away, turned the pages of a siddur quietly, raising his
voice occasionally, keeping his eyes down. Elya wondered that
the words of the prayers did not leap off the pages and burn in
outrage, and then: What have I to say? I am here silent in
his presence, I have taken the words of the *mazzikim*—the
word of the demons themselves!—that they will try to save us.
How can I live under such conditions? *To Thee, O Lord, I
called, I appealed to my God: What profit would my blood be,
if I went down to the grave? Will the dust praise thee? Will it
declare Thy faithfulness?*

Prandra, far back in the women's section, was far away.
:*They are getting up . . . preparing to saddle the horses . . .
they seem terribly cheerful. . . .*:

:*I hope you know what we're doing,*: Khreng said.

:*The Rabbi himself tells us when to move,*: Prandra said
calmly.

:You have more faith in him than he has in us.:
:There is no other choice.:

Men rose to pray, swaying with fervor, and sat down again, rose and sat down again, raised their voices in curiously muffled song, picked up again the threads of the prayers. *Thou, O God, openest daily the gates of the east, and cleavest the windows of the sky; Thou bringest forth the sun from its place, and the moon from its dwelling, and givest light to the world.* . . . The dust motes swam and trembled; children whimpered and women hushed them, but did not let them out to play in the aisles as usual, or go out to the anteroom to gossip; nor did the men leave to conduct their weekly debates on Talmudic exegesis; they glanced at each other furtively, and did not ask whether they were leaving and why not.

But Prandra rose quietly and went down the staircase to the lobby. To move at all was like pushing through shoulder-high sand, the air had become so thick and clotted; she expected obstruction. In Reb' Elya's terrified mind she had glimpsed a shadow of what was to come.

Reb Zalman opened the curtains of the Ark and its carved doors, took out the Torah Scroll, and brought it to the lectern: its silver crown glittered, the bells on the crown's rim tinkled, the readers gathered round, it was unrolled. . . . Prandra, breathing hard, reached the lobby and waited at the door to the sanctuary.

The outside door was ajar; a cat wandered in, a common short-haired animal, brindled. She looked at it: it gave her a quiet yellow stare for three seconds and leaped for her eyes. She picked it from the air and threw it out the door quite gently, for her. "Qumedon likes to play," she said, and smiled grimly.

The Rabbi of Lublin came forward to read the first part of the week's portion.

Reb' Elya knew that his words did not have their proper shapes, that the sounds did not reverberate from the beams and timbers, and yet they reached some depth of the brain where images grew. . . .

AND THE LORD SPOKE UNTO MOSES SAYING:

COMMAND AARON AND HIS SONS, SAYING:
THIS IS THE LAW OF THE BURNT-OFFERING . . .

in the breast of every man and woman a small spark was
struck from the stone fragment which had been lodged there,
leaped to the dried-out tinder stored during thousands of years
of insult and repression

THE FIRE OF THE ALTAR SHALL BE KEPT BURNING

a little flame kissed the altar of every heart, for Zevi-Hirsch
was dead, the signatory of a thousand, a hundred thousand,
hundreds of thousands beyond

THE FIRE UPON THE ALTAR SHALL BE KEPT BURN-
ING THE FIRE SHALL BE KEPT BURNING UPON THE
ALTAR CONTINUALLY

Reb' Elya began to tremble

MY OFFERINGS MADE BY FIRE fires leaped and licked
among the spirits of the Kostopoliers, and the pale disciples,
smiling, nodded and swayed

FROM THE OFFERINGS OF THE LORD MADE BY FIRE,
WHATSOEVER TOUCHETH THEM SHALL BE HOLY

the demon rabbi swept into the second part of the week's
portion, Reb Zalman's privilege, and the men of Kostopol did
not move or blink, but sat like stone ovens harboring fire

A SWEET SAVOR UNTO THE LORD

they were given a vision: Count Rosnicki lusting for the
silver of the Torah crowns, their gold-threaded coverings

WHERE THE BURNT-OFFERING IS KILLED
SHALL THE SIN-OFFERING BE KILLED

saddling horses, gathering peasants with scythes

• • •

WHEN THERE IS SPRINKLED OF THE BLOOD THERE-
OF

Elya's heart fought like a bird in its rib cage

WHERE THEY KILL THE BURNT-OFFERING
SHALL THEY KILL THE SIN-OFFERING

the readers on the beemah took one step back from the
Scroll

THE BLOOD THEREOF SHALL BE DASHED AGAINST
THE ALTAR

as if it had been spattered with blood, as if it were being
consumed by fire

AN OFFERING MADE BY FIRE UNTO THE LORD

the unearthly voice rose howling like a chimney of fire

IT SHALL BE THE PRIEST THAT DASHEST THE
BLOOD AND THE FLESH OF THE SACRIFICE
THE FLESH OF THE SACRIFICE, SHALL BE BURNT
WITH FIRE
IT SHALL BE BURNT WITH FIRE

Reb' Elya's lips quivered and moved without a sound, fire
moved from man to man and the heat of their passion
scorched him, the count came riding, smiling, calling out
laughingly to his cousins and his men . . .
Stupid, stupid, said voices in the ears of Khreng and
Prandra. Make no plan, have nothing to do, and you do nothing, stupid!

You, Reb' Elya, know no Names
you, Reb' Elya, are an ignoramus
an ignoramus!
He knew a thousand names for God, but none of the most

powerful commanded by great saints and towering scholars to
bring down the right arm of the Lord, His pillar of fire, His
burning bush

MOSES POURED OUT THE BLOOD

  it rose pounding into the heads of the men

DASHED THE BLOOD AGAINST THE ALTAR

  the riders were in the marketplace and Prandra, slipping
into the sanctuary, dared not admit a thought for fear of the
demon
  "Yes, the demon," whispered Khreng
  Watch, Ungrukh said the demon

MOSES TOOK OF THE BLOOD

  the Qumedon delivered his strength to the men of Kostopol

MOSES PUT OF THE BLOOD

  the Qumedon gave them his malice

MOSES DASHED THE BLOOD

  and Elya, gathering his horror, his passion, his intelligence
in one skein, one half second of mountainous despair, for in
all those thousands of years those hundreds of thousands lay
dead, saw with complete clarity that the men of Kostopol
would wind their tallithim about the necks of their tormen-
tors, in spite of scythes and pitchforks, break up the pews and
lecterns for weapons, trample the Books—and then the King
of Demons would withdraw his strength and the fire would
grow veins outward, and the blood flow along them to Lublin,
to Warsaw and beyond
  threw back his head and howled "NO! NO! NO!" his
whole being a bursting artery of fear and love, "Dear Lord
God, King of the Universe, remove this abomination!"
  Without a thought Khreng and Prandra pressed the switches
of their remotes.

The count and his followers swarmed stamping across the lobby and into the sanctuary.

Khreng and Prandra crouched free in their bodies, fire-red in the flaked yellow light, and roared in pure pleasure, like forges, like dragons, like earthquakes, and leaped in unison three bounds over the lecterns scattering pages, straight on the Qumedon. Converging with Elya, who had sprung out in the first violent act of his life. All four vanished in a gulping implosion.

"Demons!" roared the count and his men, in one instant turning queasy with fright. *"Mazzikim!"* whispered the congregation, and trembled. Chava and the children screamed with horror.

As the Master of Demons disappeared, his works undid themselves. His disciples and his horse reverted to their elements. But they had this much life in them: the six disciples jumped up on tiptoe with heads thrown back and whirled, crowing like cocks, for a quarter of a minute before they crumbled in heaps of earth-clotted twigs; and the horse, tethered in the inn yard, reared on its hind legs and brayed once, powerfully, in idiot discord and then turned transparent, dust sifted into the whirlwind. A great echo pulsed outward from it, rebounded and died.

The count, with cousins and farmers, backed away from the sanctuary; the congregation hurried out, pulling one another by sleeves and fringes, gathering Elya's family shivering among them.

Under the blazing noon sun, the metallic bell of the sky, they turned, twisted, peered everywhere. "What happened? Where are they? How?" They looked to the sky and the sun, to earth, trees and houses, and found no sign.

Over the southern horizon an odd cockle, a buckling of the sky's surface, was obscured by the sun.

Khreng and Prandra, tossed in a heap with Elya, stood up and found themselves in a bubble. Its surface, luminous semi-transparent silver, shifted and mottled like soap-film; under their feet its stuff was not quite solid, of a firmness created by a force-field; it had a slithery feel. Beneath their pads, through it they could see Earth, a distorted ball as in a fisheye lens, the moon, a pale concave disc; above and around them a stunning collection of nebulae magnified by the warp of the field: spiral, barred, globular. It was a fearful panorama; it was meant to be so. The heavens between these lights were as blue as Espinoza's globe. But there was no contact with Espinoza.

Elya was only half-conscious, and they lifted him between them, made a seat for him with their bent knees and a back with their entwined arms so that he was supported by a magnificent red throne of living plush; but it did not mean much to him, for he opened his eyes, took one wild look around, screamed and wrapped his tallith round his head. "I am in Gehinnom," he whispered through its folds.

They could not deny it. They too were intimidated. Their hair rose, their hearts beat faster; the earth under their feet, through the translucent film, was far away but not too far away to pull them down crashing; the nebulae above and around looked near enough to drag them as hideously burst and frozen bodies into their great orbits.

They breathed good air, their hearts beat time, but the space they were enclosed in seemed timeless.

Elya was well rooted in time. He pulled the cloth half-away from his face, enough to free his mouth though he kept his eyes shut, and said, "Kostopol? Chava and the children?"

Prandra could not keep her eyes from circling the surface of this sphere which had no door and was a mind-splitting window to the universe. "The demon leaves them," she said. She hoped it was so. It was hard to reassure him: she was unwilling to frighten him with more esp, and without Espinoza she would have to pull the language from Elya's mind and feed it to Khreng as well.

Qumedon appeared, suspended before them. A spinning unradiant star, three meters across, nothing-colored, a few points of fire swimming within it like fish in a bowl, in its center a luminous globe small enough to hold between the hands.

Firepoints struck their minds:

YES YOU ARE QUICK AND CLEVER UNGRUKH AND YOU ARE INTERRUPTING MY GAME

The bright globe darkened a little, and the huge bubble

began to swing slowly, like a pendulum. Earth and moon went here and there beneath them.

Khreng and Prandra bent their heads and closed their eyes. "Stop, please," Prandra said. The bubble slowed and settled.

"Where are we?" Khreng got back his breath and his stomach. "What is this place?"

YOU ARE IN THE CENTER OF THE VORTEX THE GLOBE I AM CARRYING IS ITS CONTROL THIS PLACE IS TIMELESS

"Is there only one of you in this sector?"

THERE IS

"You are a creature of such power"—Prandra clenched her teeth trying to keep fear and contempt out of her mind—"why do you choose a small village and a few lost strangers to play games with?"

DO YOUR CHILDREN NOT PLAY WITH SMALL ANIMALS?

"My children don't play with people."

The Qumedon shrank quietly in one supple transformation and became a naked man. Without skin. Sitting cross-legged in the air holding the bright globe in his hands; beautiful in complexity, terrible in implication, he was a triumph of Qumedon mastery, no stupid animal of dust and wind. A red glisten of muscle laced in purple veins and pulsing scarlet arteries, shimmering blue-white in the fibrous sheaths between muscles and over the tendons of his intricate hands and feet; within his breast a heart beat *lubdubb,* his eyes were fire-points.

A smell of meat filled the place. Beyond control, Khreng and Prandra found saliva jetting into their mouths.

NICE FAT PEOPLE ON THIS PLANET

Elya, between the two of them, shrank with terror.

Khreng spat his mouthful at the feet of the living model and snarled, "We do not yet kill or eat one, Qumedon!"

Qumedon moved the network of muscles in mouth and neck into laughter, tossed the ball into the air and caught it. The bubble trembled.

WHERE DID YOU GET A TASTE FOR MEAT, UN-GRUKH? DID FIREMASTER GIVE IT TO YOU WHEN HE CREATED YOU FROM RED LAVA?

"Say what you mean!"

Laughter. OR WAS IT I WHO PICKED A PRIDE OF LEOPARDS OFF SOLTHREE AND CHANGED THEM ONLY A LITTLE, DROPPED THEM ON A PLANET TO SEE WHAT WOULD HAPPEN?

They swallowed that information in an unhappy lump without asking themselves if it were true. It was clearly within his power. "Firemaster has more effect on our lives than you," Khreng said.

YOU ARE NOT ON UNGRUWARKH, AND HERE I CREATE THE EFFECTS.

Was he more forceful as a creature of unimaginable power who reflected the shape and texture of the cosmos—or as a flayed saint with the humanly evil mind of the persecutor?

I LIKE THIS PLACE, UNGRUKH. THAT IS WHY I PLAY MY GAMES HERE.

"Far away from Qumedon," Prandra said, risking jets of fire from those eyes.

YES. I'M A PERSON WHO BRINGS NEW IDEAS TO MY PEOPLE AND FOR THAT THEY WILL TOLERATE A LOT.

Everything? Without limit? Prandra became aware that the questions she wanted answers for, swelling nodes in her brain, were being contained by all this talk. But the Qumedon was turning his intensity toward the shivering Elya.

RABBI, YOUR SHOCHET, REB NACHMAN, SLAUGHTERS AND SKINS MANY ANIMALS. DO I LOOK WORSE THAN THEY?

Elya whispered, "Ashmedai, a demon and a dead cow are not to be compared."

More laughter emerged between the white teeth among the naked muscles, and the Qumedon began to weave a skin, a tissue of capillaries, fibers, laminated cells, its surface horn-colored, puckered like an old man's and dotted with moles; sprouted white crinkled hair on his head, with side-curls, mixed-grey brows and beard, body hair, provided himself with black breeches, black-and-white *tallith katan,* yarmulkeh, Cossack boots, tallith; cradled the globe in one arm against his heart as if its light were the white fires of space between the black-flame letters of the Torah Scroll. His eyes were nothing-colored. The Rabbi of Qumedon.

Elya turned pale.

YOU STOPPED A POGROM? MAZEL TOV, I'LL FIND ANOTHER GAME. I DON'T HAVE TO LIVE ON THIS PLANET, YOU DO. . . . YOU THINK IT'S SAFER HERE WITHOUT ME? The telepathic voice, an astonishing homely Polish-Yiddish, was good-humored, almost gentle.

"When was it safe?" Elya said hoarsely. "My father died in a pogrom."

STAY ALIVE A HUNDRED YEARS, ELYA, MAYBE A FEW MORE . . . SEE THE SLAUGHTER THERE'LL BE.

"A hundred years ago and more," Elya whispered, "Bogdan Chmielnicki killed my people by the hundreds of thousands during the Cossack Rebellion."

THIS WILL BE TWENTY-FIVE TIMES GREATER THAN THAT ONE—the fleshy lips curved in the white beard —YOU COULDN'T IMAGINE. . . .

Prandra said quietly, "When you say such things, I think even your own people must not care much for you."

The Qumedon's laughter was dark. EVEN THE KINDEST OF US LIKES A GOOD GAME. The laughter rebounded and circled the walls of the bubble. IRONY IS ALWAYS GOOD; YOU LIKE IT YOURSELF, RABBI—AND AT THIS LEVEL IT IS SUPERB. YOU HAVE SAVED KOSTOPOL!

Prandra began to tease out a thought beneath the whirling helix of laughter.

Elya raised his eyes. "And that killing, will that be your work?"

YOU THINK MEN AREN'T CAPABLE?

Elya closed his eyes and tears slid between his lids. His spirit shrank into a hard tight ball of anguish.

"Rabbi!" Prandra thought he was drifting into the abyss once more.

Elya opened his eyes and regarded the Qumedon. "Ashmedai, if you know so much, tell me if my people will die forever in that slaughter."

Prandra wound a thought firmly around the deep center of her being like fine wire on a spindle. "Your people are alive seven hundred and fifty years from now," she said. "After that I can't promise." Her voice sank to its deepest velvet.

"Qumedon, is it Thursday when your shuttle breaks down? That day when you make no move?"

Firepoints grew in the eyes.

"You burn me out too like the ESP of the *Ruxcimi*?" she spoke very quietly. "That is an impulse, I think. Too bad to bring such attention to yourself."

IF I KILL—

Very quietly. "You manipulate fear and hatred very well, but do you know everything about reasoning? Perhaps you are only a novice joker."

—YOU ANIMALS—

"Must think for ourselves, because Firemaster, you know, gives no answer.

"I see the power of this Qumedon, and I ask myself: why does he let us live, when he can kill us with a thought? Because he needs us. Needs *animals?* We have a shuttle, and even Qumedni, with all their powers, need ships to cross the universe and shuttles to land . . . but if he can use our shuttle, he does not need us. Can you use our shuttle?"

Silence.

"Your energy field disrupts GalFed instruments? Some such thing? I know very little about those matters. Still, the vortex draws energy from the mother ship and Qumedon carries his personal energy source in his shuttle. Espinoza says this. The source feeds both him and his engines. Probably if it does not operate fully, he can still draw enough for himself for a while, but not enough to get him back to his ship. He realizes this on Thursday and perhaps is not sure what to do. And he takes notice of our landing. He cannot come to us and say: Ungrukh, I am in trouble, I send you up the vortex, leave a message with my people the Qumedni to rescue me. Why not? Because he burns out a valuable ESP—an act which likely upsets coexistence with GalFed—and maybe this game he's planning is a little too bloody even for Qumedni who are their own law. . . ."

YOU HAVE A LOT TO SAY TO THE MAD RENEGADE QUMEDON.

"All he can do is say: Look, I am a creature of a thousand powers, if you want to live you must do as I say—and he plays his game to please himself, to show off, to frighten us. . . .

"We believe in your great power, Qumedon, but still you

are not offering to let us live—I hate to say so, but even if you are rescued, your people don't look on you too kindly. There's no way to avoid that.''

THEN WHY SHOULD I BOTHER KEEPING YOU ALIVE WHEN YOU WILL ONLY BETRAY ME?

"Tsk, he's in a bind," Khreng said. "He can't decide whether to save himself and go home in shame or stay here and die with his pride."

Elya, who did not understand a word but knew a bargaining session when he saw one, sat quietly in a crouch with his shawl wrapped around him.

SOMETIMES IT IS BETTER—

Prandra moved her head in a gesture she had learned from Reb' Elya himself. "It's always better to be alive today."

Khreng said, "I think—"

And the bubble turned upside down. And warped, pinched, squeezed. They tumbled, screaming; Qumedon rolled with them, clenched around his glowing ball.

Outside a blundering roaring vibration gripped and clawed, emitted sounds, colors all over the spectrum, blue, violet, aquamarine, screaming ultrawhines and bass rumbles out of the very pit of matter

what?

THE VORTEX HAS PULLED IN

what?

alien creature?

hand, octopod, or

?flower with fire-petals bluing down the center into a black pit of suction

clasping the bubble like a hand and

turn off the vortex! Khreng/Prandra mindscreamed

NO MY ONLY CONTACT WITH THE

then change time, change time!

Qumedon was no longer a rabbi, but the cloud of primary energy enveloping the globe. Khreng, Prandra, Elya slipped and slid with it in hills and valleys over those petal-fingers of terrifying intensity burning through the field, the globe in the Qumedon darkened all light what? disappeared where? and

brightened as the filmy sphere blew out to its former shape with an odd quavering warble. Silence.

•   •   •

"What in the Blue Pit is that?" Khreng picked himself up off Prandra, whom he had knocked flat. She was too weak to think, only lay panting.

The Qumedon seemed to be trying to pull itself together. Its fires were deep crimson, feebly wavering.

Khreng turned to Elya, who had somehow managed to sit up on the bubble floor, and was coughing. Or laughing.

He threw back his head and choked with laughter. "Oh, Ashmedai, if that's not the work of God there must be far greater demons than you!"

"Rabbi, are you hurt?"

"How could I be hurt when I'm consorting in hell with the demons?"

"Don't depend on it," Khreng said. "Qumedon, tell us what that thing is."

. . . I DON'T KNOW . . . The Qumedon's voice was as vague as its body. THE VORTEX PULLED IT IN I'VE NEVER SEEN ANYTHING LIKE THAT . . . SOMETHING FROM ANOTHER UNIVERSE. . . .

Prandra was a little lightheaded. "Perhaps it is Firemaster's apprentice!"

"Don't be fatuous," Khreng said. "Listen, Qumedon, if your vortex pulls in one more thing like that, I think you soon have no place to stay . . . and, Prandra, if you let me speak, I believe I can make a sensible suggestion. If the Rabbi is set free and we are guided up the vortex, it is very simple to send a message to the Qumedni that one of their people lands on Sol Three to explore and is trapped when his engines fail. It is not necessary to say anything else—regarding ESPs or games— and it is a way out of this impasse."

WOULD THEY BELIEVE YOU?

"You can believe us because you esp us. You know we cannot be liars and a radio message cannot be esped. When you are among your people, you make your own arrangements. You are very skilled at deception." In spite of himself Khreng's voice tailed off into a rasp of sarcasm.

Silence. The firepoints rippled and glittered in their aquarium of energy. The bubble trembled.

Prandra whispered, "I think if you stay on this planet your

energy drains away till you are some shriveled black little thing like a burnt-out star. . . ."

The firepoints intensified, their mouths went dry.

SAY WHEN YOU ARE READY

Before they could react or speak: LISTEN UNGRUKH I HAVEN'T ASKED YOU MANY QUESTIONS SO PER- HAPS YOU WILL ANSWER JUST ONE

It sank and rested gently on the floor of the bubble.

WHAT ARE YOU GOING TO DO ABOUT ESPINOZA?

"What do you mean?"

HE WANTS YOU TO KILL HIM

Prandra said sharply, "I don't esp that."

YOU ARE NOT YET A CLASS-ONE ESP WHAT DO YOU THINK ALL THOSE LOVELY DREAMS MEANT . . . THAT PATHOS THAT POOR BODILESS BRAIN-IN- A-BOTTLE ROTTING IN A RUNDOWN MUSEUM?

"He—"

HE BELIEVES HE HAS ONLY TO ASK THEN YOU WILL BREAK THE BOTTLE AND LET THE BRAINS RUN OUT AND NO ONE WILL BLAME YOU BECAUSE YOU ARE SAVAGE CATS FROM A PRIMITIVE PLANET AND DON'T KNOW ANY BETTER, the patterns of fire swirled like arrows representing ocean currents on a map, I KNOW YOU WOULDN'T DO SUCH A THING BUT SINCE YOU ARE DOING ME A FAVOR I AM WILLING TO REPAY . . . UNGRUKH . . . IT WAS ON NO IMPULSE OF MINE THAT THE ESP OF THE *RUXCIMI* DIED. . . .

Prandra kept her mind carefully clear and still. Khreng said stiffly, "Thank you, Qumedon, we manage our own affairs."

The Qumedon blinked out and was gone.

"Irony is always good," Khreng said. "Maybe we give up Firemaster and start worshiping the devil. . . . Come, Rabbi, you are going home." He helped Elya to his feet.

"Really?"

"Yes."

Elya stood on the shifting surface, wondered what thoughts to think and what to make of them. He reached under his tallith to scratch his head. Was he to thank these beings? How? and whom? He looked from one to the other of the red *mazzikim,* their savage teeth and claws, lashing tails and char-

black chevrons. *Keteb miriri?* Khreng gave him one calm
blink. *Machlat?* Prandra's eyes were warm and clear as a summer sunset. He nodded. "Thank you, creatures of God."

"Where? Where?" The people of Kostopol looked and
found no sign.

"I am here," said Elya. Among them in the marketplace.
The count and his men withdrew to one side of him, his congregation to another. Chava and the children threw themselves
upon him with hysterical weeping.

"Elya! Elya!"

"Where have you been?"

"I have been among the demons and I seem to be well." He
sighed. "I think."

"You're not—you're not—"

"I am not a demon rabbi, children—only the same Elya,"
he said, though it was not true. "It was the false Lubliner that
was the demon, Ashmedai himself."

"We know that, Elya—and you were with him, among the
demons—in Gehinnom?"

"It seemed so."

"And was it terrible?"

"I have no words to tell your."

"Then how did you defeat them? What Names, what
spells?"

"I defeated no one. God spared me." He sighed again. "I
hope He did the same for the Lubliner, the true one."

"Somebody says his carriage broke down when he was setting out here yesterday. . . . He'll have to go straight home
now, he can't stop over with Passover coming. . . ."

They turned silent. Kostopol had been cut off from its
promised glory and seized by demons instead.

"You seem strange, Elya," Chava whispered.

"What can I be, Chava? I've been frightened and I'm tired
and sad." He gathered the children under his shawl. What
could he say or tell? Mystics in wise books might claim a
demon is this or that, but his own were indescribable. And as
for what he had learned—Let it be a lie, Little Father, King of
the Universe! Let it be a lie, what Ashmedai said. . . .

"Rebbeh—" The count came to him, reddened, rubbed his

neck. "I don't know what has been happening."

"I'm not sure myself, Count, believe me." He turned to his congregation in their shawls and their beards, feasted his eyes on those worn and humble faces. "Rabbosai, we have to finish the service. . . . I think we should begin reading Torah again, with a little less fire and blood. . . ."

There was nothing much to say to Espinoza. Prandra opened her mind and let him replay the scene for himself. Strapping herself down for lift-off, she said, "Is everything that Qumedon says true?"

:Yes. Everything.:

"And nothing can stop that slaughter? Nothing?"

:No.:

"Then we save our own lives, but I think we do nothing much for Kostopol."

:Prandra, you said it yourself,: Espinoza sealed his own fate. *:It's always better to be alive today.:*

They warped outward.

—ACCEPT COURSE CHANGE OR WAIT ONE ORBIT? the radio asked.

"We don't lose much time," Khreng said. WAIT AS MANY ORBITS AS YOU LIKE, FIJI. THAT COURSE CHANGE LEADS DOWN A QUMEDON TIME VORTEX. . . .

When that was settled, he rubbed his head under Prandra's chin. "My old woman, I'm sick of dog food and contact lenses and civilization. I want sleep." He flung himself back on the couch belly-up.

Espinoza, the man without skin, flesh, bones, nerves, heart, lungs, limbs, genitals, said, *:Times I called you eisenkop I never meant you had an iron head. Maybe one day you'll wish you did. You too, ESPrandra. . . .:*

"Espinoza!" Prandra rumbled sleepily.

:Yes?:

"You stay with us, be with us as long as we need you?"

:Yes.:

"That's good. . . ." She folded her limbs over her body, curled her tail about herself neatly; rising on waves of sleep, she considered, slowly and hazily, the shapes of minds, the

organic structures that began them, the ideas and emotions
that fulfilled them, wondered how a Qumedon's functioned
and what with, whether a mind-model could ever be built, how
. . . She had time for five minutes of her life's work before she
drifted off.

Seven hundred and fifty years spiraling downward the men
of Kostopol sang:

> "This is the Torah
>   that Moses set before the
>   Children of Israel
>   the Children of Israel . . ."

Reb Nachman carried it in its tinkling crowns and glittering
threads down from the beemah, around the synagogue, men
reached out to touch it with their fingers and kissed them;

> "Long life is in its right hand
>   and in its left hand honor
>   it is a Tree of Life
>   it is a Tree of Life
>   its ways are pleasant ways
>   and all its paths are peace . . ."

Let it be a lie. Elya his spirit a teardrop, his mouth a blessing,
took the words of the most loving and gentle of all rabbis,
Israel Baal-Shem, Master of the greatest Name, in silence took
the words, made them into a song and sang it:

> Much, much have I learned bim bam!
>   much have I been able to do bam bim!
>   but there is no one to whom
>   I may reveal it bim bam bim!

BEST-SELLING
Science Fiction
and
Fantasy

☐ 47809-3	**THE LEFT HAND OF DARKNESS,** Ursula K. LeGuin	$2.95
☐ 16012-3	**DORSAI!,** Gordon R. Dickson	$2.75
☐ 80581-7	**THIEVES' WORLD,** Robert Lynn Asprin, editor	$2.95
☐ 11577-2	**CONAN #1,** Robert E.Howard, L. Sprague de Camp, Lin Carter	$2.50
☐ 49142-1	**LORD DARCY INVESTIGATES,** Randell Garrett	$2.75
☐ 21889-X	**EXPANDED UNIVERSE,** Robert A. Heinlein	$3.95
☐ 87328-6	**THE WARLOCK UNLOCKED,** Christopher Stasheff	$2.95
☐ 26188-4	**FUZZY SAPIENS,** H. Beam Piper	$2.50
☐ 05469-2	**BERSERKER,** Fred Saberhagen	$2.75
☐ 10253-0	**CHANGELING,** Roger Zelazny	$2.95
☐ 51552-5	**THE MAGIC GOES AWAY,** Larry Niven	$2.75

MORE SCIENCE FICTION!
ADVENTURE